SLAUGHTER ON THE SEA!

There was a sudden thunder of tortured, over-stressed bulkheads from the burning ship. I whirled in time to watch the flames clawing frantically, hysterically toward her arcing mast-heads, even brighter and more revealingly than before . . . and one stark glimpse of the life-boat, now only seventy yards ahead of our slowly closing bows with the huddled, pathetic press of bodies etched black against the reflection from the burning sea.

Suddenly the freighter capsized. Monstrously. Tumbling faster and faster sideways to meet the water in a roaring, hissing agony. High, gouting spurts of spray and smoke and steam and . . .

. . . and then the light went out.

Also by Brian Callison
Published by Ballantine Books:

TRAPP'S PEACE

AN ACT OF WAR

A SHIP IS DYING

THE JUDAS SHIP

BRIAN CALLISON

TRAPP'S WAR

BALLANTINE BOOKS • NEW YORK

Library of Congress Catalog Card Number: 75-23947

ISBN 0-345-29104-2

This edition published by arrangement with
Saturday Review Press/E.P. Dutton & Co., Inc.

Manufactured in the United States of America

First Ballantine Books Edition: September 1980

Prologue

'By God but it's dark, Mister.'

Trapp grinned in a pleased sort of way, moving towards the wheelhouse door. 'Night's black as a Sudanese stoker's ass.'

Which it certainly was.

Right up to the moment when the salva of starshell ignited with a fuzzy *plop* directly above the *Charon*'s bridge and simply confirmed that you couldn't rely on anyone's discretion any more. Not when you were steaming less than thirty miles sou' sou' west of a beleaguered island called Malta, in the middle of the night.

Or not when you happened to be doing it in the middle of 1942, anyway.

So the captain just tacked a bitterly resigned 'Ohhhhhh SHIT!' on to the end of his previous remark, while accelerating towards the purely psychological protection of the canvas-clad starboard wing. He also registered petulantly, before reflex action submerged him below eye level, that you still couldn't make out one detail of whatever had surprised them. Not concealed, as the anonymous threat now was, by an even more Stygian blackness out with the periphery of magnesium-frozen sea.

Perhaps, under the circumstances, the first conclusion which formed in Trapp's mind couldn't have been considered surprising. In fact any war-conditioned British seaman finding himself the centrepiece of such a gut-wrenching display of pyrotechnics might well have evinced a similar reaction.

'U-boat! Surface action by a bloody *U*-boat, f'r cryin' out lou . . .'

1

Which meant it would take, maybe, twenty seconds
more for that distant gun crew to identify, pinpoint,
depress on target and . . .

Thirteen . . . fourteen . . . fifteen . . . ! Trapp
started to screw himself around to stare back at the
wheelhouse. The mate's face hung suspended in the
rectangle of the door, a sickly white blob with a black
hole in the middle, blinking up at the lights in the
sky with brown, frightened Greek eyes which already
had the awareness of death in them. Then the hole
was erased as the little man closed his mouth and tried
to swallow, just before Trapp roared hugely, 'DOWN,
Mister! Geddown an' pray it's not . . .'

. . . seventeen . . . eighteen . . .

The first high explosive round hit the *Charon* at the
precise moment in which a second thought struck the
captain. The possibility was so awe-inspiring—so un-
thinkable—that Trapp even altered course in the middle of his warning to First Mate Theofylaktos
Papavlahapoulos.

He said sincerely, 'No, Pappy. After what we've
been doin', jus' you pray to God it *is* a U-boat out
there . . . an' not the Navy. Not the *Royal* Navy, any-
how!'

And then shrapnel and razor-edged fragments of
ship were slicing through *Charon*'s antiquated bridge
front while, at the same time, the still vertical first
mate started to scream in a bubbling, inhuman sort of
way . . .

. . . but it *was* a very odd thing to say, on reflection.
That bit about the Royal Navy.

Especially by a war-conditioned British seaman.

When under attack.

Of course, Trapp had never been a man to say the
conventional thing. Or even to do the conventional
thing, for that matter. Maybe that was what was
wrong with him—the flaw which had reduced him to
being what he now was, and which meant he sailed
haughtily through the middle of a world war without
actually being on anyone's side at all.

A sort of unilateral neutrality. Except that Trapp

was the only subscriber to the arrangement. The only person who recognised his own particular status as a non-participant in World War II.

Probably the only person who even *knew* about it for that matter.

One thing was abundantly clear.

That invisible warship out to starboard either didn't know, or just didn't care. And when you're on the exploding end of a maritime engagement then the finer points of argument somehow become a little academic and irrelevant.

So Captain Edward Trapp, self-employed neutral, just hugged the dirt-engrained deck of his ship and listened bitterly to his first mate's agony keening above the roar of escaping steam from a fractured windlass line, and sensed the *Charon* sheering to starboard out of control because the shrapnel which had colandered his wheelhouse had, presumably, carried on aft to pass through his helmsman as well.

And, for a few brief moments, allowed his mind to wander back to an earlier war at sea, when a very young Midshipman Edward Trapp, Royal Naval Volunteer Reserve, had stood nervously on the bridge of another old ship. And listened with growing fear and pride while the captain of that tired, inadequately armed merchant cruiser had said quietly; 'Order the convoy to scatter, please. Signal to Admiralty, plain language . . . AM PROCEEDING TO ENGAGE ENEMY BATTLE CRUISER. MY POSITION ONE HUNDRED AND TWENTY THR . . .'

Only the captain never did finish his signal, because the first salvo from the German ship exploded right on top of that hopelessly gallant man, long before the British guns came even remotely within range. And the only clear memory young Trapp ever had was of the navigating officer and the gunnery officer fusing together in an expanding, bloody smear just before the blast lifted him in feathery fingers and laid him gently down again, one clear cable's length astern of the racing, condemned ship.

Where he floated, quite comfortably, and watched through tear-swollen eyes as salvo after salvo of high explosive rumbled in from the distant horizon, shredding and incinerating and tearing his shipmates limb from limb amid a still-steaming inferno of disintegrating steel.

Until the antiquated, under-armed merchant cruiser finally lay over on her side in bitter defeat, while those far-away ants who preferred the alternative of drowning under the layer of coal dust which smeared the sea around her scrambled down her scarred flank —but Midshipman Trapp was really quite relieved that they were saved all that trouble when a solitary German shell found its way into her main magazine and she started to blow up in one last, long column of climbing water and fire . . .

Buoyed by the cushion of his lifejacket, sole survivor Trapp floated all that day, and throughout that night. And through all the next day and night as well. And he wanted to die but he couldn't keep his head under water long enough to drown, because it takes a brave man to do a thing like that, and Trapp was still only a little boy then, and very frightened.

And then, on the third day, a raft with a bit of a man still clinging to it drifted by, and Trapp reckoned the half man wouldn't mind floating for a while instead so they changed places, only the other chap wouldn't go away and kept following Trapp's raft for a long time after, which Trapp wholeheartedly resented because there were a lot of tiny fish and other sea creatures and Trapp just couldn't bear to watch what they were doing to his inescapable companion . . .

Until, eventually, the other chap got smaller and smaller and finally disappeared altogether. And young Trapp resented *that,* too, because it wasn't very nice to impose yourself on someone and then, just when he'd got used to your company, leave him all alone again. Not even if you did take rather a long time to do it.

By the tenth day he had started to hate the Royal Navy. And the German Navy. And the bloody war.

On the twelfth day a reddish-coloured fish skipped clean out of the water and landed on the raft, right in front of Trapp's eyes. He watched it for several minutes, flipping and struggling breathlessly, and hoped it would escape because the effort of moving was all a bit too much, just for the sake of staying alive. And then it stopped flopping about and simply lay staring back at him with bulbous, reproachful eyes and a shiny, heaving belly.

He whispered sadly: 'Sorry. But you really *do* push your luck, don't you, Fish?'

And then he ate it. Still gasping. It kept him alive for another seven days.

He was picked up by a passing ship on the nineteenth day. It was a German raider. They were very kind to him. They fed him, helped him learn to walk again, they even let him write a letter home.

And then they locked him up. For nearly two years. By the time the Armistice was signed Midshipman Edward Trapp, RNVR, had developed a pathological abhorrence of anything or anyone who had even the remotest connection with war and wanton waste.

It ended the first phase in the moulding of a highly individual, and extremely bloody-minded merchant seaman.

The second round from the gloom outwith the starshell's incandescence passed clean through *Charon*'s high, spindly funnel without exploding. It did, however, carry away a further steam line—this time the supply pipe to the old coaster's long-ago-shiny brass whistle.

Trapp stayed flat on the deck for a few more moments, getting angrier and angrier as yet another high pressure screech was added to the bedlam around him until, unable to restrain himself any longer, he spat one resounding lower-deck obscenity into the night, scrambled unheedingly to his feet and hurled his oil-stained uniform cap in the vague direction of whoever was bloody well shooting at him.

Or the *Charon*, anyway. Which meant at him, too. And at Chief Engineer Al Kubiczek, ex-US Navy mechanic, now deserted. And at Second Mate (Uncertificated) Chafic Abou Babikian, ex-Lebanese as-

sistant brothel keeper and pimp with an unlikely
affection for navigation, western classical music and
angelic little boys . . . and at Gorbals Wullie, ex-
Barlinnie Prison and currently the hardest, most intractable and most cretinous specimen out of all the
stateless, motherless, piratically anti-social drop-outs
who made up what could loosely be called the crew of
the Steamship *Charon*.

'Good boys, all of them,' Trapp brooded bleakly.
'Seein' there's not one of 'em I'd think twice about
leaving battened down below when this decrepit old
bastard finally dives.'

Apart from Pappy, maybe. There'd always been
something a bit special about his relationship with the
little mate, dating back to their halcyon pre-war days
when there was always a cargo of guns or a few
anonymous passengers to be smuggled ashore for one
of the many local North African sheikdoms . . .

Then he stumbled over First Mate Papavla-
hapoulos, jammed awkwardly across the wheelhouse
door, and felt an unaccustomed sadness because he
suddenly realised that Pappy was very quiet now.
Ominously quiet, in fact, for a normally voluble
Greek. And *especially* quiet for a voluble Greek who,
presumably, had a hole in him . . .

But the extent of his concern for the rest of his crew
did indicate just how cynical Edward Trapp had become. And how bitter.

Life had mutilated him too much. There was nothing left, now, of that young boy who'd sobbed so un-
restrainedly on a bobbing life-raft. Just because he'd
eaten a bug-eyed, reproachful little fish . . .

Not that Trapp had become so disillusioned all at
once, not even when he'd surfaced after two years in
a limbo of endless prisoner-of-war camps. Certainly
he'd sworn, there and then, that he would never, ever
fight another war. Not for anybody. But there were a
lot of returning warriors who felt like that, at the time.

He'd started to become greedy, too. Which, again,
wasn't so unusual. A great number of Allied prisoners
struggling to exist in a Germany being starved into

submission developed the same weakness. By the end
of the war a cob of black bread or a litre of acorn
soup had become a priceless possession. Trapp discovered very quickly that to acquire meant to survive.
It only took him a little longer to find that personal
survival was, by definition, incompatible with concern
for his fellow men.

Young Edward proved more than adaptable. When
the hospital ship finally landed him in Post-war Dover
he was tanned, broad-shouldered and quite remarkably fit. While many of the repatriated POW's had to
be carried down the gangway on stretchers, weakened
through malnutrition, Midshipman Trapp, RNVR,
strode briskly on a course for the nearest Salvation
Army canteen.

Even though he still clutched a bulging parcel of
surplus bread and *Würsten.*

He hadn't been able to eat all of it himself. He'd
changed a lot since the day when he'd apologised to a
fish . . .

Of course, it wasn't really Trapp's fault. In his own
way he'd become just another casualty. Only most of
the sick who returned recovered in the fullness of
time, whereas Trapp never did—or maybe he just
didn't want to. Perhaps he drew the wrong conclusion
from the fact that over four hundred men went to war
aboard that armed merchant cruiser, yet only he came
home.

So he started to ignore the rules at first. And then
quite blatantly to break them. For instance he didn't
even wait to be demobbed. Just stuffed what was left
of his uniform behind a toilet on Dover Station,
changed into a rather badly cut suit he happened to
find in someone else's luggage, then offered a derisive
two fingers in the direction of HRH King George V,
Their Lordships of the Admiralty and a Britain Now
Fit For Heroes.

Three days later ordinary seaman Trapp was outward bound for Shanghai aboard a listing, rusted old
freighter which had probably only survived the recent
hostilities because the Germans reckoned she was due
to sink either way and save them a torpedo. The con-

ditions on that coffin ship would have persuaded any
lesser men than Trapp back into the ways of right-
eousness before any permanent harm was done but,
ironically, they only served to emphasise to him that
his was the true path to fortune.

He jumped ship in Hong Kong. She went to the
bottom like a cement-filled bucket the very next morning, dragging all remaining hands down with her. For
the second time in his short life Fate had steered
Trapp on a safe course past sudden death.

He became finally convinced that he had one extremely valuable asset which placed him on a higher
plane than other more vulnerable men.

That his destiny, no matter what he did or even to
whom it was done, would undoubtedly be—to survive.

Only there did seem to be times when the tech-
niques of survival proved rather more difficult to apply
than at others.

Like when the third shell from the night exploded
less than a good spit astern of *Charon*'s taffrail,
and Trapp felt the whole bloody ship sort of ride up
aft, then surge shudderingly ahead like a surf board
on the face of a breaker.

Caught off balance he went down on one knee, hard
across the little Greek's chest, but Pappy still didn't
utter a sound. Not even in irritable acknowledge-
ment of Trapp's reflex, 'Sorry, Mate!'

Then, like switching out a cabin light, the spluttering glare from the starshell extinguished abruptly
and darkness clamped once again over the honey-
combed bridge.

But not before the captain observed that Pappy's
right eye was staring accusingly into his, only it wasn't
sparkling any more like it used to on those occasions
when the mate talked about a tiny fishing village facing the golden sands just outside Kastrosikiá.

And then he noticed where Pappy's other eye had
been. It seemed appropriate that the blackness should
come back again after that—considerate to Pappy, in
a secret sort of way.

Trapp sniffed hard and stood up. Slowly, so that

the quiet man in the wheelhouse door wouldn't think he was offended by his appearance. He tried to swallow an odd obstruction in his throat but was surprised to find he couldn't, because that suggested emotion and the captain knew it couldn't be that.

So he just stood there trying not to think about Pappy any more, and listening dully to the roar of the steam and the nervous shouts from aft, and blinking hard for no apparent reason . . . and then a second starshell erupted into a shocking, relentless dazzle, and Edward Trapp became himself again.

A survivor *par excellence*.

By hook or—given a preference—by crook.

Which was precisely what he had become, shortly after avoiding a second premature demise within that rust-weakened tomb that just hadn't been able to stay afloat any longer.

It wasn't far from Hong Kong to Macao. And Macao, at that time, provided the spawning ground of international crime. The magnet for gun runners, opium dealers, gold smugglers and all the other enthusiastically perverted drop-outs fleeing from postwar retribution. It became the symbol of the exciting, adventurous, inscrutable East—the very epitome of those robust, romantic, disease-ridden days of the Tongs and the China Pirates and the River Gun Boats.

And Edward Trapp became, in turn, intoxicated with the lawlessness of it. Entranced. To him this was his golden land of opportunity where the survivors became kings, and the meek dead.

He didn't die. Yet, in an odd way, he never quite became a king, either. Perhaps it was because there were too many good things still flickering into occasional wakefulness deep down inside him. For instance he discovered, with a certain sense of frustration, that he could never kill a man in cold blood—a definite drawback for the young, get-up-and-go executive in Macao society. And also that he had a rather untimely sense of humour which didn't exactly encourage friendship from those who could have assisted his career—like the time when he won ten tons of weed killer from a down and out ship's captain, and could only turn his asset into cash by sticking 'Fertiliser' labels over the previous legends, then selling it to a local Fu Manchu to dress that gentleman's opium poppy fields with.

The Poppy Blight descended on China that year. Everyone's poppy fields imitated the Gobi Desert during a dry spell and Fu Manchu was temporarily fooled. It was the only thing which saved Trapp the immediate discomfort of having his skin peeled from his torso in one inch strips.

It also convinced him even further that he would survive.

But he still got the hell out of Macao in plitty dam quicktime. Chop, chop!

Just make bloody *sure* he did.

Which proved to be yet another example of Trapp's incomparable sense of timing. Two days later Fu Manchu, having learned in a roundabout way of his protégé's infidelity, vented a small part of his oriental frustration by kidnapping the unfortunate ship's captain, Trapp's current Chinese mistress and a visiting commercial traveller whose only link with Trapp had been that he'd had a drink at the pier with a chap who was leaving in a hurry.

Most parts of the trio's dismembered corpses were dumped from a truck into the front garden of the British Consulate the next morning. Smack in the middle of the croquet lawn and damn uncivilised, even for a blasted yellow chap.

Oddly enough, things never again seemed to work out quite as smoothly for Edward Trapp.

During the next few years he drifted aimlessly, usually clinging petulantly to some berth or other aboard clapped-out old freighters until their mates got fed up with Trapp's intractable bloody-mindedness and deposited him ashore for someone else to salvage. Between engagements he dabbled in the various skills of smuggling, pimping, conning and, as always, of surviving.

By the mid-1930's there was nothing left of Trapp's dream. There was only a stocky, hard-as-nails seaman with a chip on his shoulder against the whole lousy world and a tongue as rough as a moored hulk's bottom.

He was a prickly, but curiously likable rogue. And as inflexible in his principles as a stoker's boot sole.

And then his last chance came. Born by avarice, out of mistrust.

Captain Trapp, as he then considered himself, received the offer of his own command. It was from a small, somewhat seedy syndicate of three Egyptian business gentlemen who had a ship and cargo but no one to drive it, seeing their last skipper had suffered a fatal collision with a firebar, wielded by a still-anonymous member of her crew.

The ship was the *Charon*. And that was the first snag. Trapp had never, ever laid eyes on such an ancient, run-down, shored-up, rust-scaled monstrosity of a maritime junk heap since the time he'd plundered an 1897 wreck off the Taipan coast—and he'd done *that* in a diving suit, seeing she'd sunk through old age and was lying on the bottom.

As Trapp remembered it, she had borne a striking similarity to his first command. Only that sunken wreck had been in slightly better condition.

The second snag was the *Charon*'s port of discharge, and her cargo. A beach in North Africa, and a consignment of fourth-hand guns which could still kill anyone they were aimed at. And the Legionnaires who patrolled that particular area, just waiting for gunrunners like Trapp, were rather inclined to shoot first and jump on your corpse later.

He was a bit offended, too, by the attitude of the Egyptians. In the way that they insisted on his staying aboard while they took the stuff ashore and negotiated final terms with the local sheik. Almost as if they didn't trust their own captain to return with the money. Inferring that he, Edward Trapp, might shanghai his own *cargo,* f'r cryin' out lou . . .

And then he had his Idea.

Naturally it meant that the cargo would be perfectly safe. Apart from any other considerations, one of

Trapp's unbending principles was of loyalty to his employers. Of course he fully intended to land both them and the guns in any part of the Mediterranean they might direct, and he was damned if he'd touch so much as one solitary round of .303 ammunition.

But it was only reasonable that he should be allowed some small gain from the transaction too, wasn't it?

Like . . . well . . . stealing the *ship,* f'r instance?

So he did. Just as soon as the first fusillade of rifle fire echoed across the still waters from that distant beach, which did rather suggest that his late Egyptian employers wouldn't be returning that evening anyway. And, moreover, were extremely unlikely to lodge any future claims as to the legal ownership of the SS *Charon.*

And thus Edward Trapp, survivor, became a man of substance. A self-employed master mariner with allegiance to no country and the whole of the Mediterranean as his oyster. He even had a ready-made crew and, while he never could prove for certain that it was Gorbals Wullie who'd retired that last skipper with a firebar from astern, he made very sure the same fate never caught up with him.

But anyone being aware of Trapp's destiny would have known *that* much already.

And things were happy and successful, in a sordid kind of way, aboard the *Charon* as she shuddered tentatively from one illicit destination to another with only an occasional stabbing or shooting or splash in the wake during the middle watch to disturb the harmony of her crew. While Fate, as ever, steered Trapp on a safe course to avoid retribution at the hands of the authorities.

Until Adolf Hitler sent the *Wehrmacht* into Poland, and the one thing which Trapp had sworn long before that he would never become involved in, occurred.

Most of the world went to war. Again.

Apart from the not particularly patriotic crew of the *Charon,* who unanimously declared themselves neutral and just carried on as before. Though in fairness to them, most of that particular crowd would have had great difficulty in remembering exactly whose side they should have been fighting on anyway.

And as Trapp reasoned with First Mate Papavla-hapoulos: 'Either way we got to steer clear of war-ships, Pappy. So we might as well be doin' it on our own account an' puttin' a bit've profit aside at the same time.'

But Trapp's principles were still as rigid as ever. Nothing he did should jeopardise the British war effort. Any black market whisky or chocolate or but-ter he picked up along the secret places of the African coast would go straight into Allied hands . . . for a price. So even the morality of it all was undisputable. From a renegade Englishman's point of view anyway.

And that was why the island of Malta, almost on her knees under the Nazi blockade, woke up regularly to find that yet another consignment of luxuries was being surreptitiously bartered from a truck which had spent the previous night waiting in a little cove just down past Vittoriosa. While any senior British officer who may have had a little more information than Trapp would have liked to think, only glanced toler-antly at the faces of those who needed every spark of cheer they could get, and then deliberately turned away.

And so Trapp's non-involvement in World War II proceeded. Right up to the moment when a starshell exploded. And a little Greek sailorman lost part of his head . . .

As soon as that second starshell went up Trapp snarled a vicious 'Bastards!' then eased his bulk past that of the dead Greek's and into the wheelhouse itself. Gradually he could feel the ship slowing down, butting sullenly into the short seas which came more and more on to the bow as the *Charon* kept swinging to star-board.

. . . forty-two . . . forty-three . . . forty-four . . . He still couldn't distinguish a bloody thing out there but the hairs on the nape of his neck told him they were running out of time. Fast.

Trapp's mind coldly visualised every move made

aboard that unidentified threat beyond the light. Smoking brass shell cases clanging to her deck . . . Reload. New rounds in the trays, oil-bright under the flare-spill . . . Breech blocks slamming into position . . .

Razor-edged shards of glass crunched under his feet as he knelt urgently beside the helmsman, now huddled untidily between the wheel and the scarred lining of the after-wheelhouse bulkhead. More glass particles glistening redly from a grotesque welter of lacerated flesh. A terrible anger swept over the captain in a great boiling flood . . .

The engine-room telegraph clamoured shockingly. Unexpectedly.

He swung round to stare uncomprehendingly at the dial. Someone down below had rung her from FULL AHEAD to STOP without any orders from the bridge and, already, he could sense the slackening vibration as the control valve of the antiquated steamer was screwed down.

. . . fifty-one . . . fifty-two . . . Gunlayers' eyes nestling familiarly against the foam sponge cups of faraway sights. Hands caressing the training wheels. On . . . On . . . ON . . . *Achtung Geschütz-bedienung . . . !*

Trapp lunged for the voice pipe to *Charon*'s engine-control platform. Snatching at the whistle he dropped it heedlessly on its retaining chain and blew violently, feeling the veins pulsing in his forehead with the strain. Far below his feet the second, terminal whistle emitted a thin, reedy scream of desperation. He blew again, angrily, then cupped the mouthpiece to his ear, listening impotently for the surge of reciprocating clamour that indicated a reply from the machinery space.

And it came reluctantly. After a long hesitation.

'Engine-room.'

Trapp transferred the pipe to his mouth, resentfully aware of an intense gratitude that somebody—anybody—was still at the other end. He snapped coldly, 'Bridge . . . An' who the hell ordered "Stop engines"? I need full speed an' I need it now. *Jaldi!*'

The sardonic, bitter laugh which echoed back to

him could only belong to one man. Chief Engineer Kubiczek.

'Christ, Captain, you think this bucket's some kinda *real* ship? Flat out down the face of a wave an' with the wind astern we only make eight knots . . . Those bastids shootin' at us can bloody swim faster'n that.'

'You give me full power, Chief. That's an order, dammit!'

Kubiczek's voice was laden with hopelessness. 'So break out the goddam oars, Trapp. We blew a steam line on deck somewhere. I'm losin' pressure like it was goin' out of fashion, gauges down to twenty pounds an' still falling . . .'

Trapp felt Kubiczek's anguish mirrored in his own belly. He gripped the pipe like a vice. 'We gotter contract, you an' me . . .'

'Shove your lousy contract, Trapp . . .' Kubiczek seemed to hesitate a moment, then he said quietly, and with no cynicism at all. '. . . Sorry, Skip. But me an' my boys, there's nothin' more we can do down here. We're comin' up.'

The captain let the voice pipe fall and stared dully through the jagged, imploded square of the wheelhouse window. All of a sudden there wasn't any future out there anymore. Not for Edward Trapp, ex-professional survivor. No more voyaging to darkened shores, no more thrilling to the tension of the smuggling game, no more bazaar haggling over a sling of whisky or a ton of diverted Africa Korps stores . . . No more Pappy Papavlahapoulos with the bright eyes and the excitable loyalty . . .

. . . only a long-forgotten memory now, for Trapp. A memory of another old ship which couldn't fight back, and of men abandoning and dying as salvo after salvo still homed in on her. But not even that could ever be the same as the coming death of his *Charon*. Because that other ship went down with dignity and pride and great courage, while all Trapp could offer would be screaming, retching oblivion to a polyglot crew of stateless misfits . . .

. . . seventy-seven . . . seventy-eight . . . seventy-nine . . .

He turned from the window and stepped over the man in the door once again. The eye seemed to follow him, that one good Greek eye, and he wondered distantly if it really did reflect Pappy's resentment at the way Trapp's greedy incompetence had killed him. It was an eerie, spine-tingling sensation for the captain. Almost as if, somehow, he was a condemned man awaiting death under the accusing Cyclopean stare of a victim already visited.

And then a very odd thing happened to Edward Trapp.

When, swinging away abruptly, he saw men on the after deck. Dim, shadowy figures working with unfamiliar harmony around the solitary, dirt-engrained lifeboat abaft the funnel.

Conscious of a growing sense of disbelief he watched silently, reluctant to acknowledge, even to himself, that a crew of such squalid, squabbling self-interest as made up the complement of the *Charon* could ever display the sort of discipline under stress which they were showing. The sort of discipline to make any ship's master stiffen with pride.

Which was disconcerting, to say the least. Because pride, however suspect, was an emotion which had deserted the captain a long time ago.

Until Second Mate Babikian caught sight of him and hesitated as the boat swung smoothly outboard. The teeth flashed nervously against dark skin and the Lebanese gestured: 'We make ready, Cap'n. But we not abandon till you say we must.'

And thus Trapp discovered that—aboard a scrap-iron ship, where human dignity had long ago been smothered under a scum of callous indifference to the needs of other men—he had finally found the one thing which, perhaps, he'd been searching for all his life.

He really was a king at last.

Only it was too late, now. Far too bloody late!

When, for the first time since the night had exploded, a sleek grey shape slid menacingly into the fading halo of light, and everyone could make out quite clearly the arrogant flutter of her White Ensign above the precisely-trained turrets of a British Fleet destroyer.

Simply confirming—as Edward Trapp had gloomily acknowledged when that first shot exploded from the night—that habitual blockade-running into wartime Malta would eventually prove disastrous.

And most certainly inconsistent. With the gentle art of . . . Surviving.

Chapter One

The phone rang piercingly, momentarily drowning even the crump of bombs from the north side of Valletta and the sharper, more co-ordinated percussion of the anti-aircraft fire. Even down there in the underground bunker we could feel the tremors, little shocks under our feet as several more sandstone houses and Maltese women and children ceased to exist, but nobody bothered to look up anymore. A few days before, on the 26th of July, the island had stood-to for its two thousand-eight hundredth alert.

And anyway, we were all looking at the telephone.

The admiral picked it up himself. He listened for a few moments then, replacing the receiver, turned to face us. I knew, before he spoke, that it was bad news.

'I'm sorry, gentlemen. *Eagle* has been confirmed as lost. She went down in seven minutes.'

I thought sickly, 'Oh God!' but I didn't say anything. Lieutenants don't. Not in a roomful of senior Army, Navy and Air Force officers who've just received a kick in the guts. Then someone, I think it was Captain (S), murmured quietly, 'Then thank God they've still got *Victorious* and *Indomitable* to maintain their air cover.'

After a few moments' hesitation someone else at the rear of the ops room opened the door and they all filed silently out. The PEDESTAL conference was over anyway, and there didn't seem to be anything left to say. Only the waiting had to be endured now, and they'd all done rather a lot of that recently, on the island of Malta.

I stayed because I'd been told to. Before the conference began. Though I think I would have done anyway. After six weeks of kicking my heels in the centre of the Mediterranean's bull's-eye I'd have gate-crashed Winston Churchill to get another ship.

A Wren third officer stuck her head round the door and hesitated as she caught sight of the admiral, standing now with his back to us and hands clasped pensively together while he gazed up at the general operations plot on the wall. I shook my head warningly at her and she gave me a funny, sad smile before withdrawing again.

She was quite pretty, I noticed absently, but I wasn't in the mood for anything right then. Except, maybe, a hammer and tongs row with an admiral.

The snag was that I didn't quite know how to start it. I didn't even know why I'd been told to wait, for that matter; so I just stared up at the plot as well, noting the neatly chinagraphed names of OPERATION PEDESTAL's escort force.

It was a list which read like a connoisseur's selection from *Jane's Fighting Ships*—the battleships *Nelson* and *Rodney;* cruisers *Manchester* and *Cairo*. *Phoebe, Kenya, Charybdis* and *Nigeria*. Thirty-two destroyers . . . they were out there, forging living history, while all I was being allowed to do was sweat the war out in irritable frustration.

Because the next phase of dying had started too, now, with the loss of *Eagle,* and I couldn't help wondering how many more of those neat legends would have to be erased before the remnants of PEDESTAL's original fourteen merchant ships could steam to their berths in Grand Harbour.

And God only knew how desperately Malta needed them, just to survive. Only two merchantmen had got through in the past few weeks—two out of seventeen forming the VIGOROUS and HARPOON convoys—and now shortages were critical. Food, ammo for the ack-ack batteries. Diesel fuel for the boats of the 10th Submarine Flotilla operating from the island. Avgas for the few remaining Spitfires . . .

. . . I noticed there was one tanker listed on the plot, just one, and I didn't need to be an admiral to know she'd be the primary target for every *Luftwaffe* sortie to hit Bomb Alley in the next few days.

Her name was the *Ohio*...

Her crew must have been brave men...

The admiral turned round and saw me gazing at the plot. Maybe he read something in my eyes, or maybe he was just a very understanding man, because he smiled slightly and said, 'You're out there with them, aren't you, Lieutenant? In spirit.'

I didn't smile back. 'I'd like to be. But in a practical, rather than an abstract sense, Sir . . .' I hesitated, then added defiantly, 'I've been hanging around for six weeks now, since they bombed me out of my last ship, with nothing to do other than censor matelots' mail. If the Navy had left me in the Merchant Service I'd at least be at sea.'

'You were a Reserve Officer. You realised that your commitment would be to the Royal Navy in time of war, Miller.'

'Yessir! And not—with respect—to His Majesty's Post Office!'

He didn't say anything for a moment. Just looked at me thoughtfully with those penetrating grey eyes then, abruptly, turned and gestured at the plot which overshadowed us. When he finally did speak again it was quietly, almost absently.

'Probably the most powerful escorting force ever assembled during this war, Miller. Over forty warships. Forty . . . And with only one purpose—to smash a way through for the convoy. Forty ships, to protect fourteen . . .'

He swung back to face me and I could see the lines of strain etching tributaries across the weatherbeaten temples. 'Yet even now I'll count myself damn lucky if three, even two, of those merchantmen ever reach us.'

I said 'Yessir' because I knew he was right, and there didn't seem to be anything else to add. And anyway, I knew there had to be a punch line—and then it came.

'So tell me, Lieutenant, how in God's name . . .' The admiral took a deep breath and shook his head disbelievingly, '. . . an unarmed eight-knot coal burner with no intelligence reports, no routing or mining information, no radar and not even a damned radio . . . how could she *possibly* maintain a contraband run between this boxed-in fortress and the North African coast with the regularity of . . . of a Birkenhead *ferry,* dammit!'

I muttered, 'Well it can't be done, can it? Not unless she also happened to be a coal-fired submarine. *With* a permanently drafted guardian angel, naturally.'

Then I found out that he really was a very understanding man, because he didn't even lift an eyebrow at the outright insolence. He just said, ever so quietly, 'Oh, but it *has* been done, Miller. Consistently. Over the last fourteen months!'

While I saw the look in the admiral's eye. And there wasn't any humour there at all. Not of any kind. Certainly not the kind to invent phantom smugglers sailing blithely through shot and shell aboard some impossibly antiquated Steamboat Annie.

So I whispered, 'Good God!'

Weakly.

And, for the very first time, the admiral smiled.

I caught my first glimpse of the smuggler two hours later.

She'd been brought in earlier that morning and now lay secured outboard of a burnt-out hulk which had been a fairly old ship even before the Stukas got to her. Since then the Navy had stripped everything salvable from her decks—and she *still* looked in better shape than Trapp's blockade-buster.

Certainly every bit as seaworthy. And the bomb casualty was already sitting on the bottom of the harbour.

But I had a job to do, for the admiral. A rather special, and very satisfying job.

I picked my way across the heat-distorted deck of the host wreck towards the *Charon.* The all-clear had gone a few minutes earlier and now the only reminders of yet another raid were the ambulance and fire bells from the centre of the city and a column of

smoke rising almost vertically into the cloudless sky
over the Naval dockyard. On the wharf behind me
the shirtless crew of a 3.7-inch AA gun were heaving
spent ammunition cases over the sand-bagged walls of
the gun pit in a desultory manner which suggested
they'd done it all so many times before.

But the *Charon* held all my attention at that moment, in a hypnotic, disbelieving sort of way. I stood
gazing over her; feeling a grudging admiration for
whoever Trapp was, because anyone who could even
sail a boat as decrepit as that from Africa to Malta—
apart from dodging every warship in the Med while
doing so—just had to be a real seaman. As well as an
irresponsible, money-grabbing, buccaneering chancer
with an undisputed death-wish.

She was, maybe, two-fifty feet overall, shelter
decked from counter for about half her length forr'da.
A high spindly funnel aft towered over the number
two hatch, battened down under a patched canvas almost as dirty as the deck itself. Roughly midships was
her open bridge though someone had, at one time,
erected what might be called a wheelhouse to protect
the watchkeepers—before blast had restored most of it
to its original spartan air-conditioning. A lower well
deck forward surrounded number one hold, with huge
rust-eroded freeing ports along the scuppers, rising to
a tiny foc'slehead with part of a shot-away windlass
still clinging grimly to the scarred deck. The battered,
buffeted sheer of the stem was as vertical and uncompromising as a surveyor's plumb line.

Every square inch of that maritime caricature was
either rusty or just ordinary filthy. The up-and-down
wooden masts had shakes in them you could have
stuffed a cabin boy's fingers into, while what laughingly passed as wire stays had so many broken strands
they looked more like petrified angora wool supports.
There was a hole roughly the size of a four-inch Naval
shell right through the funnel, and it was about the
only neatly finished thing on the whole bloody boat.

Apart from one other item, the most grotesquely
irrelevant part of that hideous steamship . . . because
right at the head of the gangway, facing you proudly

as you came aboard, was the tiddliest, smartest name-plate I had ever seen in my life. Gleaming, hand-cut brass letters mounted on a bright-varnished mahogany board which would have given the captain of a battle-ship a recurring twinge of pride, announced with utter shamelessness that you were now stepping foot on— God help all those who sail in her—the Steamship *Charon*.

Named, with the ultimate in pure irony I thought, after that bluejacket of legend who used to ferry the souls of The Damned across the Styx.

To Hades.

Reluctantly I dragged my eyes away from her and walked towards the brow between the two ships. The armed guard, a couple of bored-looking ratings, came to attention as I approached and, after a token glance at my ID card, allowed me to cross over with a sort of 'Fools rush in where Angels fear to tread' shrug at each other.

I hesitated in front of that beautiful nameplate, took a deep breath, and stepped on to the skin of grime which concealed the *Charon*'s deck I did hope she wouldn't sink before I could leave her again.

Almost immediately a door in the accommodation opened a crack to reveal a suspicious eye. I stared penetratingly back at it and, after a moment, the door swung wider and a man stepped over the coaming. He was big, stocky and weatherbeaten as a clipper's figurehead, with hands like brown soup plates and an aggressively jutting jaw. There was something else there, though—a competent wariness, almost an im-pression of dignified resentment at my presence aboard—and I wondered if the crew of the *Charon* were in any way impressed with the gravity of the situation they found themselves in.

I had an uneasy feeling that at least one of them wasn't. Which didn't make the job I had to do any easier.

I said shortly: 'Captain Trapp. I'd like to see him.'

The eyes inspected me calmly and I started to feel an uncomfortable awareness of other eyes, equally scrutinising, peering at me from secret parts of the ship. There was a distinct impression, somehow, of being in another world. A world where sudden violence and intrigue went hand in hand with an odd sort of rebellious, exiled camaraderie.

A world where I and other conventional people like me just didn't belong.

The man shrugged and, quite deliberately, turned away. 'He won't want to see you though. Not with you bein' Navy, an' all.'

I jammed my foot in the door before it finally closed and decided there and then to adopt the more informal approach of the Merchant Service. 'Then he'd better change his bloody mind, Mister,' I snarled grimly. 'Before I have this gash bucket decontaminated by the port health authorities. With a fucking match!'

Abruptly the figure in the doorway stopped dead and I could see the suppressed tension in the set of the broad shoulders. Ever so slowly he swivelled to face me again.

Trying to control the nervous tic at the corner of my mouth I reflected bleakly, 'Now you've *really* asked for trouble, dimwit . . .' but I still shoved my face against his, gripped the rim of my steel helmet firmly to deploy as a surprise back-hand if needed, and added with all the viciousness I could muster, 'So get the captain down here, sailor. On the double!'

Just for a moment the big man's eyes stared into mine with an expression of . . . could it possibly have been *disapproval,* for heaven's sake? From any seaman shipped aboard a degraded, down-at-heel hulk like that? And then, with distinct relief, I detected a glimmer of surprise—or was it a grudging respect, even?

'You're yelling at him, Mister. I'm Trapp . . .' He glanced briefly at the intertwined braid on my epaulettes, '. . . an' maybe I ought to tell you, if you wasn't a reservist, I'd've heaved you right back over the side. Tiddley Navy rig an' all.'

I snapped succinctly: 'If I wasn't a reservist, Trapp, I'd be aboard a proper ship right now. Not playing errand boy to a contraband-running copy of a Port Said clap barge!'

I saw the big hands clench involuntarily, but he still spoke with icy control. 'I'm non-aligned. This is a neutral ship . . .'

'She's a contraband-runner. Under close arrest in an Allied port in time of war. And that means you're in trouble, Captain. Right up to your non-aligned neck.'

We stood there, toe to toe, glaring at each other with an almost comical ferocity. I don't think either of us heard the rising wail of the sirens as Valletta tucked its head down for yet another alert. In fact I was only dimly aware of the guns opening up from the southern end of the island when Trapp spoke again.

'You run back an' tell your bosses they got no authority to hold this ship. Tell 'em it's the Royal Navy that's in trouble, Mister—opening fire on a neutral freighter, killing my first mate an' another poor sod who was only doing his job . . . boarding me and uttering threats . . .'

Out of the corner of my eye I noticed the crew of the ack-ack gun on the wharf erupt into frantic activity. A voice roared, 'Raid alarm . . . Take post!' while the Layers swung easily into their seats, hands already reaching for elevating and traversing dials.

Trapp ignored them all, just as though they didn't exist. As if the *Luftwaffe* didn't either, for that matter.

'. . . this ship flies no Flag, belongs to no country, Mister. She's a free trader an' so am I. In business. Buying and selling. Just now I got a cargo of whisky, Dutchman's gin, coffee and eighty-five cases assorted tinned fish—an' if the Navy's so bloody keen to do something for the poor bastards living on this island then they can dip into the pockets an' *pay* me for it . . . not shanghai it like grey funnel bloody pirates . . .'

From the wharf. 'Hostile . . . forty plus . . . low level, bearing wun niner fife!'

I said coldly: 'You're a parasite, Trapp. An exploiter. You've made a business out of war, a . . .

a profit. Only now your luck's run out. The war's caught up with you and your drop-out crew, and this bloody atrocious junk heap you call a ship.'

A sudden growl of aero engines from seaward. I saw Trapp's eyes just at that moment though, and hesitated. There was outrage there, and plain greed, but there was something else too . . . an earnestness, a sort of fanatical belief that he was right and the rest of the lousy world was out of step.

The growl from the sea became a de-synchronised drone, increasing in intensity by the split-second. I became aware of the two ratings of the armed guard running for the shelter of the burnt-out accommodation inboard of us while crisp, controlled commands snapped clearly from the gun pit nearby.

'Single Messerschmitt Wun Wun Oh,' from the TI.

The barrel of the 3.7 already swinging downwards and towards the entrance to the harbour. 'On target.'

'Fuse six.'

'Fuse six . . . set.'

I said tightly: 'Time to take cover, Trapp,' then wondered where the hell we could anyway, aboard a tissue paper boat like the *Charon*.

He shook his head, teeth bared in a ferocious, mocking grin.

'It's *your* bloody war . . . *Lieutenant*.'

I started to dive as the roar grew to a thundering howl. One glimpse of the twin-engined bomber blasting towards us across the harbour, so low I could see the prop-wash ripping feathery scuds of spray astern of it, then I was huddling desperately against the angle of the *Charon*'s bulwarks, fingers splaying into the mess of rusted filth which filled the scuppers.

But I'd been through it all before. They took exactly three minutes to sink my last ship.

The blood-curdling shriek of Daimler-Benz at three hundred and sixty miles an hour . . . More planes— dozens of bloody aeroplanes high in the sky above me, all mixed up with the puff-ball bursts of flak . . . every gun on Malta loosing off in an ear-shattering concussion . . .

From the wharf. Hugely . . . *'FIRE!'*

Crash!

A second aircraft banking low and hard across my vision, smoke streaming from its starboard engine . . . the shocking screech of Stukas peeling off over the centre of Valletta . . . an enormous explosion from somewhere inland. *Crash!* And again, the 3.7 next door . . . CRASH!

I felt the prop-wash battering down on me as that first Messerschmitt slammed in over *Charon*'s bulwarks, bomb doors gaping like an eviscerated belly and the twin underslung cannons in her nose winking little spurts of yellow light . . . holes appearing ridiculously in wavering parallel lines across the scaling deck . . . Trapp! Where in God's name was *Trapp* . . . ?

I rolled over, face upwards—and found him. Still standing, he was shaking his fist at the already departing aircraft while, even above the pandemonium, I made out the foulest lungful of international oaths any man could ever muster.

Slowly I climbed to my feet. The guns were still firing and the island shuddered to the detonations of German bombs, but after seeing Trapp's reaction to the rest of the world's idea of civilisation I didn't care anymore. Not now. Because I suddenly remembered why I had been sent aboard the *Charon* in the first place. Aboard the one ship which didn't want to have anything to do with unprofitable things. Like defending liberty, and country.

I started to laugh. Trapp turned towards me with a face as black as thunder and, though I knew he'd never see the joke or the irony of it, I couldn't keep the edge of mockery out of my voice.

'Oh, but it is your war now, Trapp. Yours and the *Charon*'s. That's what I was sent to tell you.

'. . . 'cause you've been drafted, Trapp. Called up. You and your ship and the crowd of misfits you call a crew. Called up . . . to fight for your country. Without even a profit in sight.'

Chapter Two

'Well?'

'He says you can go and fu . . .'

I stopped, remembering where I was. 'Trapp won't do it, Sir. Claims that, even though he is British by birth, he's still over the age for compulsory military service.'

The admiral didn't look particularly surprised. Only sardonic. 'No latent twinge of patriotism then? As you say, the man *is* British.'

I muttered, 'Hah.' Bitterly.

'And did you tell him what we want him to do for us? The somewhat . . . ah . . . unorthodox employment we have in mind?'

I couldn't keep the irritation out of my voice. 'No, Sir. Largely for security reasons. Trapp is obsessed by the profit motive and I wouldn't chance his selling the whole idea to Jerrie . . . not that they'd ever be crazy enough to believe him, mind you.'

'You think the proposition that outrageous, Miller?'

'I think it's the most ridic . . .' Hesitating I stared pointedly at the braid on his arm but he only raised a quizzical eyebrow so I continued heavily, 'I suggest that the operation—even using the best man available, along with a specialist ship—is at best suicidal . . . To send Trapp over there, and that grotesque fugitive from the breaker's yard which he calls a boat, seems ill-conceived, utterly impractical and doomed to failure. Sir.'

He didn't look at all worried. Just pleased. 'Then we can only trust that our friends on the German Naval Staff will dismiss the possibility with equally logical contempt.'

I shrugged. 'Trapp's already dismissed it. Even after I suggested that his only alternative was jail, as a suspected enemy agent . . .'

My voice trailed away doubtfully. For some reason the admiral still seemed inordinately pleased with himself—a reason which I, at that moment, apparently wasn't going to be invited to share. He caught me looking uncertain and smiled encouragingly.

'You don't think it worries him. The prospect of detention?'

'The intractable bast . . . He actually challenged us to jail him, dammit! Said complacently that he'll sue the Admiralty for illegal detention as soon as the war's over. Through the Swiss courts or somewhere. Reckons his damages'll exceed anything the *Charon* can earn in twenty years.'

I didn't think the admiral was too concerned, though. He just seemed to stare reflectively into space for a moment until, glancing up abruptly, he snapped briskly, 'Right, Miller! Get down to the dockyard. I've told them to prepare rough drawings so they'll be expecting you—but you'll still need to push 'em hard. Bloody hard, in fact.'

Determinedly I stood my ground. As far as I was concerned I'd already spent more than enough time on a lost cause. Especially one as hopeless as that one. 'Sir . . . I must request that you send me back to sea. I'm neither an admin bloke nor a planner, and PEDESTAL's still got a long way to steam . . .'

He stood up and placed his hand on my shoulder reassuringly. 'Get this *Charon* operation off the ground and I'll personally ensure that you get a sea-going appointment, Miller. You have my word on that.'

I looked at him gratefully, feeling the first glow of hope for four months. Until I had a vision of an utterly unrepentant and unyielding master mariner jumping up and down with self-righteous rage when even a whole aeroplane was shooting at him, let alone a junior Naval officer, and my heart sank.

Bitterly I muttered, 'There's still Trapp, Sir. I haven't a hope of changing his mind . . .'

The hand patted my shoulder encouragingly. 'For-

get him. You just see that the *Charon* is ready in all
respects for the job we propose, and her crew made
up from the Fleet.'

'And Trapp?'

He rubbed his hands in an almost anticipatory gesture. 'Perhaps you should leave the captain to me. Eh,
Lieutenant?'

I nodded trustingly. Happily. Personally I didn't
give a damn anymore, as long as Trapp was taken out
of my hair.

After all—I did have his word on the one thing *I*
wanted.

And he *was* an admiral. And therefore, a gentleman.

I didn't spend very long at the dockyard.

We all stood round a table gazing in stunned silence
at the rough drawings of the *Charon*. Her lines and
sections, on paper, looked even more like the jotting-
pad dribblings of a mentally deranged cartoonist. What
we proposed to do to her lifted the whole thing straight
to the heights of total insanity.

The Chief Naval Architect shuffled in embarrassment. 'I'm sorry, gentlemen, but the ship really *does*
look like that. My assistant checked the measurements
personally. Three times.'

I indicated the red overlay numbly. He shrugged
apologetically. 'The proposed modifications and . . .
ah . . . additions. The admiral was quite adamant
about his requirements.'

Someone asked in a wondering tone: 'But will she
be able to float, with all that in her?'

The Chief Naval Architect closed his eyes for a
moment. 'Not even if we filled the rest with cork shav-
ings. But, according to our calculations, she can't
anyway . . . theoretically she never could, in fact.'

The Chief Naval Constructor sniffed irritably. 'Of
course the whole damn thing's out of the question!'

The Commander (Supply) muttered: 'Can't be
done. None of it.'

The man from Ordnance smiled pityingly. 'She'll
sink first time we run trials. It's utterly impossible.'

I said firmly: 'When will she be ready then?'

'Week on Thursday do you?'

'Thank you very much, gentlemen.'

I left. Closing the door quietly behind me.

'You want volunteers for special service,' the lieutenant from Appointments and Personnel echoed incredulously. 'Special service aboard *that?*'

'The admiral does, Micky,' I corrected. 'Personally I couldn't care less if you have to draft them with an armed guard. It's quantity I need to get me off the hook, not quality.'

I did feel a slight twinge of conscience about being so callous but, on the other hand, I reckoned that—as the *Charon*'s future crew weren't likely to survive more than a few days after she sailed—it would be bad planning to allow the cream of the Navy to go down with her.

Micky shrugged. 'Course you realise you'll finish up with all the hard case throw-outs that every first lieutenant in the Med Fleet's been praying to get killed in action . . . or even in a bar brawl down the Gut, for that matter, an' the hell with his ship's good name.'

I smiled a superior smile. I had an admiral on my side. 'Not me, chum. Soon as this lot's organised I'll be back helping you find me a hand-picked berth aboard a proper ship.'

I opened the door and winked at him. 'Like a bit of advice, would you. Straight from the horse's mouth?'

He stared at me gloomily. And he only knew part of the fairy story.

'Whoever you select for the job as number one of the *Charon*,' I said sincerely, 'make sure an' pick someone you *really* hate.'

It was only when I got outside that the thought did occur to me.

I mean—nobody could hate anybody. Not *that* much.

'I'm a tactician, not a blasted magician, Miller.'

The Staff Planning Officer glared balefully at me and I tried to look sympathetic. 'Sir, I realise it's a pretty rotten problem. But the admiral seemed to be rather keen . . .'

'The admiral *seems* to be losing his grip, dammit!'

I turned to go. 'Yessir. Perhaps I should pass on your opinion and see if he won't . . .'

'Come back here, Miller.'

The SPO's voice was like a whiplash. I had the distinct impression that I'd lost another friend. 'Sir?'

He gave me a forced, man-to-man smile and almost managed to prevent the hatred showing in his eyes. 'It's merely that we're a little pushed for time just now . . . ah . . . Lieutenant. Seems a pity to organise something in detail which . . . well . . . which appears to be . . . ah . . .'

'Doomed, Sir?' I suggested helpfully. 'Long before any of those plans you'll have to work out can even be implemented.'

I could see a little vein in the side of his head beginning to pound.

'Yes, dammit!'

'But I can still tell the admiral that you *will* go ahead and prep . . .'

'Out, Miller. Get OUT!'

I closed the door gently behind me and leant against it, feeling waves of blissful relief sweeping over me. So I'd almost made it off this bloody awful prison of an island at last. Now all I had to do was to keep pushing the work ahead, which wasn't going to be difficult seeing I had the full weight of an admiral's whim as a lever. Hell, the old boy had even agreed to handle the recalcitrant Captain Trapp for me.

I was as good as back at sea, where I wanted to be. And where my encounter with the SS *Charon* would only be a fading, slightly disbelieving memory of a soon-to-be-erased nightmare.

But then I started to tremble for no apparent reason. It was a weird sensation, almost as though I'd felt the icy touch of a yet unrevealed but hideous spectre.

Almost as if I, too, was one of those Damned Souls. Awaiting passage across the River Styx—to Hades.

I felt it again, that unnatural shiver. As soon as I set eyes on the *Charon* for the second time.

It might have been the way she lay there so forlornly, moored alongside that derelict, burnt-out wreck so that even the low evening sunlight was barred from her shabby, neglected decks. Two ships huddled together in the aftermath of battle. One already dead, the other pathetically awaiting the enemy's *coup de grâce*.

I noticed that the armed guard had been increased since I'd left earlier. As I approached the brow a gunnery branch petty officer stepped forward and saluted. A further ten ratings were spaced along the wreck's outboard alleyway for the length of the *Charon*. They were all big seamen, they all gripped their rifles with grim self-control, and every last one of them looked as if he'd dearly love to throw his weapon away and sort out a certain ship's crew in the more traditional bluejacket manner—with fists, boots, bottles and fire hose nozzles.

Across the space between the two dilapidated vessels, and roughly man for man with the Navy, lounged the crew of the SS *Charon*—and, whatever I'd previously expected, I found out then that they were ten times more outlandish and outrageous. Without any doubt Trapp had gathered together, in one ship, the scruffiest, most cosmopolitan, most insalubrious crowd of piratical hooligans ever to be dredged from the gutters of the international slums.

My opinion of Trapp took a remarkable uplift. Not because of his taste in ships' companies but because of his obviously unmatchable ability to survive even among such a homicidally-inclined rabble, never mind weld them, however sketchily, into any semblance of a crew.

The PO said tightly, 'Can I help you Sir?'

I thought wishfully: 'Yes please. You could tow the bastards out an' sink them . . .' then I hesitated. It had only just occurred to me that I didn't even know why I *had* come, in actual fact. What incomprehensible reasoning had steered me in the direction of the problem ship I'd just spent all day trying to get rid of?

There was something about her, some perverted fascination, which held a ghoulish attraction for me—or
was it in the strangely obscure, buccaneering Captain
Trapp himself . . . ?

I waved my ID card. 'I'm Miller. Attached to Flag
Officer's Staff.'

'Yessir. I know about you.'

He gave the impression of a tolerant man who'd
had just about enough. I jerked my head at the old
freighter. 'Trouble with the natives, PO?'

'They're mad. The whole bloody pack of 'em. Lu-
natics—jeerin', sneerin', throwin' stuff. And we got
express orders not to go aboard . . .' His eyes bright-
ened suddenly, as if with a vision of delights unattain-
able. 'Maybe one of them'll try an' make a run for it
ashore soon, though. I'd like that. Jeeze but I'd like
that a lot. Especially that Scotch git—that one there.
The one they call Gorbals Wullie . . .'

Just as he spoke I saw the little man with the cloth
cap and the weedy, undernourished frame climb
lithely up the rusted ladder to the *Charon*'s shelter
deck and flourish two fingers directly towards me.
'Hey youse . . . officer lad wi' the fancy suit. C'mon
ower an' let's see if you're such a hard man wi'out
yon heavy mob ahent ye!'

I sensed the PO's fists clench longingly but I just
stared stonily back across the gap between the ships.
'I see what you mean; only hasn't Captain Trapp tried
to stop them, or doesn't he give a damn either?'

The jeering Gorbals accent continued scathingly:
'C'mon, Jessie. C'mon ower an' gie's a square go at
ye, Nancy boy!'

A leading seaman next to us said pleadingly: 'Let
me go, Sir. Please? Jus' two minutes, that's all I ask.'

The PO Gunner snapped: 'Keep your feet on this
deck, laddie . . . Trapp's not here, Sir. Master-at-
Arms took him ashore half an hour ago. That's when
the others started gettin' stroppy.'

The little man in the oil-black cap started to prance
about, waving his fists hysterically. 'Poofy officer . . .
Poofy officer . . .'

I noticed the Army gunners watching interestedly

from the gun pit of the 3.7 on the wharf while the rest of the *Charon*'s crew seemed to give up their own particular running battle with the armed guard, starting to drift untidily aft towards the gangway. I thought wearily: 'Oh Christ but I'm either going to have to fight that Wullie idiot, or bloody shoot him . . .'

'. . . Poofy officer . . . Poofy officer . . .'

And then it finally happened. The *Charon* being what she was, it just had to happen.

When the little man's arm jerked suddenly and something glinted in the fading sunlight as it curved towards me. I heard the smash of glass as the bottle shattered against the steel bulkhead behind me, and felt the sharp slice of fragments spearing into my cheek.

It also proved the last straw laid on a very long suffering camel.

As the leading hand roared an uncontrollable *'Bastards!'* and started off at a berserk gallop while, beside me, the PO's voice snapped an unheeded, 'Stand *fast* there, you lot . . . !' before it was submerged in the clatter of joyously discarded rifles as the armed guard finally became unarmed and surged as one man towards the brow between the two vessels.

I felt the blood trickling down my collar and thought miserably, 'This *bloody* rotten disease of a ship . . . ,' then I caught sight of the expression on the petty officer's face as his disciplined world and career suddenly collapsed in ruins about him. And then he too started to grin a huge, uncaring grin of utter happiness while unbuckling his webbing revolver holster with urgent fingers.

'I already lost my PO's rate twice, Sir,' he chortled like an anticipatory bear, 'an' bugger me if neither of them times was half as bloody worthwhile as this is goin' to be . . .'

I heard his polite, 'Excuse me if you please, Sir,' hanging in the air before, roaring with delight, he finally disappeared into the centre of the melee at the head of the brow. Then the Artillerymen on the wharf started to cheer and jump up and down with the sheer hysteria of it all while, aboard every ship in Malta's

Grand Harbour, little knots of war-weary sailors gathered in whistling groups hanging over gun pits and bridge wings and outboard rails.

Taking my blood-spattered cap off I placed my steel helmet and gas mask ever so carefully beside it. Then I hitched my shorts up and turned back to scrutinise the cursing, struggling, grunting riot of bodies with great discernment. But I was looking, quite specifically, for an oil-stained cloth cap with a voluble, irrepressible little bastard of a Scotsman underneath it.

Until a somewhat harassed-looking able seaman wearing the remains of a Royal Navy collar and a shred of blue jumper came hurtling backwards out of the scrum, while a wiry figure shrieking weird Highland oaths followed to pancake aboard him in a magnificent airborne glide, fists already pummelling like steam pistons.

Whereupon I murmured: 'Sorry, Your Majesty. About my being an officer.'

A bit guiltily, mind you.

Before I, too, started to run . . .

Chapter Three

The pretty third officer Wren hesitated before she opened the Ops Room door and looked at me curiously. 'I know I shouldn't ask,' she said awkwardly, 'but has the PEDESTAL convoy arrived already?'

I leant against the wall gratefully. It was a long corridor and I didn't feel terribly energetic any more. I did feel a bit hurt, though, that she hadn't recognised me from my last visit to the admiral—or maybe the blood and the cut eyebrow and the torn-away epaulettes had something to do with that.

'Not as far as I know,' I muttered cautiously. 'What makes you think so?'

Her wide, heartwarmingly attractive eyes flickered uncertainly from the graze on my knee to the rapidly darkening bruise on my left cheekbone. 'I wondered. You know—if the Germans had been . . . It's just that you look so, well, battle-weary. And miserable.'

I reflected hopefully: Keep it going, Miller boy. Nothing like sympathy to undermine a girl's moral code . . . 'Actually I *have* had rather a bad time of it, dear,' I whispered brokenly. 'But as long as there's a war on I've got to keep goi . . . !'

'Yeah, well you jus' keep on going through that door, then, Sir!'

I turned and met the somewhat less heartwarming stare of the Regulating CPO in charge of the shore patrol. 'The admiral 'specially said you was to see him right away,' the chief growled, 'and I likes to see that the admiral gets what he wants, Sir. Maybe you should, too—an' make the court martial easier on yourself, if you see what I mean.'

I gathered from the sudden flinty comprehension in

37

my Wren's eyes that brief romance had once again deserted the corridors of Naval Headquarters, Malta, so I just said gloomily, 'How's the final tally for the armed guard, Chief PO?'

He stared back at me accusingly. 'Three in base hospital—one with internal injuries, one fractured skull an' one razor slashed—four more with minor things like fractures an' concussion . . .' Abruptly the granite features blossomed into an unexpected, conspiratorial grin . . . 'Mind you, see what they did to them other fellers. And did you kick the hell out've that little Scotchman or didn't you, Sir. The wee yobbo won't get a spoonful've porridge into that mouth of 'is f'r a week at least.'

My late love clapped a horrified hand to her lips and let out a muffled *'Oh!'* while I toyed with the handle of the admiral's door, searching desperately to postpone the inevitable.

'And what about the guard commander, Chief?'

'Crocker?' He grinned again. 'Bloody but unbowed. Third time unlucky for Arthur, though. I'd reckon twelve months' detention an' loss of rate after this shambles . . . You better go in, Sir. We'll hang on out here.'

I nodded heavily. I did hope Petty Officer Crocker had enjoyed himself. I hoped that a lot. Because it looked as though it would have to last him a long time. But one thing seemed certain—that whatever else happened to me I, like PO Crocker, was undoubtedly finished for ever with Captain non-aligned Trapp and the *Charon.*

And that blessed release, in itself, was worth a great deal of suffering.

I took a deep breath, gave my Wren a last wistful little smile, and turned the handle.

'Well, Miller?'

The admiral looked me up and down distastefully while I stayed to rigid attention and tried hard to swallow. 'Sir, I realise I've been an embarrassment and can only suggest that, if you send me back to sea immediately, it might save a lot of troub . . .'

'What the *hell* are you mumbling about?'

I ground to a halt and blinked at him doubtfully.

'Sir?'

He snapped irritably, '*Charon*. Any delays likely there?'

I said hesitantly, 'Not from the dockyard at least. No, Sir.'

He seemed to relax and I began to feel uncomfortable. This reception was the last thing I'd anticipated.

Hurriedly I added, 'There was a bit of trouble with Trapp's crew. But I don't doubt someone's told you *that* much already.'

I suppose, on reflection, that I may have sounded a little aggressive. But the admiral's response still shook me rigid by its savagery.

'They did. And you can put a stopper on that damned self-righteous resentment, Miller . . . that "trouble" of yours was nothing short of a full-scale riot. Three ratings were seriously injured, Trapp now has another shot in his anti-Navy locker and, perhaps more regrettable than anything else, a first class Gunnery Petty Officer is now under close arrest . . .'

I stared at him, aware of the blood draining from my face as, sitting back in the chair again, he gazed at me bleakly for several moments before adding, 'And you will carry the responsibility for that disgraceful incident, Miller . . . but in the Navy's time. Not yours.'

I didn't answer. I couldn't trust myself to. I could only stare at him in bitter defiance, knowing full well that I was in the wrong but equally unprepared to accept that he—as originator of the whole rotten mess— was in the right.

Maybe it was then that I first started to understand just a little of why Edward Trapp had become the man he was and, in a reckless sort of way, to feel a closer affinity towards him. A mutual resentment against those impersonal pressures of the establishment which seemed, in their turn, to generate a frustrated desire to strike back at conventional values.

The admiral bent abruptly and stabbed the intercom on his desk. 'Send Trapp in. Right away.'

He glanced up at me, and there might have been

tentative sympathy in the grey eyes, only I wasn't prepared to see it. So he shrugged imperceptibly, then
said: 'I've kept him waiting for over three hours. I
don't suppose he'll like me very much either.'

Then the door slammed open, and Trapp strode in.
Or rather, steamed in. Like an attacking battle-
cruiser.

'You in charge, are you?'

'More or less. Of Naval matters, anyway.' Smooth as
silk.

'In that case I want . . .' Trapp caught sight of me
and hesitated, eyeing my dishevelled rig. Then he
smiled sourly. 'I heard you was back aboard *Charon*,
Mister. Now I know you was.'

Viciously I reflected, 'So does that Wullie bastard,'
but just glared back at him frostily without answering.
Undeterred he returned to the attack.

'I demand legal representation. I'm goin' to sue you.
And I want repairs effected on my ship . . . or d'you
deny she was fired on by the Navy while going about her
lawful business?'

The admiral raised a quizzical eyebrow. 'She was
fired on, yes. We had no friendly ships expected in that
area, so the captain of that destroyer was perfectly
entitled to shoot.'

'Right at me? International law demands a shot
across the bows, Mister . . . Not into 'em.'

'Not in a war situation—and would you have
stopped, anyway. Unless you'd suffered a certain
amount of damage?'

Trapp hesitated again, then grinned unashamedly.
'No.'

The admiral inclined his head fractionally, acknowl-
edging Trapp's rather unexpected outspokenness. I
wasn't quite as impressed, though. 'If we're going to be
all that candid, Trapp, let's cut out any pretence about
your being engaged on "Lawful business", right?'

He turned, but kept the grin switched on. 'The international courts may not agree with you, Mister.'

From behind us the admiral's tone, when it came,
was the purr of a cat playing a mouse. 'Oh, but I rather
think they will, Lieutenant Commander.'

Perhaps because of my irritation I didn't absorb the full content of what he'd said. But it didn't register with Trapp either. Not for a moment.

'Then we'll have to see, won't we? 'Cause right now I'm lodging an action against your Admiralty—not only for compensation over the damage my ship received when illegally fired upon, but also f'r loss of profits while under wrongful arres . . .'

And, all of a sudden, Trapp ground to a halt and blinked. Then he slowly swivelled to face the admiral. Slowly, and almost nervously.

'*What* did you say, mister?'

'I said "I rather think the courts will". Agree with us, that is.'

Trapp shook his head warily. 'I mean the other bit— the lieutenant commander bit, an' you know it.'

I watched the admiral in fascination. Like a rabbit watches a snake. Only I had the funny feeling that, this time, Trapp was elected Bunny. The admiral nearly managed to look surprised.

'But . . . ah . . . surely you can't have forgotten, my dear chap.'

For the first time I saw Trapp looking bewildered. It was a thoroughly satisfying experience, even though I couldn't understand what the admiral was driving at any more than Trapp did. Or did he . . . ?

'Forgotten . . . what?'

'That you, in common with Miller here and myself, are a Naval Officer. And have been for the past twenty-odd years . . .'

I found myself staring in incomprehension as the admiral leaned forward for the *coup de grâce*. He was gentle with it. I think he realised, from the shock on Trapp's features, that he would have to be.

'Do you remember the events which took place after you were repatriated. During November, 1918?'

Trapp said worriedly, 'It's a lot of bloody nonsense . . .'

'Do you remember?'

'AYE . . . I took a ship the next day. Outward f'r the Far East. So what about it, eh?'

'You didn't leave much time to settle your affairs in Britain, did you?'

Trapp shrugged impatiently. 'Time? For what, Mister?'

The admiral played with a sheet of signal paper before him. 'To attend your demobilisation centre, for instance?'

Trapp grinned sourly. 'Demob . . . Christ but I'd had enough, Mister. Enough of the Navy, an' little men with supercilious faces . . .'

Then he stopped speaking abruptly. And both he and I stared in slowly dawning realisation at the man before us, who nodded almost apologetically.

'Exactly. And because you never offered your resignation, your name was never removed from the Royal Navy's List of Reserve Officers . . . Your promotion, over the years, has been entirely automatic—Lieutenant Commander Trapp.'

Trapp said, 'Christ!' again. Dead shattered.

I couldn't help it. I started to laugh. Deep down inside me.

I was still trying to control myself when the armed shore patrol came in to take him away, still refusing energetically to have anything whatsoever to do with the Royal bloody Navy.

His bloody Navy too, now.

Lieutenant Commander Edward Trapp's, I mean.

The admiral didn't send for Trapp again until the following afternoon. While I hadn't entirely been able to shake off my resentment at carrying the can for the *Charon* riot, I had to admit that I found I could live with it a lot more placidly. My troubles, compared to the abruptly-drafted Lieutenant Commander Trapp's, would fade to minor irritations the moment I was granted my release from Malta.

Trapp's were just about to start. When he found out *why* the Royal Navy had so persuasively recalled him to Active Service.

Very active Service, I reflected guiltily. Until the inevitable caught up with him. And to do that—as far as the *Charon* was concerned—the inevitable wouldn't even have to travel very fast.

Certainly not as fast as the admiral was going to have to talk—to persuade Trapp, even with the weight of King's Regulations behind him, to sail away and commit suicide.

And then the door opened and Trapp slouched in. Looking very bleak indeed. Though it didn't seem proper, somehow—not for a Naval officer still to be dressed in faded denims, a stained reefer on which the gold rings had now deteriorated to a matt, salt-eroded green, and filthy plimsolls laced with strands of cod-line.

The admiral murmured politely. 'Good afternoon, Commander.'

I noticed he'd commenced with the abbreviated form of address inferring that, whatever else was discussed, it wouldn't be whether or not Trapp *was* a member of His Majesty's Armed Forces. And to my surprise Trapp appeared to have resigned himself to his new role with remarkable aplomb.

'Afternoon, Mister.'

'Sir,' the admiral prompted gently. 'I'm afraid you aren't allowed to call me "Mister" any more, Commander.'

Trapp hesitated a moment then shrugged philosophically. 'Aye, aye . . . Sir.'

'Changed days, eh, Trapp?' I couldn't resist the dig, not after the way he'd shown his contempt for me and my uniform the first time I met him. Slowly he turned, and looked me up and down with cold precision.

'*Sir*,' he snapped. 'I got two an' a half stripes that says ordinary lieutenants call *me* "Sir." D'you read me loud an' clear—Lieutenant?'

I caught sight of the expression on the admiral's face. There was an unmistakable warning behind the half-concealed smile. 'Loud and clear . . .' I muttered bitterly. 'Sir.'

'Oh, that's nice,' Trapp said, looking pleased as a cat with two tails. 'It makes it all seem worthwhile, some'ow.'

'Just you wait until you've heard the rest of it,' I thought viciously. 'Then see if you still think so . . .'

'Talking about things bein' worthwhile,' Trapp continued smoothly, turning back to the admiral. 'How long did you say I've been on the Navy List . . . ah . . . Sir?'

'Since nineteen eightee . . .' The admiral frowned abruptly then, without any malice whatever, started to smile broadly. 'Trapp,' he barked, 'You are a calculating rogue, dammit. An avaricious, profiteering scoundrel!'

Trapp grinned back quite delightedly, 'Yessir. An' I reckon the Navy owes me twenty-four years' back pay, bounty and allowances on the strength of it.'

But I might have guessed Trapp wouldn't take long to figure that out. All there was left to do now was to break the news to him about the particular way in which he'd have to earn his right to collect.

OPERATION STYX, the admiral had christened it. I reflected, with great satisfaction, that it was a hell of an appropriate name. Considering where it was virtually guaranteed to end.

'I want you and your ship to do a job for me,' the admiral began smoothly.

'How much?' Trapp said, then added hurriedly. 'Charter fees for the *Charon,* I mean . . . seein' she wasn't even in the Navy in 1918.'

'Enough. A reasonable daily rate, I promise you.'

'*Daily* . . . ?'

It was the admiral's turn to hurry. 'The background to the proposal first, I think. And then we can go into more detail, Commander.'

'She's a good ship. Expensive to run, though. The maintenance alone costs a few bob, remember.'

I thought, '*Hah.*' Savagely. Personally I'd seen more maintenance carried out aboard a total loss on the Goodwin Sands; however the admiral ignored Trapp's sales pitch and continued without comment.

'The present military situation in North Africa is, from the Allied point of view, extremely grave. At the moment the British 8th Army is barely holding Rommel along a line . . .' he allowed his finger to hover over the plot, then stabbed decisively, '. . . here. Between Tel El Eisa and El Alamein. D'you follow?'

'We believe,' I supplemented after a nod from the admiral, 'That the Afrika Korps are preparing right now for a final offensive. A push right through towards Alexandria and the Delta areas.'

Trapp frowned. 'That's Army tactics, isn't it? How do they involve the Navy, here in Malta?'

'Because Rommel depends, like every other military machine, on his supply lines, Commander. And this island is virtually the only Allied territory in the Mediterranean from which we can still operate against them. Both the RAF anti-shipping strike aircraft and the 10th Submarine Flotilla depend on Malta for a base.'

'Which makes this little bit of rock pretty vital, eh?'

The admiral looked at him and said quietly, 'If Malta falls, Commander, then we have lost our keystone to the defence of the Middle East.'

I didn't say anything. There didn't seem very much to add. Finally Trapp gave a faint shrug. 'So what do you want me to do? And the *Charon?* Bring stuff in . . . but legal, this time?'

'*Charon*'s too small. There wouldn't be enough . . . and we need fuel most desperately right now. We, all of us, can only survive if even one tanker can fight its way through within the next few days.'

Trapp's eyes were hard. 'And is there one coming?'

I had a chilling vision of aircraft peeling off to the attack, legion upon legion of black, screaming dive-bombers hurtling seawards above a tiny, spitting group of ships while, right in the middle, one ship in particular steamed doggedly on through climbing, cordite-stained columns of atomised spray. And of men falling at their stations aboard her before other men dragged them aside and took over their ports. And when *those* men were hit, then other volunteers were transferred from the wheeling escorts . . .

'Yes, Commander!' I muttered, gazing at the PEDESTAL legends on the wall and seeing one in particular. '. . . there *is* one tanker coming. Very soon.'

The seaman in the dishevelled rig frowned momentarily. 'Then how *do* we fit in? Me an' the *Charon?*'

'While Malta still holds,' the admiral said, 'we must take every opportunity to use it as a base for attacking the enemy supply route to the Middle East theatre . . . And you and your ship, Commander, could very well provide one of those opportunities.'

This time Trapp really looked mystified. The admiral nodded meaningfully at me and I took a deep breath. 'You're to work on your own. Hitting those same supply lines of Rommel's. But operating close inshore to the North African coast . . . where it's too shallow for submarine penetration.'

Trapp stared hard at us, as if anxious to see the joke as well, then he started to grin doubtfully. 'Me? And the old *Charon* . . . ? Acting like we was a *warship,* f'r Chrissakes?'

Only neither of us smiled back and, gradually, his grin faded. 'You have to be kidding, Admiral,' he growled. 'But as a matter of pure interest—d'you intend I should throw rocks, or maybe you want me to ram Jerrie. At all of eight knots.'

'Neither.' The admiral spoke very quietly. 'Because when you leave here, Commander, *Charon* will *be* a warship. A very special kind of warship, I promise you.'

'In fact, a Q-Ship,' I supplemented, watching him closely. 'Still the *Charon* from the outside, an inoffensive little freighter. But inside—behind drop-down plates and canvas screens . . .'

'Guns!' Trapp muttered. 'Concealed bloody guns!'

I grinned tightly. 'Damn right. Only by then it'll be too late to find out. For your target, anyway.'

'. . . anyway, *Sir.*' Trapp reminded me absently.

I stopped grinning. 'Sir,' I snapped. But it was still worth it. To encourage him a bit.

'And supposing they've got guns too. Those targets of yours?'

'They won't have. The big supply ships we can already cope with, using daylight strike aircraft. What you'll be after are the small coastals who are sailing at night and keeping their heads down during the day.

Mostly Arabs and maybe a few Italians . . . Dhows, caiques, clapped-out traders like your . . .'

'Like my *what?*' Trapp grunted ominously.

'Nothing,' I amended hastily, 'Sir.'

'Then why not use a proper warship in the first place?'

'Too obvious. They'd be looking for her after the first action, even if the *Luftwaffe* weren't tracking her before she got there.'

The admiral spread his hands. 'Whereas *Charon* will blend into the local shipping scene. To their pilots you'll just be another of Rommel's supply coasters.'

Trapp shook his head. 'Not to their Navy though. I know that coast, Admiral, and there's a hell of a lot of fast patrol boats operating out there still. Say they board and search me?'

I shrugged. 'You've been taking that chance for fourteen months already. It took the Royal Navy to catch up with you in the end.'

'Yeah. Only in those days I din't have a boat full of artillery—with War Department markings all over it. I might've been able to talk my way out, even then.'

'And this time you won't have to, Commander. You were in the last war. You must remember the Q-Ship drill?'

'Let the enemy think you're abandoning. Part of your crew actually does, in fact. Then, when he thinks the *Charon*'s been left by a panic-stricken crowd and moves in for a closer examination . . .'

'Weapon covers off, hull-plates down, gun crews closed up, already on target and . . .'

'Bang!' Trapp murmured contemplatively. 'Before they can even say *Ich verstehe nicht.*'

'Precisely.' The admiral glanced at me hopefully. 'You have all the advantages of surprise, Commander. And your knowledge of that coast is second to none while, as you appear to have been entirely self-supporting during your recent . . . ah . . . trading venture, presumably the fuel and logistic sources are still available?'

'Aye. But they'll be expensive,' Trapp answered automatically. 'Them Wogs don't have no patriotism—

and they never were daft enough to join the Reserves, ours or anyone else's.'

Which proved, as far as I was concerned, that the Algerians and Libyans had a lot more sense than I gave them credit for. The admiral caught Trapp's drift though.

'Funds will be made available. And naturally we won't anticipate certified receipts . . . within reason.'

Trapp looked at him calculatingly. 'And the *Charon?* I'll have substantial loss of profits to recover. While the capital depreciation's goin' to be terrible on a trip like that.'

'Especially when Jerrie catches up with you,' I reflected cynically, 'and blows the bottom out of Trapp's Wartime Enterprises, Incorporated!'

'Eighty-five pounds per day. Bareboat charter monies payable up to the date when the *Charon* ceases to exist.'

'Sir?' I cautioned quickly.

The admiral coughed. 'Ah, ceases to exist as a unit of His Majesty's Navy, of course.'

'Sir,' Trapp said earnestly, 'for that sort of money you couldn't attack Jerrie with a rowin' boat an' a crossbow. Now f'r one-sixty a day against a twelve month charter—three months in advance an' the rest guaranteed irrespective—I could do you an' His Majesty proud. And *still* be more competitive than a lend-lease destroyer.'

'Commander Trapp,' the admiral murmured gently, 'under the circumstances I have every right to confiscate your ship without any recompense whatsoever . . .'

'Eighty-five it is, Sir,' Trapp interrupted hastily, with the air of a man giving away everything, '. . . plus fuel, vittling an' crew wages—with a six months' guarantee. Even if the charter's cut a bit short.'

'*Three* months!' the admiral stated positively, which was still throwing two and a half months' money away for a start, according to my assessment of Trapp's prospects for survival. 'And as your crew will consist of Naval personnel, naturally we make arrangements for their payment.'

Trapp seemed a little disconcerted. 'You want me to

sail with a proper RN crowd in the fo'c'sle. A mob of tiddley, polish-everythin' bluejackets?'

I remembered Appointments and Personnel's estimate of the types he'd actually get and smiled inwardly. 'Not quite, Sir. But I guarantee every man on your draft will be hand picked from the Fleet by his first lieutenant personally.'

'Well it's still not on.' Trapp shook his head doggedly and I could see the admiral's turn to compromise was at hand. 'I already gotter crew who knows the *Charon*. An' they're an aggressive set of black-hearted bastards anyway. It'll do 'em good to take up fighting professionally, 'stead of just as a hobby.'

I smothered another grin as I saw the look of horror in my admiral's terribly British eye at the vision of . . . well . . . of His Majesty's Armed Merchant Cruiser *Charon* steaming unsteadily and at a snail's pace to war while carrying Trapp's band of bloody-minded cutthroats as her official Admiralty complement. But the admiral also had single-mindedness of purpose.

'Very well,' he agreed tightly. 'But you will still carry Naval gun crews and—most definitely—one of my officers as your number one, both to act as gunnery officer and to advise you on matters of strategy when required. Is that understood, Commander?'

Trapp seemed a bit too pleased with himself for my liking but I was busy right then in feeling a deep and terrible sympathy for whichever ill-fated drop-out from the Admiralty promotion list got lumbered with the first lieutenant's berth aboard *Charon*.

The captain of the Royal Navy's newest warship nodded in a way which suggested the negotiations hadn't quite finished. 'Understood, Admiral. Only, seein' I'll have my old crowd back with me . . .'

'Now what are you getting at, Commander?'

'. . . and the profit's goin' to be trimmed back to the bone . . .'

'*What*, dammit!'

Trapp leaned forward and looked enormously logical. 'I'm thinking of all them Ayrab dhows going to the bottom, Sir. And all the valuable gear that'll go down with 'em. Unless we tries to save it, like . . . sort of a fringe benefit, d'you see? A kind've bonus on results.'

Ever so slowly the admiral rose to his feet and shook his head disbelievingly. When he answered it was quietly, but with great deliberation.

'What you are proposing Trapp, is that I should endorse—on behalf of the British Admiralty—a request from you for permission to sail as . . . as an Elizabethan privateer. Give you a . . . a commission in *piracy,* in fact . . .'

Trapp nodded happily. Shame didn't appear to be one of his weaknesses. Personally I didn't know whether to admire him for his outrageousness or show aloof contempt for his greed—but he *did* have a good point for a man who obviously abhorred waste. About all that stuff going to the bottom . . . The admiral turned to me almost appealingly.

'I don't want to hear another word, Miller. Regarding the *Charon's* activities after she's sailed. Not unless she actually sinks something—preferably one of the enemy.'

'No Sir,' I said.

'Yessir,' Trapp agreed respectfully. 'There's just one more small point, if I might be so bo . . .'

'Then make it, Commander,' the admiral snapped. 'Quickly.'

I grinned just a little spitefully at Trapp. It was nice. To see someone else pushing their luck a bit too far. He just blinked back though, a bit flintily, almost as if remembering the way I'd sneered at him the first time we met.

Then he said: 'You're bearing in mind that the *Charon's* still basically goin' to be a merchant ship aren't you, Sir?'

'Yes.'

'Then that first lieutenant you're giving me— shouldn't he be a bloke with a bit o' Merchant Navy sea time in his discharge book as well?'

'What are you getting at, Commander?'

Trapp shrugged. 'It's just that . . . well, I think I might 'ave just the right sort of chap in mind. To sail as *Charon's* first mate, alongside me. He seems tough enough, an' handy with 'is fists . . .'

I started to get a nasty feeling. While those icy fingers were suddenly stroking my spine again. A premonition.

'A good seaman and gunnery officer . . .' The admiral nodded, ever so thoughtfully. 'But sharp with his tongue when required. And very aggressive, Commander. Quite ideal, as you suggest.'

I said anxiously, 'No, Sir. Please! You promised . . . I have your word.'

He smiled gently. 'And still do, Lieutenant Miller— to send you back to sea as soon as OPERATION STYX is under way.'

'Can I have 'im then, Sir?' Trapp had a pleading gleam in his eye. 'Aboard the *Charon*. In charge of my lads?'

'I have an obligation to Miller, Commander.' The admiral smiled at me again. A gentlemanly, generous smile.

'Of course you can. As from this moment.'

Chapter Four

And so I went back to war. Aboard the Steamship *Charon*.

Or perhaps *with* it. Starting the very next morning . . .

He was waiting for me at the head of the gangway. Just under that outrageous name board which was the only clean part of Trapp's ship.

'Ah'm Wullie,' he said. 'Gorbals Wullie. D'ye remember me, fancy man?'

I thought, 'Oh God but here we go again,' noticing, with gloomy satisfaction, the bruised and swollen mouth which gave him an even closer likeness to a wiry, glowering ape. Only there was a shifty malice in the little Glaswegian's eyes which put him on a different level to the true anthropoids. A more dangerous one.

Apart from which, gorillas didn't wear cloth caps. But then again, they couldn't sneak up astern of you on a dark night and heave you over the wall with a seaman's knife between your shoulder blades for ballast. Wearily I accepted that—if I ever hoped to sleep soundly aboard that bloody awful parody of a warship—I was going to have to make an impression on Gorbals Wullie. Probably with the heavy end of a marline spike.

Otherwise the crew of the *Charon* would dispose of me quicker than the German Navy could. And I didn't reckon Jerrie was going to waste a lot of killing time either, once we started shooting at what was left of Erwin Rommel's seaborne supply lines.

I dropped my suitcase at the seaman's feet. 'Take

this up to the mate's cabin,' I snapped, 'and tell the captain I'm aboard.'

He didn't show a flicker of surprise. Obviously the *Charon*'s crew had already been told of their new employment. All that was needed now was a bit of persuasion to indicate that the alternative of open mutiny held even less attraction.

He did grin though, and shook his head with great deliberation. 'Ah'm no' much of a lad at takin' orders. No' frae poofy officers anyway.'

'Or thinking up original insults,' I reflected, glancing outboard towards the replacement Naval guard and noting that they were doing precisely as I'd instructed earlier—by pretending not to watch. They wouldn't be available once we sailed, and I'd a fair idea that the Royal Navy's gunnery draft to the *Charon* might not feel terribly protective anyway. And certainly not towards the officer class.

I said mildly: 'That's a pity, sailor, because you're taking them from this one . . . so pick it up.'

Gorbals Wullie tried to grin again but the pain from his split lips must have jogged his memory so he changed half-way to a defiant glower.

'Och, youse can get stuffed,' he growled resentfully, seeming to crouch in anticipation while, at the same time, balancing automatically on the balls of his feet. If I'd had any doubt before, about his challenging me, I didn't any longer.

Then suddenly I had the same uncomfortable sensation I'd felt the first time I'd boarded the *Charon*—that eyes were watching me, critical eyes from all the secret places around the ship. Almost as if this meeting with the *Charon*'s leading hard man wasn't at all by chance . . .

I gazed at the menacing little yobbo coolly for a few more moments before placing my steel helmet on the cover of a winch and carefully hanging my respirator bag above it. Turning back I said very clearly, 'Pick it up. Now.'

'Fuck you!'

I blinked at him nervously then allowed my eyes to drop to the case, shrugging as though it didn't really

matter anyway. Meekly I bent forward, hand reaching
towards the handle . . .

His boot came in viciously, arcing low towards my
groin. I sidestepped as planned, my weight already
distributed in anticipation while allowing my out-
stretched hand to continue upwards and parallel to the
kick. All it needed then was a little added momentum
through a firm grip on his ankle and the mutineer-
elect was performing an involuntary pirouette to finish
up facing away from me.

Then I kicked him, as hard and as malevolently as I
could, propelling him in a funny, half-staggering gallop
until the edge of the hatch coaming caught his shins and
he went down across the boards with a muffled growl of
fury.

'The case,' I remarked conversationally. 'Pick it up,
there's a good lad.'

Awkwardly he climbed to his feet. There was a
smear of blood where the corner of his mouth had
opened up, only it was his hand I was more concerned
with right then—the hand, and the immaculately
honed cut-throat razor balanced so expertly with the
steel angled back across the knuckles, delicately poised
for the crosswise slash of the true gutter pro.

'Ah'm goin' tae cut ye, fancy man . . . Now ah'm
goin' tae mark yon jessie face so's ye'll aye remember
Gorbals Wullie!'

Cautiously he started to sidle across the raised hatch
cover towards me, half crouching with that oil-stained
cloth cap flat-aback like a mocking halo framing the
thin, spiteful features. I thought savagely, 'What a
bloody lousy way to fight a war . . .' until, just as his
body tensed for the drop down to deck level, I went in
low with my shoulder, catching him off balance for the
second time—and probably the last.

He was quick, though. Too bloody quick! The stroke
of the blade was like an icy pencil line running diago-
nally across my hunched back but, surprisingly, no
pain—not right then. Only a sudden terrible rage at
the *Charon* and the cretinous human flotsam who sailed
in her, and at a certain admiral for the way he'd abused
his promise.

Then we were sprawling together with the blued steel of that obscene weapon slashing in jerky, uncontrolled arcs only inches away from my eyes while I clung in terrified desperation to the bony, twisting wrist. I felt the shock of outraged agony as his teeth closed on my forearm then I'd brought my knee up into his groin in a last convulsive effort to hurt the rock-hard little bastard.

He let out a muffled gasp and his body arched under me. I managed to get my other hand to the wrist which flourished the blade and wrenched violently, bringing my knee up again and again into him. Suddenly he let out a sickening shriek while the razor skittered in a spiralling arc towards the edge of the hatch.

I yelled, 'Pick it up, you bastard!' and hit him full in the mouth. He twisted his head away and spat defiantly. 'Ah'll no' take orders frae a . . .'

So I hit him again, twice, then dragging myself to my feet hauled him up with me aware, as I did so, of the slowly increasing pain from my slashed shoulder. Already I was trembling violently, partly with rage but with shock, too, and the fear that very soon I wouldn't be able to hold him in check.

I drew my fist back very deliberately, just to let him see it coming. Just for a moment the hard eyes stared nervously into mine, maybe searching hopefully for some sign of gentlemanly irresolution then, not finding any, Gorbals Wullie muttered painfully, 'Och . . . It's no' as if I give a damn either way,' and, to my enormous relief, seemed to shrink fractionally in defeat.

I shoved him away, forcing myself to look arrogantly contemptuous while all I really felt was a little boy desire to run away and hide. As I did so I became uneasily aware of men moving quietly from the accommodation, circling around us yet still watching warily. Almost waiting. Only what more was there to anticipate . . . now?

Two men in particular caught my eye. Standing apart from the rest of the *Charon*'s crew they seemed to direct their hostility towards Gorbals Wullie rather than me. One was a slim, dark young Arab with an oddly effeminate air while the other, obviously an engineer, was a thick-set European type with a battered, amiable face and once-a-long-time-ago-white overalls.

Uncertainly I eyed the now utterly dejected Wullie as he trailed over and reached for the suitcase handle. Only something—some indefinable mood from the audience—seemed to trigger a tiny warning bell in my mind and, conscious of the growing pain from the wound in my back, I forced myself to step casually from the hatch and lift my respirator bag by the strap.

Suddenly the little Glaswegian hesitated before lifting the suitcase, then straightened up. When he turned towards me his expression was a sheepish grin of pure embarrassment. Awkwardly he dragged his filthy cap off and sort of gripped it in one fist while the other came up in what was undisputably a proffered handshake.

I watched him bleakly as he came towards me while the grin got even wider in an unexpectedly generous attitude of conciliation. Not quite certain of how to handle this new approach I just stood waiting, still holding the respirator case loosely by its web strap.

No one else aboard the *Charon* moved. Not even seeming to breathe.

The scruffy little seaman shrugged diffidently. 'Och but Gorbals Wullie's no' the man tae bear a grudge, mister. Here's mah hand on it . . .'

Beside me the man in the white overalls jerked into life. The American accent was sharp and urgent. 'Watch out, buddy. F'r the guy's CAP . . .'

But I'd already seen the other arm swinging up and across towards my face as Gorbals Wullie lunged at me across the space between us. And, at the same time, caught the bright glint of stainless steel almost lost in the oily camouflage—from the line of safety razor blades sewn ever so professionally into the battered peak of that innocuous headgear.

With a desperation born of pure terror I grabbed blindly while pivoting away from the slash. Somehow I caught his shirt sleeve and I literally hauled him forward and past me, starting to swing simultaneously

with the dangling respirator case. It curved round in a
wavering, pendulous orbit until it finally overtook him,
slamming into the small of his back with a dull, terribly
heavy *thud*.

It was as if I'd clubbed him with a ball and chain.

And then started on the rest of the *Charon*'s crowd
too, judging by the stunned disbelief on their faces.

While Gorbals Wullie let out one appalling shriek of
agony and cartwheeled forward in a tangle of nerveless
arms and legs to crash upside down against the rail and
sort of hang there, head lolling and with the bloody
foam smudging grotesquely over the slack, inverted
face.

Swivelling back to glare at the semi-circle of watch-
ers I ignored the sticky warmth of blood soaking
through the shoulder of my shirt. 'Right, you so-called
hard bastards . . . ,' I snarled, hating them like I'd
never hated men before, '. . . as from now I'm the first
mate, first lieutenant—first any other bloody thing you
c'n think of—aboard this stinking, dirt-infested corpse
of a ship, an' if any one of you doesn't like it, then
now's his chance to bloody say so!'

For what seemed a very long time they just stared
back at me mutely. Greeks, a couple of West Indians,
a tall angular Arab and a trio of unshaven Europeans.
Then someone laughed nervously from the back of the
crowd and gradually they started to grin uncertainly.
One of the West Indians jerked a thumb towards the
still dormant Wullie and winked admiringly at me.
'Man,' he beamed happily, 'you got a backswing on
you like a kick from a mule an' that's for sure . . .
Mister Mate, Suh.'

I forced myself to stay on my feet without wincing.
'What's your name, sailor?'

'Joseph, Suh. Able seaman Joseph. I never had no
other second tally.'

'Well you take that man below and see to him. Can
do?'

He nodded and looked pleased. 'Can do, Suh.'

'And . . . Joseph?'

'Yessuh?'

I kept my face straight. 'When he can get to his feet

again . . . tell him I still want that suitcase taking up
to the mate's cabin.'

I made myself stand until they dispersed, hauling a
vomiting Gorbals Wullie somewhat unsympathetically
towards the fo'c'sle accommodation. Suddenly I felt a
lot better. A movement beside me made me turn,
maybe a bit nervously, until I found it was the two
men who'd stood near me earlier. The battered engineer in the overalls grinned and stuck his hand out.
Remembering it was he who'd warned me the last
time someone else tried to shake hands I didn't have
any hesitation about taking his.

'Al Kubiczek,' the American said. 'Chief engineer've
this bucket. The pretty guy here's Chafic. Second mate,
would you believe?'

I grinned shakily back. 'Aboard this ship I'd believe
anything, Chief . . . and thanks.'

'No need. Wullie's a good guy at heart, just kinda
anti-social at times. Maybe you should kick him around
the deck regular. Good f'r the soul—not that the shifty
little bastard's got one to speak of.'

I said hopefully, 'Maybe I'd better ration my pleas-
ures. It could get to be habit forming . . .' then something made me glance upwards, towards the shrapnel-
scarred bridge deck, and I stopped talking abruptly.

Because a man lounged over the rail above me. A
man who looked like he'd been there all the time. Had
seen everything that had happened and made no attempt whatever to stop it.

'I see you started work already, Mister Mate,' Trapp
beamed unashamedly, 'Welcome aboard His Majesty's Ship *Charon.*'

I only had one more thing to do before I changed
into working rig. I did it when nobody was looking,
concealed by the outboard side of the bridge super-
structure.

I emptied the eight pounds of Valletta sand out of
my respirator case. The one I'd paralysed Gorbals
Wullie with.

A bit guiltily, perhaps. But, well, I'd rather figured
that when in Rome . . .

We moved round to the Admiralty Dockyard later that morning. They directed us to what must have been the most remote, discreetly tucked-away berth in Valletta; largely for security reasons—the *Charon*'s whole value as a Q-Ship would have been compromised if word of her rather unorthodox refit got to the enemy —but also, I figured, because the Royal Navy didn't want people to think she was anything to do with them in any capacity at all, not even for scuttling as a sacrificial blockship should the Germans attempt to enter Grand Harbour.

After we'd secured alongside I watched moodily as the shipwrights and ordnance experts climbed tentatively aboard—mostly glancing about them with a sort of disbelieving reverence, as if entering some previously unimaginable and ancient tomb—then tried to skulk aft towards what was laughingly known as the chief officer's cabin while attempting to look like just another casual visitor to the ship.

But not entirely successfully. Clambering up the ladder from the well deck I came face to face with my late adversary from the Staff Planning Office.

He glared at me suspiciously until recognition slowly dawned. 'Isn't it . . . ah . . . Miller? And aren't you that damned . . . ?'

I glowered back. 'Yessir.' Anyway, 'Damned' was a pretty accurate description, though not in the way he meant it.

'Only now they tell me you've actually been appointed as number one of this . . . ah . . . this . . .'

'Sir.'

The SPO smiled. It was a beautiful, seraphic smile. 'Then I fear I have to admit that I was wrong, Miller,' he said with great humility. 'Whatever I may have thought, I know now that the admiral was *not* losing his grip!'

Entering my cabin I slammed the door savagely, staring around with sheer distaste. Roughly half the size of a small cupboard, it was panelled in nicotine-stained teak enclosing an atmosphere of garlic, brilliantine and human sweat. There was a high bunk with scarred weatherboards, a yellowed wash basin with blue ceramic flowers and a jagged hole in the bottom, and a single verdigris-welded porthole which filtered the bright Mediterranean sunlight to a dirty brown opacity. And a very little else—apart from encrusted dirt.

Hauling the filthy, age-compacted mattress from the berth I opened the door again and, carrying it at arms' length, heaved it straight over the rail where it floated below in a slowly widening film of oily Technicolor. I watched it for a few moments, feeling the gloomy and probably pretty short future hanging over me like an inescapable black cloud, then I muttered, 'Oh bugger the Navy!' and turned inboard abruptly.

To come face to face with the thin, menacing features of Able Seaman Gorbals Wullie.

Who murmured, quite feelingly, 'An' that's what ah said too, Mister Miller Sir. Eight year ago—afore ah deserted frae the *Royal Oak* . . . Dae ye want the sootcase in yer cabin then?'

I checked that the cap was inoffensively secured on his head before my eyes dropped suspiciously to his hands, but there was nothing in them. Only the suitcase. I snapped warily, 'On the bunk,' and he nodded before disappearing through the door.

A moment later he stepped back over the coaming and I met him with an icy stare. 'So you're a deserter too, are you. From the Navy.'

He turned his head briefly and glanced at the *Charon*'s decks, now swarming with bluejackets and dockyard mateys. When he looked back at me his expression was rueful. 'It disnae seem like ah was an awfy successful one . . . ah'll away an' get a bucket then.'

He must have seen the query in my eye because he hesitated, looking a bit embarrassed, then grinned. 'Yon Greek mate we had—he was an insanitary wee bastard . . . ah'm no' havin' you cleaning out that pigsty yoursel', Mister Miller.'

I resisted telling him I didn't have the slightest intention of doing it myself anyway, because it was probably the nearest thing to an apology anyone had ever received from Gorbals Wullie. But then again, not everyone won his sincere respect by belting him all over the boat with eight pounds of Maltese sand.

So I watched him go, still jaunty as hell with that lethal cap tilted stylishly over one eye and an air of utter indestructibility that defied the entire weaponry of the Royal Navy, the *Kriegsmarine* and any other poofy outfit who fancied their chances against a proper hard man.

And suddenly, for the first time in days, I found myself smiling just a little bit. While that black cloud which stretched ahead did seem to have at least one tiny break in the gloom.

But only one. It still looked pretty damned impenetrable everywhere else.

And then, unexpectedly, the future appeared to take a sudden turn for the better. At least as far as I was concerned, anyway.

When the enemy beat Trapp to the punch, and declared war on the *Charon* first.

By dropping a large, superbly aimed bomb on her. The very next day.

They came in at two levels that morning; the Stukas high from the northwest while, just above the wave tops, the twin-engined 100's and the Reggiones blasted towards Grand Harbour and the Dockyard in a die-straight, all-or-nothing bomb run. The enemy knew that time was running out for them. Perhaps the greatest irony of all was that we realised exactly the same danger applied to Malta as well. Both sides—Axis and Allies—were trying desperately to hang on.

But this particular raid was a classic of the hit and run technique—the sirens, the opening staccato of the anti-aircraft barrage and the first roar of desynchronised aero engines blending together in an unbroken sequence which didn't leave any of us aboard *Charon* much time to do more than stand and watch it coming.

Hell, I didn't even see *that* much. All I knew was that one moment I was standing together with Trapp and two of the Naval ordnance people in the open square of number two hold, wrestling with the impossible problem of how to strengthen *Charon*'s time-eroded frames enough to prevent her falling apart in a cloud of rust dust the first time we fired our main armament, then the next thing was a disembodied voice roaring 'Air raid . . . Take cover!' Before the patch of blue sky above my head was crisscrossed with wheeling, diving shapes, black cruciform silhouettes emitting an occasional sparkle as the sun glinted on Perspex canopies and the near horizontal spinners of the yellow-bossed Stukas.

One of the ordnance blokes glanced up nervously and muttered, 'Perhaps we'd better adjourn the meeting temporarily?' while the other winked at me and said laconically: 'Why? Seein' we're probably aboard the last place in Malta they'd ever want to hit anyway, Charlie.'

Trapp glowered at him. 'You jus' get on with the job, Mister, an' have a bit've respect f'r one of His Majesty's ships. No square-headed Jerrie aviator's goin' to waste men's time aboard this ship. Time's money to me an' I'm damned if . . .'

I think I was the only one who actually heard the bomb coming. The one with the *Charon*'s name on it. First there was the scream of the diving Stuka—masked from view at that moment by the hatch coaming, but steadily rising up the scale of audible intensity until the mind froze with the certain horror of what was about to happen. Then, as I screwed my eyes tightly closed with the paralysing terror of it all, the deck beneath me rocked slightly under the slipstream as the Stuka's automatic dive brakes pulled the plane out just above the *Charon*'s spindly funnel while the scream of its wing-tip sirens muted instead to an even higher pitched whistling screech . . .

Someone wailed in a shocked, anguished tone, 'Oh Christ.'

Maybe it was me. I never did find out.

Either way I was half-way down to the wooden tween-deck boards, shoulder to shoulder with a similarly reacting Lieutenant Commander Trapp, Royal Navy, when the bomb actually hit us. And all the time I was diving my mind kept hammering mockingly,

'What the bloody hell's the point, Miller boy. You're dead already 'cause there's no damn place to hide from a direct hit . . . they even got you secured in your coffin *before* they bloody smash you apart . . .'

There was a *twang* like the severing of a gigantic harp string from above. Abruptly the howl of the bomb dissolved into a chilling series of crashes interspersed with the squalling of rending steel. Something smashed into the upstand of the coaming and I opened my eyes again in the same millisecond of time while the run-away projectile glanced screechingly off a steel supporting column, ricocheted in a berserk blur from one side of the hold to another, then finally—all in the space of a human heart beat—drilled clean through the wooden boarded gap between Trapp and myself to vanish vertically into the *Charon's* lower hold.

And then silence. An impossible, blanketing silence.

I stared dazedly at Trapp across the splintered hole which separated us. 'I didn't explode . . .' I whispered accusingly. 'It didn't . . . bloody . . . explode.'

While one of the ordnance men started to shudder convulsively with the shock of it all, and Trapp gazed gloomily down the hole saying. 'But it still could, Mister. Explode, I mean . . .

'. . . Seein' how I never had no clocks in my cargo. Yet there's something ticking like a bloody metronome down there. Right under us.'

A crowd was already forming around the hold as I urgently assisted the shocked gunner up the vertical ladder and on to the deck.

The lightning raid was almost over already and, as I stuck my head above the coaming to draw a gulping, shaky breath of air, I caught sight of the last enemy plane—an Italian Reggione fighter bomber—streaking past us, almost brushing the surface of the harbour with a cannon-blasting Spitfire clinging remorselessly to its tail like a predatory guard dog. Then, just seaward of the entrance, bits started to break off the Reggione until, trailing a sudden plume of black oily smoke, it dug one wingtip into the water and cartwheeled for two hundred yards in a series of skipping, cavorting gouts of foam and blazing Avgas.

Someone grabbed my arm and hauled me over the coaming. I found myself looking into the brown, nervous eyes of my junior partner, Second Mate Babikian, and snapped tightly, 'Get everyone ashore damn quick, laddie. We've got a hot bomb down below.'

A few of the crowd started to move away immediately but others seemed to be less inclined to take the warning. I noticed with a faint surge of surprise that most of the stayers belonged to the *Charon's* crew. In fact only a couple of the Greeks had joined the general drift towards the gangway and the safety of the wharf, the rest just hung around looking bloody-minded and I reflected irrelevantly, 'God knows what they'll do to the Jerries but they worry the hell out've me!'

Babikian murmured hesitantly, 'Pleese? You men all go shoreside to be safe.'

A real leader of men, him.

Wullie—it had to be Gorbals Wullie, naturally— growled truculently, 'Och, it's no' gone off. How can we no' haul it up an' ditch it ower the wall then?'

I stared at him. It didn't quite seem to be the appropriate time for a dissertation on the pro's and con's of do-it-yourself bomb disposal—apart from which, even if we did manage to get it over the side, when it exploded it would probably lift the *Charon* clean out of the water and deposit her somewhere around the centre of the bloody island.

Which was the silver lining to my particular cloud, on reflection. As long as it didn't do it while I was still aboard. Then a new arrival shoved his way through the SS *Charon* debating society and I recognised, with a feeling of relief, the sensible battered features of Al Kubiczek.

Until *he* also said, quite unconcernedly: 'Maybe she's a dud, huh? Far as I know it was deflected by the mainmast stay, then bounced around the deck like an eight ball on a pool table . . . an' if that didn't trigger it then I'd figure nothin' would.'

I took a deep, controlled breath. Never, in all my life, had I envisaged being involved with a group of men who substituted sheer misguided optimism for reasonable, logical get-up-and-go when it came to deciding on the best course of action regarding an unexploded bomb.

Every muscle in my body was taut as a wire stay while I waited for the explosion which would smash me, Trapp, the *Charon* and the rest of her impossibly intractable complement into a timeless, searing oblivion.

'Chief,' I said, ever so slowly and reasonably. 'There is a highly explosive device right underneath your feet. It is not a dud, it is a delayed action bomb which, once its timing mechanism has started, will undoubtedly detonate within the very near future . . . and it has already begun to tick. Apart from which, after the impact it's taken, it's probably unstable as hell on top of everything else. . .'

A movement in the hold below made me stop abruptly and glance down. For a few blissful moments I'd clean forgotten Trapp until—as I stared disbelievingly—I saw him casually lever one end of the splintered hatch board to one side then sort of hang, face down, with his upper half suspended over the empty lower hold.

And over the bomb.

I yelled involuntarily: 'Leave it, f'r God's sake! Just clear the ship and call in the disposal team, Captain . . .'

His voice, muffled but ominously unimpressed, drifted up to us. 'I c'n see it now, Mister. Lodged neat as you please in the McIntyre Tank atween the floor plates an' the intercostal.'

'Then come topside and get the crowd well away . . .' I glanced around desperately, nobody was even looking like moving yet. 'I'll have to go ashore and get hold of the BD people. This is going to need a special priority from the admiral . . . but for God's sake get them off the ship, *Sir!*'

Trapp called, 'Oh, Aye.'

Thoughtfully.

I groaned desparingly.

And started running.

The wharf was deserted as I charged down the gang-way, heading for the nearest phone. A little knot of dockyard workers hung around the corner of an engineering shed about eighty yards away and I thought I saw the helmeted head of an Admiralty policeman converging on the scene behind them. I skidded to a stop and looked anxiously around for any sign of transport approaching, then it occurred to me that, at this time, only those men who'd been aboard *Charon* could have known about the bomb.

Suddenly I caught sight of a glint of chrome in the shadow of the shed. Running over I found an ancient Alvis open-seat tourer discreetly parked around the corner—presumably her owner didn't encourage ostentation in case someone asked too many questions about where the petrol for the machine came from . . . or, more specifically, which Admiralty fuel dump.

Still with every muscle in my back knotted in anticipation of the inevitable explosion I vaulted into the driver's seat, saw with relief that the keys were still in her, and pressed the starter. Behind me the *Charon* continued to rust away with quiet dignity, only a tiny knot of aggressively suicidal figures gesticulating around her number two hatch to break the calm of that Mediterranean scene.

The Alvis roared into life. I eased off the handbrake, threw one last glance towards those shipmates whom I was presumably about to lose any moment now, then roared away from her with an odd feeling of regret . . . Perhaps because—for the first time since I'd become involved with them—I was aware of an inexplicable affection towards that archaic hulk and the piratical, procrastinating brotherhood of renegades who formed her crew.

It took eight minutes of shouting, swearing and threatening before they finally connected me with the admiral. He snapped angrily: 'Now what, Miller? I left orders that this conference was not to be interrupt . . . !'

I said, 'We've taken a bomb aboard. Unexploded time delay . . .'

'Right. Clear the ship. I'll give you priority.'

The phone went dead in my hand. I stared at it resentfully and muttered: '*You* clear the damn ship. Even the bloody *Luftwaffe* can't!' Then leapt back into the Alvis and, fighting the temptation to curl up and hide until I heard a loud and final explosion, slammed her in gear and tore back towards the *Charon*.

So now it was *my* turn to be bloody-minded. And I intended to evacuate that floating disaster area even if I had personally to heave every last man over the side. Including Lieutenant Commander Edward Trapp, Royal Naval Reserve and mercenary extraordinary.

In fact—especially Lieutenant Commander Trapp. With great and long-suppressed satisfaction.

Either that, or go up with them. It was really only a question of advancing the *Charon*'s sinking time a little—and it would save me the discomfort of living in that hell hole of a cabin only to get shot-up or torpedoed or roasted alive in blazing cordite, somewhere off the coast of North Africa.

I rocketed through the still-watching dockyard men with horn blaring then accelerated down the wharf towards the ship. Surprisingly she was still there and looking even more derelict to my distorted imagination as I screeched to a halt, leapt out . . .

Then stopped. Dead. And just stared.

There was power to the cargo winch now. I could see that much by the wreaths of escaping steam which escaped from every ill-maintained gland to cling around the lower half of its operator, Able Seaman Joseph No-other-tally. The rusted running wire led from the winch barrel, up over the derrick head block and back down again, past the concentrating figure of Second Mate Babikian, to disappear from my sight into the square of number two hold.

Where the bomb was.

I whispered, 'No. Please . . . Not with a *winch* f'r . . .'

Then I began to run. Again. On legs which suddenly felt like cement-filled tubes.

They'd opened up the lower hold completely. Now the tween deck boards lay piled in a corner and the

bright sunlight streamed into the bottom of the ship, a
natural spotlight on the black, droplet-shaped cylinder
which lay jammed awkwardly between two steel
frames.

A rope strop had been taken round the lower end of
the fins, leading to the lifting wire of the derrick. Two
manilla guide lines had also been passed through the
bomb release eyes and a grimly determined Chief Engineer Kubiczek held one while Gorbals Wullie, cloth
cap secured laconically to the after end of his skull,
waited with obvious impatience for something to
happen as he toyed with the other.

Which it undoubtedly would, I reckoned, the moment they took the strain on that winch.

Trapp, arms akimbo and feet straddled firmly apart
in the best position to watch what was happening—
over the fuse-cap of the bomb itself—glanced up
briefly and grunted: 'Back already, eh Mister . . . ?
Heave away, Second Mate. Take the strain nice an'
easy, mind.'

I yelled urgently, 'NO! Belay that last ord . . .'

Only I was too late, because Babikian had made a
funny, circling motion with his raised arm while Black
Joseph completely vanished in billowing clouds of
steam as he let in the winch clutch and the antiquated
machinery clattered frenziedly into life. Abruptly the
wire itself jerked taut as a bowstring and started to
thrum under the strain from the jammed bomb.

For a few moments nothing happened, except that
the rusted wire seemed to stretch thinner and thinner
as the clatter of the winch muted to a strained growl of
frustration. Trapp scratched his head speculatively
while Wullie placed one foot on the casing of the
bomb and tried to shove it from side to side to free it.

I felt the cold sweat of sheer terror coursing down
my face as I leant over the coaming. 'Trapp, for God's
sake, man . . .'

He looked up impassively, 'Cap'n Trapp, Mister.
An' I know what you're goin' to say, anyway.'

The winch gave a rattling, victorious quarter trun and
the wire sang in agony. I gripped the flaking coaming
until my knuckles showed white. 'Now you've been

given a direct order, Captain. From the admiral—to
evacuate this ship until the disposal people can deal
with the job.'

'Aye? And did he say anythin' about the insurance?
Like who pays if that bomb goes off before your Navy
experts get round to fixin' things?'

Gorbals Wullie gave up kicking the bomb and
started searching round for something, probably a
lever—though it might have been a bloody sledgeham-
mer for all I knew. I snarled, 'If it goes off now, you'll
not be here to collect anyway, Trapp.'

Trapp shrugged. 'In that case it won't matter about
the insurance, will it, Mister?' he said with devastating
logic. 'But jus' now I got my business assets to consider. I got a lot've capital tied up in the old *Charon*,
plus a three month charter from a very reliable firm
so . . .'

The still straining winch burst into sudden, shocking
life as the strain abruptly eased. I had one frozen
vision of that explosive-packed cylinder jetting backwards out of the grip of the frames, then it sparked
across the steel deck with a nerve-paralysing screech,
clanged reverberatingly against the outer plates of the
hull, missed Gorbals Wullie by the thickness of a
skin of paint and finally swung in ever-decreasing spi-
rals with the shiny brass fuse-cap half an inch above
the deck.

Trapp said, 'Din't I tell you then?' with enormous
satisfaction.

Wullie looked aggrieved. 'Yon wee bastard's dangerous. Bluidy near scuppered me, so it did.'

The chief put his ear to the slowly revolving bomb
and then grinned reassuringly. 'I guess we fixed it
good fellers. It's stopped ticking.'

I yelled, 'Oh *Jesus!*' then, hating them all for leaving me no alternative, I grabbed the startled second
mate by the arm and spoke as firmly and as plainly as
I could.

'We've got maybe seconds, maybe minutes, Babikian. There's a car on the wharf—you get that
bloody bomb out've there and lowered shoreside . . .
now get a *move* on, laddie.'

I was down the gangway, in the driving seat of the
Alvis and reversing frantically before the derrick, still
with the suspended bomb, swung ponderously outboard. I vaulted out and tried to steady it as it slowly
descended, guiding it into the back seat.

There was a sudden shout from the *Charon* and I
swung in fright until I saw Gorbals Wullie and Chief
Kubiczek charging down the gangway towards me.
Wullie tripped on the bottom step, cartwheeled in a
cloud of dust then bounced smoothly upright again,
legs still going like pistons. 'Haud on, Mister. Us
lads'll gie ye a hand.'

There wasn't time to argue. And it was their bomb
anyway. I snapped, 'So get in the back seat an' steady
the bloody thing. GENTLY!' then slid in behind the
wheel and started her up with a throaty roar.

The chief yelled, 'Hang on, pal. Unless you want to
take the goddam ship along f'r the ride,' and I saw that
bomb was still secured to the winch wire. Wullie muttered savagely, 'Och but ah cannae untie the bastard,'
and I snarled 'Cut it, man. *Cut* the damn thing!'

He looked at me a bit vaguely. 'Ah havenae got a
knife, Sir.'

I closed my eyes. Just for a moment. Then, grabbing the cap from his head, I slashed the rope strop
with the razor blades sewn into the peak, shoved the
Alvis grindingly into gear, and took off like a Sea Fury
catapulted from a carrier's flight deck.

The bomb finally exploded thirty seconds after we'd
broadsided to a halt on a patch of cleared ground. Just
after we'd leapt out, leaving the engine still running,
and pelted crazily for the nearest cover. The blast,
when it came, bowled me head over heels and left me
spreadeagled on my back staring hazily up at the ring
of disapproving faces which formed our top-priority,
newly arrived bomb disposal squad.

The Naval lieutenant in charge said huffily, 'I must
say I think it's a bit off, old boy—messing around
with our property.'

I blinked at him dazedly. 'There didn't seem to be a
lot of choice. Not at the time.'

He turned away and clambered back into his lorry,

still looking petulant. 'Well, all the same, we're supposed to be the only chaps with authority to blow ourselves up around here. Do please try and bear that in mind from now on.'

I dragged myself upright and glared after the departing truck. 'If I want to blow myself up, then I bloody well will,' I yelled hysterically. 'Anywhere I like—at any time I like . . .

'. . . an' as *often* as I bloody well like!'

Trapp was waiting for me as I limped back aboard the *Charon*.

'That car you used,' he said firmly. 'That was your idea an' your responsibility. I hopes you don't expect me to pay f'r it, Mister.'

I stared at him. 'You bastard,' I muttered. 'You miserable, profiteering parsimonious bastard!'

'Sir?' he said. Then grinned like a great big Cheshire cat.

'Sir,' I snapped.

Then, a bit grudgingly, I started to smile too. But there didn't seem to be any logical alternative. Apart from completely losing my sanity, at least.

Not as long as I was first lieutenant of His Majesty's Warship *Charon*.

Chapter Five

And so the refit continued with squads of fitters and ordnance specialists working night and day to convert the *Charon* into probably the most unorthodox man of war since Leonardo da Vinci designed his first submarine. And that sank the moment they launched it, as far as I knew.

In terms of strict firepower we would still be comparatively impotent. In the event of a straightforward gunnery engagement the *Charon* would probably be even less formidable than a surface U-boat—ignoring the very real likelihood of her archaic hulk literally falling apart under the shock wave of even a near miss.

The only ace in our pack would be the element of surprise. That, when we were inevitably faced in the end with a real warship, by appearing to abandon an inoffensive freighter with obvious panic—which I didn't reckon was going to require a lot of acting ability, under the circumstances—those of us remaining on board would hopefully be given one brief opportunity to engage an enemy lulled into temporary complacency. To hit him hard, fast, accurately and so mortally that he wouldn't be able to reply.

And to do that, they were fitting us with two primary pieces of artillery. The first—what was optimistically referred to as our main armament—was a 4.7-inch naval gun which, to me, seemed very appropriate considering it must have been almost as old as the *Charon* anyway, except that it fired HE rounds instead of cannon balls. And it wasn't muzzle loaded.

This ungainly weapon was mounted in the specially reinforced tween deck of number two hold—where already, and all too recently, a live bomb had been battered into submission. On either side the *Charon*'s hull plates were skilfully cut away, then replaced as drop-down screens which gave us a reasonable field of fire either to port or starboard. One thing for sure—the expression on any *Kriegsmarine* commander's face when he unexpectedly saw the *Charon* collapse at the seams and found a carronade with a muzzle like a railway tunnel leering back at him instead— now that, even I grudgingly admitted, was almost worth anticipating.

Our second gun was at least modern if considerably smaller—an ex-Royal Artillery Bofors which would allow us to maintain a steady rate of fire to back up the slower 4.7 and would, in fact, be more practical for engaging the less threatening targets, those ships of Rommel's nocturnal supply fleet which were our primary objective for as long as we stayed afloat.

Camouflaging this Bofors gave us quite a problem until, eventually, it was decided to disguise it as deck cargo . . . mounted on the forward well deck and concealed under a large, roughly finished wooden packing case designed literally to spring apart at the pull of a link-pin when the order was given to open fire. A sort of giant size Jack-in-the-box with a high explosive leer.

Four heavy machine guns under dummy louvred vegetable lockers along the inboard sides of the bulwarks were added as an afterthought. For when we settled down to the specialised business of close-range killing.

Or would it be—murder? Because the one thing we didn't know yet was . . . what could we do with the survivors of those Arab dhows and coasters, once we'd attacked? How were we to prevent them from reporting back to the nearest enemy HQ and alerting every German unit in the southern Mediterranean to the fact that a disguised British Naval vessel was loose in their waters?

Unless, of course, we discouraged them from jeopardising our operation. With a bullet . . .

Several other modifications were being carried out while the ordnance installations went ahead. A new wheelhouse, appropriately weatherbeaten, replaced Trapp's original hen coop while, at the same time, they enclosed the bridge wings with timber-faced steel plates which suited me admirably as that was to be my particular action station. My somewhat basic fire control equipment consisted of a selection of slotted peep holes to give the bridge the appearance of being utterly deserted, a camouflaged range finder on each wing and a telephone connection to the 4.7 gun captain, the Bofors and the engine room.

Oh, and a steel helmet each for Trapp and myself. But there was no expense spared when it came to OPERATION STYX.

They also issued us with brand new lifejackets but, seeing they weren't bullet proof and I didn't particularly fancy their ability to extend my survival time when floating in the oggin face to face with a Schmeisser held by an irritable Nazi *Oberbootsmann,* I wasn't too impressed by the Navy's generosity.

One last item. In view of the strategy of our laying on a 'Panic Party' to abandon ship and thereby lull the Germans into that essential sense of false security —and on the assumption that we might need to do it more than once—they replaced the *Charon*'s original sieve of a lifeboat with a new one. So's it wouldn't just keep on going, straight below the surface, as soon as it was launched.

Or, as my arch-enemy the Staff Planning Officer so succinctly put it. 'That way . . . ah . . . Miller, you'll be a little less likely to run out of sailors before you finally run out of luck.'

A few days later we were grabbing a hasty tea in the *Charon*'s saloon, all of us oil-stained and spattered with rust flakes and prehistoric grime from the innermost recesses of the ship, when suddenly Al Kubiczek hesitated half-way through the mug of watery soup that formed our main course of the day, and frowned.

'You guys hear somethin? In the distance.'

I stopped chewing and listened. He was right, there was a sound but I couldn't identify it right away. A slowly swelling roar from the direction of Grand Harbour's entrance. For a few moments we just sat and looked at each other a little apprehensively, then

Trapp said, 'People cheerin'. D'you reckon it could be people cheerin'?'

Babikian smiled wistfully, 'Maybe the war is over, hah?'

I stared distastefully at the slice of dry bread and thin skin of jam in my hand. And there wouldn't even be that much in a few more days.

'Maybe someone's found a tin of corned beef,' I growled. Then it hit me in a wave of hardly-daring-to-hope excitement. 'PEDESTAL!' I shouted, scattering the chair behind me. 'It has to be the PEDESTAL convoy coming in . . .'

They watched me go with the disconcerted stares of reckless men who suddenly find they've got a real live lunatic in their midst.

I stood on the ramparts above the harbour, shoulder to shoulder with jostling, cheering servicemen all mixed up with the Maltese who'd endured so much and for so long.

Slowly those grey, tired merchantmen steamed towards us along the cleared channel with the Malta-based sweepers searching ahead of them and the Spitfires, rondels glistening against the evening sky, patrolling defiantly above. It was the island's day. The enemy weren't invited.

I counted the ships. It didn't take very long. There were only three of them—three out of fourteen. Long, deeply laden freighters quietly slipping towards the berths which awaited them so welcomingly. The *Melbourne Star* with her hull scarred and burned through steaming over the pyre of one of her less fortunate consorts. *The Port Chalmers,* the *Rochester Castle* . . .

Nothing else. No tanker. No *Ohio* . . .

A voice beside me said quietly: 'The people can eat again now, thank God. But it's cost us a great deal . . . a very great deal.'

I turned and saw the Commander (Planning) staring sadly out to sea. Then he stirred and murmured, 'I suggest you get ready to sail as soon as possible . . . ah . . . Miller. Otherwise you may not have time to get away at all.'

I stared at him. 'Sir? But PEDESTAL's here. Or part of it. Surely . . . ?'

He looked at me. His eyes were very grave. 'We're down to our last reserves of oil at this moment. We needed those food ships but by God we needed a tanker even more.'

The horizon seemed far away, and very empty. I muttered sickly, 'The *Ohio*. She's been sunk?'

The commander shrugged. 'We don't really know. But it doesn't matter. They've been forced to abandon her seventy miles away . . . it's only a question of time . . .'

I pushed my way through the happy, relieved sea of faces. None of them knew yet. Only a few of us did on that island where courage just couldn't offer quite enough.

A few of us. And another group of exhausted men who, at that moment, waited bitterly near a slowly sinking, bomb-battered hulk an impossible seventy miles from safety.

But we were almost ready. All we had to do now was to fit a replacement windlass for the one which the Navy had shot away and complete the *Charon*'s engine overhaul under the eagle eye of Chief Engineer Kubiczek who—considering he was a self-confessed deserter from the United States Navy—had still managed to inspire considerable if grudging admiration from the RN artificers working on a form of propulsive mechanism which they'd thought was as obsolete as Stephenson's Rocket.

Or maybe their respect was for Al's good taste in deserting, rather than for his skill in fabricating impossible-to-obtain engine spares for the *Charon*.

And then, talking about potential deserters, our own Naval Gunnery Draft appropriately arrived. Our ten 'Volunteers'. From the Fleet.

Half drunk, totally pugnacious, and barely recognisable as specialist ratings from anyone's Navy. Except, maybe, Trapp's.

I stood at the head of the gangway and watched with a despondent heart which grew gloomier and

gloomier as they fell, one by one, out of the back of a
lorry amid an avalanche of kit bags, black market
beer cans and mislaid uniform caps. Then gradually
the curses and obscenities faded to a stunned silence
as they caught sight of the *Charon* for the first time
and it finally began to dawn on them precisely what
could happen to a too-troppy matelot who fell foul
of his own first lieutenant.

One of them, a sort of uniformed copy of Gorbals
Wullie said, in a shocked voice, 'You mean I gotter
draft chit to *that?*'

Someone else, a big leading hand with a broken
nose and a warped sense of humour, growled, 'They
did give yer the alternative, din't they? I mean, you
could've done twelve months' detention instead, mate.'

The other man whirled round and started to climb
back in the lorry. 'I'll take it, Killick. Glasshouse'll be
a bloody pleasure after seein' . . .'

Suddenly a mighty voice from inside the truck
roared hugely: 'Get back, Clark. Get fell *IN* like I
told you!'

I thought weakly, 'Lord, but what kind've petty officer's *that*—able to keep this shower in hand,' then I
found out when Seaman Gunner Clark hurtled backwards as a foot was placed firmly against his chest and
pushed. Hard.

Then the man in the lorry swung easily down to the
ground, dusted himself off while loftily ignoring the
sprawling rating, and grinned up at me with great good
humour. 'Remember me, Sir . . . Arthur Crocker? Re-
portin' for duty aboard, soon as you give the word.'

For the moment I frowned and then, suddenly, I
started to grin back involuntarily. Because my new
right hand man had turned out to be the most perfect
candidate I could ever have asked for, in the imposing
shape of Petty Officer Crocker, RN—last observed
under close arrest for dereliction of duty while Acting
Guard Commander in that he did wilfully disobey orders and, on boarding a restricted vessel, did strike
several members of the said vessel's complement . . .

'Welcome aboard, PO,' I called sardonically. 'Most
of the crowd up here you've already met.'

The only thing I just couldn't figure was how we were ever going to get a draft of such obviously incorrigible Service cast-offs to take any orders at all, never mind form themselves into some vague semblance of an efficient fighting unit.

And supreme efficiency—which demanded goodwill and not resentment—was the only thing which could possibly save us from being blown apart the first time we came face to face with the enemy. More and more I was beginning to regret the inexcusable lack of enthusiasm I'd shown when arranging the *Charon*'s complement.

Trapp came and leaned over the rail beside me as I bleakly waited for the gunners to stumble unsteadily aboard, shepherded by the uncompromising chivvying of Petty Officer Crocker.

'Get up . . . Get bloody UP, you revoltin', footless, toad-brained shower've dead-beat idjits . . . Pick that man UP, there! That ditty bag . . . Pickit UP, UP, UP . . .!'

Seaman Gunner Clark collapsed abruptly in a drunken lunge and leant against the side of the ship being sick down the front of his jumper. Trapp nodded and, looking tremendously pleased, said: 'You did well pickin' them, Mister. Them lads is just the right stuff . . . Just the kind to fit in lovely aboard the old *Charon*.'

Which was probably the most accurate statement he'd ever made in his life. I muttered faintly, 'D'you want to talk to them or shall I?'

'They're your lot. They're Navy.'

'So are you, Sir. Now,' I grated. 'And you're the captain.'

'Oh aye, I keep forgettin'. Right then, Number One. Kindly have all hands . . . ah . . . What's the proper word f'r it?'

'Muster,' I said, 'Sir.'

'*Mustard*,' he repeated with relish. 'Then get 'em mustard abaft the bridge so's I can inspect them. Like on a proper tiddley warship.'

So I did. Eventually. Then I took one appalled glance down the straggling line of scruffy, filthy seamen who rocked unsteadily backwards and forwards, and reflected viciously: 'On a proper warship, Trapp, the captain would be so long picking out the faults he'd be a bloody admiral retired before he finished.'

I said tightly, 'New draft ready for inspection, Sir.'

Then Trapp strolled casually over and, for quite a long time, stood eyeing his new Gunnery Department with a surprising degree of distaste, considering the even more cretinous appearance of his own crowd, until finally, he tipped his cap to the back of his head and, shoving his hands into his pockets, said contemptuously: 'They said you was goin' to be bright boys. Hand picked f'r the job. Jus' the sort of men I needed aboard a Q-ship they said . . . But look at you! Jus' stand back an' *look* at yourselves . . .'

For a moment words failed him then he shook his head in utter disgust. '. . . dammitall, you're CLEAN! You're as clean an' smart a bunch of bluejackets as I've ever had the misfortune to set eyes on in all me life . . .'

I stared at him, hardly able to believe my ears. And so did the newly arrived line of maritime tramps. I noticed even Petty Officer Crocker starting to grin while the rest of them just forgot to look sullen and began to look perplexed instead. God only knew what kind of routine, stiff-upper-lip pep talk they'd been expecting—but then again, they'd never met Lieutenant Commander Trapp, Royal Navy, before either.

'But from now on,' Trapp continued grimly, 'You'll look a bit more appropriate to this ship. Them fancy neat uniforms—ditch 'em over the wall. An' them shiny glass boots—I want ter see them scuffed like an alligator's backside by tomorrow mornin'. Oh, and then there's shaving. Not one of you've got more than a couple've days' growth an' if you think I'm goin' to tolerate a crowd of soap-smellin', shiny-faced ponces aboard this man o' war then you c'n go an . . .'

I turned away. One more glance at the line of fascinated, disbelieving faces had already convinced me, beyond any doubt, that Trapp had done what no master-at-arms in the whole of the Royal Navy had ever succeeded in accomplishing.

And that His Majesty's Ship *Charon* might finally

sail with a loyal and efficient—if highly insanitary and odoriferous—crew of gunners.

The next morning I went up to Naval HQ to organise arrangements for storing the ship—if there were any stores to be had.

The attractively disapproving third officer Wren bumped into me as I rounded a corner. It was the most comfortable collision I'd ever had and, to my surprise, she even smiled when she recognised me.

'Have you heard?' she said. 'The good news?'

'The admiral's had a stroke?' I asked hopefully.

'Our tanker. The *Ohio* . . .' Her eyes sparkled with excitement. 'They've gone back on board again. And *Rye* and *Penn* are out there with her. They're going to try and tow her in.'

I was glad for her, and for the rest of the island. But I felt a terrible despondency too.

Just as I got back an intriguing packing case arrived, delivered by a closely escorted Naval truck.

The label, for discreetly obvious reasons, stated that it was consigned to *The Master, SS Charon*. Under that, someone rather less security conscious had printed in large, easy to read letters—SECRET MATERIAL. NOT TO BE OPENED WITHOUT PRIOR AUTHORITY.

'Open it,' Trapp said.

'You can't,' I answered, examining it curiously. 'Not until we're given permis . . .'

He jammed a crowbar under the sealed lid, heaved, and the binding wires burst apart like a rifleshot. 'Oh yes I can. It's easy when you got the knack.'

The contents spilled over the deck of his cabin. I looked at him, and he frowned quizzically back at me.

They were bits and pieces of Naval uniform, mostly. White topped rating's caps, thick oiled wool sea jerseys and a few matelot's jumpers. I noticed the jumpers already bore specialist badges, mostly from the Torpedo Branch.

I picked one of the caps up and blinked at it, mystified.

The gold-printed tally round the band said, rather strangely—H.M. SUBMARINES.

Miraculously a straggler from PEDESTAL also arrived that day. She came in under her own steam, sailing defiantly towards the entrance to Grand Harbour under a protective canopy of those indomitable Malta-based Spitfires and Beaufighters.

Her name was the *Brisbane Star*.

She'd steamed for several days with a great, gaping rent in her bows from a torpedo hit and a crippling maximum speed of eight knots while, apart from the carrier *Eagle,* the Royal Navy had lost both the cruisers *Manchester* and *Cairo* and the destroyer *Foresight* —all heavily armed, fast warships.

For the first time since I'd joined the *Charon* I began to hope—but only to hope—that after the *Brisbane Star*'s gallant example, and with the kind of buccaneering genius for survival which Trapp undoubtedly displayed, then I might just live a little longer than I'd previously resigned myself to.

The horizon astern of the *Brisbane Star* was still ominously unbroken. The little groups of people constantly watching and waiting along the Baracca and the Valletta ramparts talked in low, quiet tones.

But still the *Ohio* didn't come.

Another curious item turned up which gave us further grounds for furious, and vaguely uncomfortable, speculation.

This time it was an ordinary rubber inflatable raft. Not unwelcome aboard any vessel with a strong prospect of being sunk in the very near future.

Only this also happened to be the type supplied quite openly to certain warships.

And especially to His Majesty's submarines.

And finally we were almost ready. Or as ready as we'd ever be. The most immediate problem I had was going to be to weld the RN gunners into that tight efficiency we needed so desperately, and to do it as soon as possible. There could be no working up period for the *Charon*—when we sailed it would be straight into a war area and, from a security point of view, once we left Malta's coast astern we couldn't risk turning back.

It all depended on the gunners' co-operation. Or had disenchantment with the *Charon*'s insanitary novelties already set in, despite Trapp's block-buster reception . . . ?

I walked up on deck. The moon was like a great red orb over the island. Moving to the rail I noticed another man leaning over and recognised the stocky relaxed form of Petty Officer Crocker.

He smiled when he saw me. 'Evenin', Sir.'

'Evening, PO.' I hesitated. 'How are the new boys taking it? The conditions and everything?'

'You mean are they goin' bolshie on us again?'

I shrugged. 'We haven't time to fight them and Jerrie. Tomorrow we ammunition ship. The day after, we could be in action.'

He grinned and I saw him jerk his head in the moonlight. 'Listen, Sir.'

The voices came from forward. Rough as hell yet at the same time with a certain bloody-minded pride. The sort of feeling which every matelot since Nelson has grudgingly admitted when he knows that, no matter how insignificant nor how uncomfortable she may be, his ship is still the finest in the Navy.

Only he and his oppo's don't actually say it quite like that. Or sing it. No more than our gunners were singing it anyway . . .

> *This is our story an' this is our song:*
> *We been in this rust heap jus' too fucking long.*
> *So roll on the 'Nelson', the 'Rodney', 'Renown',* .
> *This stick-funnelled bastard is gettin' us down . . .*

'They're settlin' in lovely, Sir,' Petty Officer Crocker said reassuringly. 'That's pure appreciation, that's what that is.'

We took on the ammunition at the last possible moment.

I adamantly refused to let any of Trapp's original crowd near it, not after the way I'd watched them treat that earlier bomb. Hopefully enough the Naval draft didn't seem to resent this in the least and stowed the whole lot down in the magazines themselves, hoisting and carrying the forty-five pound shells with a slightly deprecating air of professional superiority.

The *Charon*'s crew apparently accepted their inferior role with great humility by putting their feet up, lying back in the sun, and occasionally remembering to look suitably frustrated by the strong sense of discipline which prevented them from helping their sweating oppo's.

As Gorbals Wullie said, in between sips of fo'c'sle-brewed lager: 'Och but it fair screws mah guts intae a monkey's fist, seein' youse Navy lads scunnerin' yersel's an' no' bein' able tae lend a haund 'cause of mah loyalty tae Mister Miller . . .'

Being cramped for accommodation space we'd been forced to rig a makeshift messdeck for the Naval gunners in part of the forward hold. The remainder formed the Bofors magazine. Obviously a paragon in adversity, Seaman Gunner Clark quickly established a handy stowage for his meagre cigarette ration on the shelf formed by the 'NO SMOKING' sign above his hammock.

Petty Officer Crocker did, however, finally display considerable and somewhat earthy irritation on discovering that the message itself was being rapidly erased under the scorch marks of Seaman Gunner Clark's stubbed-out butts.

The lower hold of number two had been converted into a makeshift magazine for the 4.7 inch gun, which was ideal for handling but also meant that its crew would go into action literally standing over several tons of unprotected high explosive. Though it was all a bit academic, really—if the *Charon* was hit in the wrong place it wouldn't matter a damn where any of us happened to be at the time.

The completion of that operation also meant we were ready to sail.

As ready as an asthmatic hospital patient would be, anyway. To go deep sea diving.

The admiral appeared strangely detached when
Trapp and I went to see him for the last time. While
the grey, lively eyes appraised us keenly there was
also an impression of remote anticipation, of concern
with other, graver matters and his hand kept straying
towards the telephone. As if willing it to ring.

He said warily, 'Any questions, gentlemen?'

I was just going to murmur, 'About a thousand, at
least,' when Trapp answered, quite specifically,
'Three. Just three problems outstandin', Sir.'

'Being?'

'First—there's a small matter of a contract, along
with my cash advance. This bein' a bit've a business
arrangement, you'll understand.'

The admiral smiled bleakly. 'Your money is ready
and waiting for you at the Fleet Pay Office, Commander.'

He picked up a document from the desk and
handed it to Trapp. 'This is your Charter Party on
behalf of the British Admiralty which I'm certain you
will find in order. Do you . . . ah . . . wish any refer-
ences regarding our creditworthiness?'

Trapp shook his head solemnly. There did seem to
be occasions when business acumen blunted his sense
of humour. 'No thank you, Sir. I reckon Herr Hitler'd consider the Royal Navy a pretty going concern
wi'out my askin' him.'

The admiral glanced at the telephone again, almost
hopefully, then nodded. 'I hope so, Commander. I
sincerely hope so . . .' He gestured towards the contract in Trapp's hand. 'Incidentally, you'll find the
Charon's insurance is covered in there at . . . ah . . .
replacement value.'

'Which is another fifteen quid've the taxpayer's
money down the drain,' I reflected morosely, but
Trapp seemed quite pleased. 'Good,' he said with
enormous satisfaction. 'Then I don't need to bother
you so much with question number two now, do I?'

'Which was, Commander?'

'Ammunition safety devices . . . we don't have
none. Nothin' to stop a premature flashin' right back
into the magazine. No flooding valves against fire

burnin' through to the explosives. Not much in the way of fire hoses, f'r that matter but . . .' Trapp shrugged happily, '. . . they're not so important now. Not seein' the old *Charon*'s insured against that sort of thing.'

'Oh Christ,' I thought, 'but how mercenary can you *get!*'

I had a horrifying vision of oil-shiny survivors retching and struggling in a wreckage-strewn hell. Bleeding, torn hands scrabbling for our only lifeboat while, above the choking, gurgling shrieks, Trapp's enormous voice roaring, 'Don't scratch the *paint* there! Paint costs a good few bob, paint does . . .'

The admiral's hand stroked the telephone. 'Thirdly, Commander?'

Trapp looked apologetic. 'We gotta crate delivered. A secret one. But it fell off the back've the lorry . . .'

'And burst open. By accident.' The admiral nodded sympathetically, obviously aware of the misfortunes which could befall curious ship's masters.

I said quickly, 'It was submarine rig, Sir. And we also received an inflatable boat.'

'I know.' He chewed his lower lip pensively then glanced up. 'OPERATION STYX is a vital one, gentlemen. It is also an extremely dangerous and unpleasant venture—you realise that and so do we. And one of your greatest threats will be through premature disclosure of the *Charon*'s existence to the German Naval High Command. Information of the kind which must come, in the first instance, primarily from the survivors of any vessel which you attack . . .'

I caught Trapp's eye and he stared back at me impassively. This was the one problem which both of us had tried to avoid facing. Until, perhaps, the time came to allow a struggling man to live—or kill him, so that *we* might continue to.

'As you have already been briefed,' the admiral continued, 'you will only enter into aggressive engagement during the hours of darkness. By dawn you must be out of the area and steaming under the guise of either a neutral or one of their own supply fleet. In that way we hope you will avoid suspicion

. . . but only if your target's loss can be accounted for by some other means. A red herring to draw the enemy's scent.'

I sat forward involuntarily. 'Like a submarine. You intend them to concentrate on searching for a submarine then, Sir? Which they'll never find because it doesn't exist.'

'Precisely, Miller. As you already know, we daren't risk a real one in those waters. But, to the *Kriegsmarine,* it would still be more conceivable than the truth. Than the *Charon.*'

Personally I reckoned anything was more believable than the *Charon.*

'You'll make a particular point of boarding suspected blockade-runners before you sink them. Especially during your first few engagements.'

Trapp grinned. 'By rubber boat, like from a sub. An' rigged out in submariners' gear with the old *Charon* well hidden by darkness . . . Them wogs'll be imaginin' periscopes all round the bloody horizon. An' Jerrie'll swallow everythin' they're told. There's nothin' so bloody convincin' as a scared stiff, eye-poppin' Ayrab.'

The temporary euphoria left me suddenly. I asked quietly: 'Only it won't always work, will it Sir? The darkness isn't always dark. There's an unexpected rift in the cloud, moonlight . . . Some of them are going to recognise the *Charon* for what she is—a surface raider.'

The admiral looked at us for what seemed a very long time. Then he said carefully: 'Then it will be your lives in the balance. Yours, and the lives of your crew . . . I feel it is only correct that the action you take must be your decision also. I will stand by you, whatever that may be.'

He glanced at the phone again. Anxiously. And I was left staring intently at Trapp and wondering just what he would do when the problem arose. Because, however philosophically he appeared to accept the situation, he was again about to be forced into the killing game . . .

And then the telephone rang.

The admiral snatched it from its cradle before I'd time to switch my eyes back to him.

'Yes?' Tense as a heavy-lift wire.

A moment later, 'Thank you. I'll be down right away.'

We heard the click as the caller went off the line but, for what seemed a very long time, the admiral didn't move or speak. Then gently, almost absently, he replaced the receiver and sat back in his chair. 'I must apologise, gentlemen. But there are other matters . . .'

Trapp jerked his head at me meaningfully and heaved himself upright. 'There's nothin' else anyway, Sir. We'll be ready to sail at twenty-one hundred tonight as planned.'

The admiral stood up as well and held out his hand. 'It seems inadequate,' he said quietly, 'but there are times when I do believe that God is on the side of the people on this island. Perhaps you will take some of that priceless advantage along with you, too.'

I looked at him and, for the first time, noticed that his eyes were sparkling with a great pride.

'That telephone call, Sir?'

He nodded and, reaching for his cap, placed it firmly on his head. The golden oak leaves around the peak glistened softly under the reflected light from the plot. The plot which had so recently listed the participants in an operation called, enigmatically, PEDESTAL.

'She was Malta's last hope,' he murmured. 'The tanker *Ohio* . . . And they're bringing her in at this very moment.'

Painfully slowly she was assisted up the swept channel, three warships struggling to prevent her being swept into the mine fields on either side. Now barely afloat, with her main decks almost awash, that gallant ship nosed stubbornly towards the wide entrance to Grand Harbour. Mortally wounded but refusing to die, virtually lashed between the destroyers *Penn* and *Bramham* in order to stay afloat, the *Ohio* still carried her vital fuel oil and kerosene cargo to its final destination.

Twice abandoned, bomb scarred, her engines and
rudder damaged beyond repair: she had a twenty-foot
rent in her port side with her decks above the impact
point torn and protruding in great, tattered leaves.
Her rails and ventilators drooped in tortured lines
while, amidships, the distorted scars of the fires
which had ravaged her showed black against the
blistered grey.

The skeletal bones of a crashed Stuka still pro-
truded from forward of her bridge . . .

I stole a curious glance towards Trapp while, all
around us, the hysterical cheers of the people of
Malta drowned even the sound of the brass band ren-
dering a defiant *Rule Britannia* from the end of the
mole.

But he didn't see me. He just gazed down at the
limping *Ohio* with an almost remote detachment, as if
this part of the war wasn't included in his contract. The
responsibility of some other, less profit-conscious firm.

Almost. Because there was something else there
too, barely discernible. A sort of regretful acknowledgment of things now gone forever. A sad realisation
that these brave moments might have been a part of
him also.

Once. A very long time ago.

We sailed the *Charon* towards her bit of the war a
few hours later.

There weren't any brass bands to bid us farewell.
There weren't even any people.

Only the dimly-seen silhouette of the tanker *Ohio,*
now empty and resting brokenly on the bottom.

PEDESTAL had ended in glory. OPERATION STYX
had begun.

In squalid, insignificant anonymity.

Chapter Six

The ML which had escorted us through the minefield left us at the departure point, only a creamy flower of whirlpooling foam under her counter visible in the velvety darkness as she sped back to the island.

One brief, 'Good luck, *Charon*,' and we were alone. From now on the Royal Navy couldn't do much to help or protect us.

I'd already laid off our course to the proposed patrol area, commencing abeam of the desolate Misurata salt marshes and gradually working eastwards through the Gulf of Sirte towards the front lines then, if we got that far, turning round and steaming back up the Libyan coast again. And again. Which was precisely what Rommel's supply runners would be doing at the same time—unless we stopped them.

Gorbals Wullie was on the wheel. I said quietly, 'Steer one-six-zero.'

He peered at me suspiciously through the darkness of the wheelhouse. 'Eh?'

I did a quick calculation in my head. No matter how many guns we carried the *Charon* obviously still navigated by windjammer methods. 'Say . . . South sou'east.'

From out on the wing Trapp's voice snapped sharply, 'Belay that! You jus' bring her to due east an' keep her that way, Mister.'

Wullie muttered heavily, 'Mak' up yer minds, wull ye?'

I said tightly, 'East. Bring her due east.'

He spun the wheel easily and the ship lumbered corkscrewingly to port. 'Onything you say, Mister Miller, Sir.'

I walked out to the wing and faced Trapp. 'At the
moment we're heading nearer to Crete, Captain . . .'
I stopped abruptly as a nasty thought crossed my
mind. 'Or the Greek Islands. By God but you're not
goi . . .'

His teeth gleamed briefly in the darkness. 'If you're
drivin' a warship an' you sights a strange vessel,
Mister, what d'you try an' guess first?'

I frowned. 'Where she's bound for?'

'Aye And where she's come from. So if you was a
U-boat commander an' you raised a freighter on a
direct line between Malta an' Jerrie-held territory,
wouldn't you 'ave a few suspicions, eh?'

'Damn right.'

'But if you was that same bristle-head an' you saw
a ship on a course atween, say Taranto an' Rommel's
stampin' grounds. And it was flyin' the Eytalian Flag
to boot . . .'

I grinned I was beginning to learn how Trapp had
been able to stay in business despite the minor incon-
venience of a global conflict. 'So we steam due east
until we hit the Axis supply route, then alter for Misurata And hope the RAF have been well briefed
about us while we're on it.'

'Isn't that what they allocated us a recognition signal for, Mister? Anyroad,' he turned to the rail and
leaned easily against it, 'we c'n always tell 'em to
bugger off. With the Bofors gun.'

'And either way,' I retorted with a straight face,
'the boat's insured. Isn't it, Captain?'

'You're quick,' he chortled into the darkness.
'Whatever else, Mister, you're very quick to catch
on.'

We started to work up the ship.

The Panic Party were already detailed. Mostly the
men who stayed aboard would be Navy: the guns'
crews under the eagle eye of Petty Officer Crocker,
with Trapp and myself on the bridge, watching and
waiting to give the word to slam into action. Only Al
Kubiczek plus one fireman in the engine-room and
Gorbals Wullie on the wheel were to remain out of

the *Charon*'s originals. The rest of them were sched-
uled to go sailing with Second Mate Abou Babikian—
a natural panicker if there ever was one.

For eight hours Crocker and myself drilled the 4.7
crew in the enclosed oven of number two hold. By
the time we'd finished even I was a lot more confident
that, when necessary, the *Charon* could give a pretty
sharp welcome to any too curious prowlers.

But only if . . .

I found Trapp still on the bridge. He hadn't been
below since I'd left him eight hours earlier. The more
I got to know the strange, extroverted seaman the
more grudging respect I formed for him. But not too
openly. I'd learnt a long time ago that Trapp enjoyed
nothing better than a good hammer and tongs argument before taking a decision—even with the cook
about what we'd have for dinner next day. Fortu-
nately for the cook he was as bloody minded as the
captain and positively gloried in the traditional daily
slanging match. Only I wasn't the cook.

So—'I don't like it,' Trapp said predictably.

I sighed. 'But we've got to have a shoot, Captain.
Hell, we can't even be sure the damn guns'll *fire* unless we try at least once.'

'But how d'you know,' he asked cleverly, 'that
some Jerrie U-boat skipper isn't leerin' at us through
'is periscope this very minute, eh? Tryin' to figure us
out . . . an' then *you* go an' start firin' off guns that
shouldn't even be there, so's we suddenly look more
like a Brock's bloody benefit than an Eytalian
supply ship.'

'And how do you know,' I retorted spitefully, 'that
this whole moth-eaten hulk won't just fall apart under
the recoil of the first round? Personally, if we're going to disintegrate through old age, then I'd rather
do it with a reasonable chance of privacy.'

And anyway—it was highly unlikely that anyone
would be watching us at just that precise moment.

Or so I thought. At the time.

'I still don't like it, Mister.'

I looked wearily up at Trapp, already on my knees

below the rail with the phone to the guns in my hand. It was the fifth time we'd nearly been ready—each time before he'd suddenly imagined something at the last minute and lost confidence. I took another glance through the peep holes and saw nothing but empty, gently heaving sea then, switching my gaze to the deck, observed the Panic Party, looking dead bolshie by now, lounging impatiently around the already swung-out boat.

'Please, Captain? It'll only take a few minutes . . . An imaginary submarine surfacing to starboard, Babikian abandons while the gunners close up. I give them tracking instructions for a little while as the U-boat supposedly closes us, and then . . .'

'Yeah, yeah.' He scanned the horizon for the last time. 'An' I thought it'd be them Ayrabs seein' phantom bloody periscopes . . . Hands to abandon ship stations. Abandoooon SHIP!'

At the same time I snapped, 'Gun crews close up!' into the phone and listened to the sound of running feet, now reassuringly confident in their drill, as the *Charon*'s scruffy gunners transferred themselves abruptly into a warship's crew.

Trapp roared irritably, 'Get a MOVE on there, Second Mate!' then ducked down beside me to leave the bridge apparently deserted. Gorbals Wullie, crouching behind the wheel, called suddenly, 'Here, is there no' something youse has forgot tae do?'

Trapp glanced at me queryingly but I just shrugged back, everything was too well planned to make mistakes at this stage. Wullie shrugged philosophically as well, dismissing the thought. 'Och well. It was just—ah wondered if maybe you wanted tae stop the ship afore yon lifeboat got lowered doon tae the watter . . . ?'

Five minutes later we lay heaving sullenly in the swell. Trapp snapped furiously, 'Get *on* with it then, Mister!'

Babikian called tremulously from the after deck. 'We go now, Captain?'

'Ohhhh bugger off,' Trapp bellowed back petulantly, then flopped down beside me again and sniffed. 'Decisions,' he muttered, 'Always bloody decisions.'

Hastily I busied myself with the handset. 'For exercise . . . Target—U-boat. Range—three thousand yards and closing. Bearing—zero-two-fife relative. Moving astern . . .'

Already Crocker would be elevating and traversing the 4.7, still concealed behind the drop-down hull sections. As I altered the range and bearing, so would he until—on my selected moment of engagement—all it required was for the plates to be released, the already laid gun to be fired and . . .

. . . and after that anything could happen. One thing was for certain—that unless we disabled our unsuspecting investigators with the first few rounds, HM Armed Merchant Cruiser *Charon* would very quickly be reduced to a blinded, shattered holocaust of exploding ammunition and burning, screaming men.

But this was only a practise shoot. It wasn't as though anything was actually out there. Theoretically I corrected: 'Target's range now two thousand-fife hundred and closing. Bearing—zero-four-zero . . .'

Trapp said abruptly, 'I do see summat, Mister. Out to starboard!'

I glared at him irritably. From astern there was a rattle of blocks and Babikian's high-pitched voice urging, 'Leggo the falls . . . I spik to you plain, hah? So you let go the falls and you not argue . . .'

No problems about the crowd in the boat acting demoralised, anyway.

Only by now Trapp was up on his knees, peering tensely through the slit beside me. I tried to ignore him, following the path of my imaginary submarine to a believable conclusion.

'Range now two thousand-three hundred and constant. Bearing—zero-eight-fife and moving abeam . . . Stand by to shoot.'

Trapp snapped urgently, 'Hold it, man. F'r Chrissakes belay every . . .'

The phone said tinnily, 'On target. Standing by to release plates, Sir.'

Gorbals Wullie yelled abruptly, 'Here! Is this no'

supposed tae be a practice? Cause ah can see
someth . . .'

Trapp swivelled towards me, face red with pent-up
emotion. 'It's a submarine,' he shouted, almost pleadingly. 'It's a real live bloody submarine, Mister.'

And then I saw it too. Surfacing like a great black
whale with the white foam pouring down its pressure
hull in spluttering, excited torrents. Only it wasn't
quite where my imaginary U-boat was supposed to be.
It was farther aft and moving remorselessly the other
way . . . well clear of our 4.7's present line of fire.

Trapp said desperately, 'If we drop them bloody
hull plates now, while we're not even *aimin'* at
them . . .'

I hit the handset switch in near panic. 'Check!
Check! Check! Crocker, d'you read me?'

'Aye, aye, Sir,' calm and unflurried.

'We have a real target. A real submarine. This is
not for exercise, Crocker. I say again . . . this is *not*
for exercise.'

There was a momentary silence, then 'Not for exercise. Aye, aye, Sir.'

A distant, appropriately panic-stricken cry from the
Panic Party. 'Please Sir. What do you *now* tell us we
must dooooo?'

Men were already streaming from the distant submarine's conning tower, running forward to where the
slender gun squatted evilly on her still sea-washed
foredeck. I grabbed for the eyepieces of my camouflaged range finder. 'She's going to engage us on the
surface. She still thinks we're a genuine sitting duck.'

Trapp was back at the peephole but his first flush of
disconcertion was wearing off. Some of the old calculating snap was back in his tone. 'You jus' lay the gun,
Mister. Otherwise do nothin', d'ye hear? No Jerrie's
going to fire on us while we're on this route, not seein'
we're flyin' the Eytalian Flag. As far as he's concerned
we're one of their own.'

Then the range finder snapped into abrupt magnifi-
cation. I had one chilling glimpse of the barrel of that
huge foredeck gun swivelling remorselessly towards
me, then I was staring in horrified disbelief at the men

who manned it, and the white-painted legend on the side of her conning tower.

'No he won't. Not under this Ensign.'

I stared at Trapp, my face tight with shock. 'Because that isn't a U-boat out there . . . It's a British submarine.'

Just for a moment he blinked back at me. Then he said bleakly, 'Then why're they gettin' ready to shoot, Mister? Or hasn't nobody bothered to tell' em to stay clear.'

'*I* don't damn well know . . .' I stopped dead as understanding hit me. 'Or maybe *you* didn't, Trapp! Bother to brief the Ops crowd that you intended to steam a hundred-odd miles east of where they think the *Charon* is.'

Glancing back into the range finder I saw that the gun was still traversing but there was, as yet, no desperate urgency on the part of the Navy crew. As far as they were concerned we were just another Eytie blockade runner, already abandoned with remarkably prophetic urgency, but still a sitting target for surface gunfire.

I said bitterly, 'Did you, Captain—advise them you'd changed their plan?'

The telephone asked anxiously, 'Sir? New firing orders requested, Sir . . .'

I snapped, 'Wait one,' then stared black at Trapp. '*Did* you?'

He moved uncomfortably. 'We c'n still flash the signal, Mister.'

'No damn good. That submarine's patrolling well away from the area concerned. She won't even have been advised we exist.'

Trapp wriggled round to gaze through the peep-hole again. The muscles in my back started to knot in anticipation of what was coming. We didn't have very long left. Then Trapp swung back.

'Lay the gun,' he snapped flatly. 'Lay the gun like I already told you, Mister!'

I felt the blood pounding in my ears. 'That's the Royal Navy out there, Trapp. *Our* Navy!'

'I *know*,' he roared back, 'An' they give me a bloody job to do, Miller. Their choice, not mine, remember? So you jus' lay the bloody gun an' prepare to engage . . . an' that's an order.'

And then the first round from the submarine ripped over us like a runaway locomotive, just above the well deck, and I knew it was already too late, however fast Crocker was. Far too bloody late for anything. But I still raised the handset and snapped hopelessly, 'Target—submarine! Range—Wun thousand-seven hundred and constant. Bearing . . .'

Their second shell exploded almost alongside the bridge and only twenty-five yards short. I felt the whole ship keel away from the blast like a shying carthorse just before we were drenched by a great gout of yellow-stained seawater, collapsing inboard with a thundering rumble . . .

Gorbals Wullie from the wheelhouse. 'Och, ye bastards!'

Trapp into the engine-room phone. Cold as an iceberg. 'You get the hell outa there, Chief. An' your fireman . . . you got, maybe, ten seconds.'

My handset. Petty Officer Crocker. Still as if it was all a bloody exercise. 'Range set, Sir. C'n you relay a bearing if it's convenient?'

The end at any moment now . . .

Numbly I started to call off the bearings to Crocker. 'Wun-two-fife . . . wun-two-zero . . . Range still constant . . . wun-wun seve . . .'

The explosion, when it came, was different somehow to the way I'd always imagined it. No flash, no pain . . . only a vaguely detached rumble, almost as if it wasn't anything to do with the *Charon* at all, then the eyepieces of the range finder seemed to go hazy and white while the British sailors around that far-away gun appeared to wither away like leaves before an enormous gale . . .

Trapp said in a funny voice, 'Howd'you do that? Without droppin' the screens?'

I blinked at him curiously. He wasn't even supposed to be there by now. None of us were. Then Gorbals

Wullie in the wheelhouse muttered in an awed tone, 'Would ye look at that . . . Aw Jeeeeeze but would ye tak' a look at *that*.'

The spray from the explosion still hung like a vaporous shroud over the submarine, drifting crosswise over her long black foredeck in hissing, rainbow fingers as the warm sun refracted through them. There didn't seem to be any gunners grouped around the weapon any more either, while the long slender barrel now pointed drunkenly towards the sea and it took me a moment longer to realise it was because the British vessel was listing over to port with the curve of her starboard tanks cutting the line of the horizon.

Then the whole of her pressure hull forward of the conning tower erupted in a great orange flash of light while a jet of yellow and black smoke belched obscenely from the conning tower itself, rolling higher and higher into the startled blue sky, and we heard the thunder of the second explosion battering towards us across the debris-slashed sea . . .

Petty Officer Crocker on the other end of the phone snapped in a finally startled voice, 'What the . . . Sir —we're on target an' waitin' for orders down here . . . F'r cryin' out loud are you *up* there still, Lieutenant?'

'We're still here, Crocker,' I said quietly. 'Cancel that last target but stay closed up to the gun . . . And keep those cover plates closed, too.'

Trapp started to get to his feet like a man in a daze. I fought off the paralysis of horror that was swamping me and grabbed for his shoulder. 'Stay down,' I muttered. 'For God's sake stay under cover.'

He frowned, suddenly irritable. 'She's gone, Mate. Christ knows how, but the poor devils have gone.'

I wriggled urgently back to the peephole. There wasn't anything left out there now. Only a sullen, oily swirl on the surface and a few bobbing, unidentifiable shapes.

'She was torpedoed,' I snarled, beginning to feel frightened again. 'Which means there's *another* submarine watching us out there as well. Only this time it *has* to be a U-boat!'

We lay there, tensely waiting, for twenty minutes.
Twenty long, mind-torturing bloody minutes.

And all that time we knew we were being watched
by a suspicious, slowly cruising glass prism. And all
that time we also anticipated, at any moment, the
smash of the deck as it reared in our faces under the
impact of another torpedo. The one which would bring
the flash, and the pain. And the noise.

But we still stayed closed up at action stations without, to that remotely staring eye, a soul being visible
aboard the wallowing, silent *Charon*. Only our tiny,
dirt-engrained lifeboat splashing aimlessly and in erratic circles like a homeless water beetle while Babikian's crowd waited too. Perhaps, in their case, for
the close range snarl of the Schmeisser which might
follow the thunder of the U-boat's torpedo.

During those twenty everlasting minutes Al Kubiczek crept back down to his beloved engine room followed, rather less enthusiastically, by his fireman. And
Petty Officer Crocker louged impatiently in the sweat
box of number two hold with his gunners while the
crew of the Bofors, virtually imprisoned inside their
flimsy wooden packing case on the well deck, must
have suffered the claustrophobic torments of the
damned.

Until, when the twenty minutes were up, Trapp
stubbed his cigarette out on the deck and said aggressively: 'Well bugger them, Mate. They've 'ad their
chance an' I gotter contract to keep up with.'

He glanced for the hundredth time through the
peephole. So did I. But there was only the empty,
sunwashed sea. And those few pathetic humps, now
slowly fanning out in an oil-expanded circle.

'Then I suggest we stay out of sight, Captain,' I
murmured, hoping to God he wasn't going to start
arguing with me again. Not this time. 'Let Babikian
come back aboard as though the ship's still completely
abandoned. Then we can appear.'

Trapp gazed at me with lofty dignity. 'Naturally,
Mister Even before you started I was tryin' to tell you
there was a U-boat out there. Now I bloody well *know*

there is . . . an' somethin' tells me he isn't finished with us yet.'

But I'd realised that much already. Because the commander of that German submarine was a patient, calculating man.

And what we did during the next few minutes could decide whether we lived, or died.

So even after a nerve-racked Panic Party had returned aboard and the lifeboat had been retrieved, I still stayed out of sight below the bridge rail and waited. Coldly, this time. With the telephone in my hand.

Until, while the already disclosed part of our crew hung uncertainly over the rails and stared anxiously out to sea—which neither looked unusual nor took any acting on their part—Trapp, now back in the wheelhouse with the telegraph in his hand, called sharply, 'Aye, he *is* still there, Mister. Comin' up astern, maybe three points abaft the beam!'

I wriggled round stiffly and gazed aft. At the same time I gripped the handset a little tighter and said, 'Target still submerged, PO. Closing from astern, starboard side.'

Crocker answered, 'Aye, aye, Sir.' Just as if we'd only that moment started work.

And then, suddenly, the cruising feather of spray seemed to sprout a finger. And the finger lengthened into a vertical, slashing column which started to boil at its root as the conning tower of the submarine rose above the surface before, like a flat-topped metal cigar tube, the rust-streaked pressure hull itself followed in a smooth swirl of creaming, draining water.

U-149 . . . There was no confusion over the origin of this newly materialised apparition.

Then we were bleakly watching a carbon copy of our previous visitor's surface drill as ratings swarmed from her bridge, a line of smoothly moving men heading for her foredeck armament while others snapped into immaculately rehearsed activity around the vicious quick-firer abaft the tower.

Trapp muttered tightly: 'Here we go again . . . Engage when ready, Mister.'

I looked up at him sickly. 'We can't, dammit! She's still too far astern to bring our gun to bear. *And* he's keeping us fine on his bow . . . odds on he's got his torpedo room closed up too.'

Trapp said, 'I'm gettin' bloody fed up with this.'

Just before there was a surge of amplified static from the U-boat and a metallic voice boomed across the water between the two ships. *'Guten morgen, Kapitän! In welchem Jahrhundert hat dieser schiff gelebt . . . ?'*

And then, outrageously, the Tannoy spluttered into coarse, electronically-echoing laughter.

Trapp flapped his hands at me. 'What's he sayin'? What's he sayin', dammit?'

The relief which swamped me was sweeter than anything I'd ever felt before. 'It's OK, Captain. They aren't even suspicious . . . just play dumb and hope none of them speaks Italian.'

'But what's that bloody bristle-tead *sayin'*?'

I didn't dare look at him. 'He's asking . . . ah . . . to what century does this ship belong.' Hurriedly I added, 'But it's a *joke*, f'r Chrissake. Just a Teutonic bit of friendly humour.'

Trapp snarled, 'Jus' you get that gun've yours screwed aft a bit an' I'll see the bastard dies laughin' . . .'

'Achtung, achtung, Kapitän! Womit kann ich dienen?'

Sharper this time. And without any humour at all. I snapped nervously, 'Say something, for God's sake. We haven't a hope in hell of hitting him while we're stopped . . . even if we were sure the damned gun'd fire anyway.'

I saw his fists clench angrily below the level of the rail, then he roared tightly, *'Italiano . . . Nicht sprechen . . . ah . . . ?'*

'Sie Deutsch.' I whispered urgently.

'. . . see Dutch.' Trapp finished heavily.

There was a momentary silence from the U-boat. Peering out I could see her crew still closed up on the guns but obviously appreciating the fresh air more than the need for purely formal safety precautions. 'Please, God,' I thought longingly, 'please make him move a little farther ahead an' the hell with trying the gun out first . . .'

But then shouted commands echoed across the water and the German sailors started to run aft again, swarming up the vertical rungs of her conning tower. At the same time a hand was raised in salute from her bridge and the loudspeaker crackled for the last time.

'*Unterseebooten Eins Vier Neun zu ihren Diensten. Kommen sie wieder . . . Glück und auf Wiedersehen.*'

'U-boat 149 at your service. Call again any time. Good luck and . . .'

'I know, I know,' Trapp snapped. 'I'm not entirely bloody ignorant.'

Suddenly she surged ahead with a white swirl of water trailing her. Then, with a roar of compressed air, the sleek submarine started to slide under the surface once again and, within seconds, there was only the whirlpooling turbulence to mark where she'd been.

For a long moment there was an almost physical silence along the decks of the *Charon*. I started to shiver spasmodically, feeling utterly drained of emotion. Then Trapp muttered, 'Worth while takin' a look where our own sub got fished, d'you reckon?'

I stared over to where the oil slick had almost blended into the empty seascape. 'No,' I said quietly. 'No point at all. And our allies might still be watching.'

Then I lifted the telephone. 'Guns' crews, secure from action stations. Hands to tea, PO.'

It was back to normal aboard HMS *Charon*. Or as normal as we could ever be.

The ship started to tremble under the thrust of her slow revving screw as Trapp rang her to 'Full Ahead'. Then he turned to me solemnly. 'So did you enjoy your tiddley exercise then, Mister?'

'Exercise . . . ?'

I started to grin at that incorrigible master mariner. 'Aboard this ship, Captain, we don't have time for exercises. We're too damn busy dealing with the emergencies!'

Chapter Seven

We saw our first aircraft the next morning, just after breakfast—or the swill of lukewarm porridge and blackened, wilting toast that Trapp's favourite enemy, the cook, euphemistically called breakfast, anyway.

It was Babikian who heard it first. I was standing in the lee of the bridge half listening to Trapp arguing as usual about whether we'd sample the gastronomic delights of 'Chips an' mince' or 'Mince an' bloody chips.'

The cook had just screamed, in a rising fury of Greek outrage, 'When I 'eld the post of Head Commis Chef at the 'Otel Majestique in Salonike . . .'

'Chef . . . ?' Trapp bellowed incredulously. *'Chef?* You was a second assistant bloody dishwasher, you was. An' *that* was only in Georgie Kyriakopoulos's bug-ridden doss 'ouse next door . . . !'

Then the second mate leaned nervously over the after end of the bridge and said anxiously, 'Pleese, Captain? I think there is an aeroplane aiming towards us.'

I took off like an Olympic runner. 'Deck party to Lounging Stations. Bofors gun crew, close UP!'

For maybe half a minute the scene aboard the *Charon* was one of utter chaos. Some hands trying to barge their way upwards to their deck posts through a tidal wave of others struggling blasphemously to breach a path below and out of sight.

Trapp roared one victorious parting salvo at the enraged cook. '. . . an' even that was before you got the bullet f'r bein' too dirty.' Then, charging up the bridge ladder like a baby elephant, snapped his usual 'Bugger off!' greeting to the sloe-eyed second mate and skidded to a halt beside me.

'Where away, Mister?'

'Two points on the starboard bow. Can't identify it yet.'

I leaned over anxiously to scrutinise the scene below. The Lounging Party—so called because their primary job in the event of air investigation was to give the impression of small-crew normalcy on deck —were now doing precisely that, despite the heavy breathing and red flushed faces apparent to a closer observer.

However, in case the impression they actually gave was the wrong one, they also stayed close to the concealed heavy machine guns under the fake vegetable lockers but—as our last-resort defenders consisted primarily of a homicidally-oriented Gorbals Wullie, a jumpy Second Mate Babikian, a lethargic Greek stoker and a bloody-minded ship's cook from Georgie Kyriakopoulos's place—I had strong reservations about the efficiency of our secondary armament.

But, on the credit side, being part of the *Charon*'s crowd they made very practical and completely authentic Loungers.

The plane droned closer until the twin-engined silhouette filled the lenses of my binoculars. 'Dornier,' Dornier,' I muttered. 'Reconnaissance plane.'

Trapp grinned enthusiastically, 'Good. Then clear the Bofors away an' we can give them a bashing f'r a change.'

I eyed him apprehensively. The nearer we got to the enemy the less neutral Trapp seemed to get— either that or he was getting more and more carried away with his already over-optimistic opinion of the *Charon*'s real firepower. That was why I'd originally wanted an experienced Naval Officer in command, one who could assess the odds and act accordingly —not barge into action every time he caught a glimpse of a Swastika, just out of some megalomaniac conviction that business was business and he had a contract fo fulfil.

In fact, sailing to war under Lieutenant Commander Edward Trapp, RN, promised to become increasingly more hazardous and nightmarish.

'Well, then?'

I shook myself out of my daze. Trapp was staring at me oddly, a bit petulantly.

I said wearily: 'We daren't risk firing at it, Captain. For one thing the Bofors can't be trained or elevated until that dummy case is removed. Plenty of time for any pilot to shy clear. And even if we got lucky and splashed him, he'd still have radioed our position and description . . . we wouldn't even *see* the next U-boat.'

The plane was drawing steadily and remorselessly closer. Identifiable without glasses now.

But Trapp still eyed it hungrily, assessing it against his own tactical yardstick. 'I dunno. There's a few thousand quid's worth've Jerrie war effort there . . .'

'Oh, dammit! Irrespective of what you think, we're not a blasted anti-aircraft cruiser . . .' Then I hesitated and added slyly: 'Please yourself, of course, only—if we don't hit him first time round and the *Charon*'s real function is compromised—then you're in breach of contract, remember. For going against orders.'

I could tell by the worried frown that I'd found his Achilles' heel. 'In breach, Mister?'

'No aggressive engagement during daylight hours. Which means no shooting at Germans who take us at face value.'

He glared at the Dornier resentfully then, coming to a decision, hung over the bridge rail. 'You lot get lounging proper. An' stop hangin' round them machine guns like they was Christmas boxes . . . where's that big ensign?'

Babikian scurried aft and came back with an armful of bunting. They spread it over number two hatch cover and the *Charon* steamed onwards with the Italian Flag plain as a pikestaff to any aerial observer.

The first pass over us was fairly high. Then we watched tensely as the plane turned almost lazily and came back towards us fifty feet above the surface, passing down our port side about half a mile away with the black crosses plain against the slender fuselage. Unsuspecting maybe, but still careful. I had a feeling that particular pilot could very well live to see the end of the war.

Or was there some doubt in his mind? Something not quite right . . .

The third time he turned he came straight for us, just above masthead height. Watching the elongated silhouette growing larger and larger, with the twin props discing opaquely in the sunlight as he closed I suddenly felt horribly exposed, while the fear that Trapp had been right and I'd been wrong all the time grew more and more overpowering.

The Dornier's bomb doors were still closed, I could see that much. But they also mounted cannon and machine guns which could turn the *Charon*'s bridge and decks into a bloody, colandered shambles instantaneously. I gripped the handset to the Bofors in one hand and started to wave with the other.

Almost pleadingly.

Trapp started to wave welcomingly too, and so did the others, as if our lives depended upon it—which, on reflection, they probably did. Whatever Italian seamen may have felt about their Nazi allies they'd have been damned glad to see them in waters where their visitor could just as easily have been British.

Five hundred yards . . . four hundred . . . Twin machine guns in her nose clearly visible now against the glinting Perspex dome . . . three hundred . . .

Gorbals Wullie waving in hysterical excitement while bawling, 'C'mon ye square-heid poofs. Get doon here so's ah c'n hae a square go at ye's. Poofy Jerries, poofy Jerries . . .'

Trapp roaring furiously, 'Smile, you bastards. Smile at them like thy was bringin' yer wages . . .'

. . . two hundred . . . one hundred yards . . .

Please God, don't let them see anything wrong . . .

The huge plane started to bank at the last moment, dropping its nearside wingtip as it thundered above us, the propwash plucking at our hair and ripping the black smoke from the *Charon*'s broomstick funnel into tumbling, shying tatters.

One frozen glimpse into her cockpit of helmet-framed white faces gazing down at us, then a clenched fist raised in brief salute and she was gone, droning along the line of our wake with the slipstream dragging and rolling the Italian Ensign across the hatch cover in billowing frustration.

We watched the Dornier silently until it faded over the shimmering horizon, then Trapp sighed in a sort of disappointed way and turned to the rail.

'An' *another* thing,' he yelled at the cook. 'Them scrambled eggs you destroyed yesterday was like bloody rubber . . .'

And so, as much by good luck as good management, we reached the Axis-held coast of North Africa.

We still hadn't fired our guns. We hadn't even dropped our hull plates and tried to.

But we'd had a great deal of practice. In the theory of being a Q-ship, anyway.

That night, after making our first landfall, we took on new stores and fresh water.

And coaled ship. Just like that. Up a featureless, sandscoured creek and right in the heart of enemy occupied territory.

We'd closed the dark, craggy coast just east of the salt marshes and anchored in four fathoms. Then Trapp and Al Kubiczek rowed silently ashore with muffled oars—a bit of cloak and dagger promise which froze my blood at the necessity for it—until, one and a half hours of nerve-torturing tension later, they rowed erratically and somewhat merrily back again, with one rowlock now squealing and screeching in oil-dry and unheeded protest.

After which, with alcoholic abandon, Trapp had steamed the *Charon,* chugging and clanking, straight for that foreign shore and brought her up, full astern, to crunch alongside a dilapidated stone quay with an impact which must have been heard in Cairo.

Already lined up on the wharf waited three creaking, antiquated Ford trucks of approximately the same vintage as the *Charon* herself—and almost as seaworthy to my prejudiced eye. Two were loaded to the gunnels with fourth grade but nevertheless adequate coal while the third positively sagged under the weight of cases, each bearing the Wehrmacht Eagle and stamped with mouth-watering legends like *Ochsenschwanzragout* and *Geräucherte Rinderzunge* and *Klops*.

Or, as Trapp grinned cheerfully: 'Grub, Mister. Jerry vittles. We dunno what they are 'til we opens 'em but it makes the dinners bloody exciting.'

There was also a group of men watching us impassively from the shadows. Tall, bright-eyed men with dark, aquiline features and Schmeisser submachine guns slung negligently across their black-robed shoulders. Desert men who, by their silent presence in this threatening, unbelievable place, made me feel very uncomfortable indeed . . .

Which was of course, why the admiral had needed Trapp so badly, as well as the nondescript, chameleon-like *Charon* which merged so well into a background where local machinery was fifty years behind the times anyway. Because no Royal Naval officer—or no *other* Naval officer—could possibly have the intimate knowledge which Trapp possessed of those desolate, half-forgotten landing points along the Libyan coast.

Apart from the cut-throat, camel-stealing, black-hearted criminal connections Trapp had so diligently established with those menacing representatives of the local Arabian Mafioso or whatever. In fact, after that first night I became utterly convinced that if we'd ordered a desert-camouflaged, good-condition Tiger tank or a *rotte* of only slightly used Me 109's then Trapp's Bedouin oppo's would have delivered with equal alacrity—the corpses of their original occupants being optional extras.

It all suggested that Rommel's major problem, as far as Trapp's hawk-nosed band of Arabian trading associates were concerned, wasn't so much getting his Afrika Korps to fight as preventing them from being stolen before they could.

Only, as Trapp whispered throatily, 'Don't take your eyes off've the ship f'r a moment, Mister. Them thievin' Ali Baba's don't 'ave no principles. No business integrity.'

From then on I just prayed that the steady income they received from supplying the *Charon*'s need was more attractive than the price they could negotiate with the Germans for a one-off, outright sale . . .

And, the next night, the seagoing branch of Trapp's Wartime Enterprises opened for business.

When we went into action.

The target was small, well down to her marks and slow enough even for the *Charon* to surprise.

We first saw her to seaward, passing across the lighter line of the horizon. Trapp, with his flair for survival, had decided to hunt from close to the shore so that *Charon*'s silhouette would be lost against the impenetrable blackness of the land. This had the incidental advantage of making any other traffic easier to see.

For myself I was only too glad to do anything which might prevent us from being recognised as a surface vessel. I still couldn't shake off that chilling apprehension over Trapp's reaction when faced with potentially compromising survivors. And perhaps the most horrible part of that grisly quandary was—that I couldn't really be sure of what steps I would take myself. Not when the moment of truth finally came.

But that was one difficulty we shouldn't have to meet that night. Not being as dark as it was. There wasn't even any need to conceal our guns as we stalked the enemy coaster, we just lowered the screens quietly from the 4.7 and cleared away the Bofors so that its crew, for the first time since we'd sailed from Malta, would be able to lay on their target all the way in.

Gradually we closed, with the tension aboard *Charon* almost a tangible element in the cold night air. Approaching as we were, virtually bows on, we wouldn't be able to train the big gun until Trapp swung us to run parallel with the enemy but, all the time, the slender barrel of the Bofors followed that shadowy, unsuspecting steamer.

No radio aerials apparent through the glasses. No need, then, to pound her to matchwood with our opening salvo.

Quiet. Deathly quiet, with only the sigh of the water under *Charon*'s vertical bow and the muffled, reciprocating throb of her labouring engine whispering us to war. Hardly anything visible on the foredeck, just the ghostly white anti-flash hooded shoulders of the gunners and the occasional soft gleam as a vagrant moonslip catches the round of a motionless steel helmet . . .

Trapp, leaning deceptively against the bridge rail, watching and only muttering the briefest of helm orders to Joseph No-Name at the wheel. Curiously I glance at him but there's no suggestion of emotion in the impassive, weatherbeaten features, no indication of the turmoil which must have been in his mind at finally being forced to come to terms with destruction and killing, and the waste which, for most of his life, he's dedicated himself to avoiding.

Then there's nervous, out-of-place Babikian standing beside his machine gun at the after deck rail. A weapon which, so far, he's only learnt how to fire from the manual and from what Crocker and I have told him.

And Petty Officer Arthur Crocker himself, with his outrageous RN draft. Probably mine, and the Royal Navy's biggest surprise package of all up to now. A crowd of matelots who out-*Charon* the *Charon*'s own crew when it comes to muttering intractability— until there's a job to do. Most of them out of sight, below us in the exposed limbo of number two hold and gloomily wondering if their bloody gun will even fire when needed.

The fat, atrociously incompetent cook at *his* gun, still wearing that filthy apron. And Al Kubiczek, virtually entombed with his sweating, cursing firemen in a steel coffin with wafer-thin walls . . . Gorbals Wullie, silent and strangely thoughtful, looking sheepishly and incongruously clean in the seaman's cap and uniform of a torpedo rating from one of His Majesty's submarines. Waiting with an unfamiliar sten

gun in his hands beside the already-inflated rubber
boat.

But not too long to wait now, though. The other
ship still steaming steadily on a converging course
with us . . .

Planning to open up on her with the Bofors alone
at first then, as she's unlikely to radio for help. Only
want her to heaveto until we've boarded. Then it's
back to the *Charon* while the poor bastards out there
get away if they can, and sink her with the 4.7 inch.
If *we* can!

Finally, get the hell out of the immediate area at
all of eight knots while praying to God no enemy
patrol craft are in the vicinity . . . maybe even following us suspiciously at this very moment over the sights
of *their* closed-up and ready-trained guns.

While tomorrow—if there is a tomorrow—there'll
be a Tunisian Ensign spread out over the hatch cover,
or a Vichy French one or an Italian, while our Panic
Party waits and our Lounging Party lounges like hell.
And while the *Luftwaffe* goes crazy searching for
das verdammt Britisch unterseebooten. . .

But that's all in theory, too. Like the rest of the
Charon's proposed war has been.

Up to now . . .

Suddenly Trapp called gruffly: 'Port twenty the
wheel . . . Midships. Steady . . . Steady as she goes,
lad.'

I gazed calculatingly at the enemy ship, now running almost abeam of us and still blissfully unaware
of our proximity. I knew that, now we'd turned,
Crocker would already have the 4.7 trained on that
other coaster's dimly seen bridge. The range wasn't
hard to judge. It was point blank.

Then Trapp snapped in a flat unemotional voice.
'Engage when ready, Mister.'

I didn't use the telephone. There wasn't any point
in secrecy any longer.

I just took a deep, uneasy breath and roared,
'Bofors gun. Twelve pounds . . . Open FIRE!'

Pom . . . pom . . . pom . . . pom! Pom . . . pom
. . . pom . . . pom . . . !

Splitting the hush of the night with an obscene,
mind-paralysing rage. Slamming our senses with that
characteristic four-beat rhythm, the one-pounder's
millisecond muzzle-flashes riccocheted from every
rusted plate and staring, apprehensive face aboard
the *Charon* . . . One flickering, Chaplinesque image of
the rating on the loading platform feeding the clipped
rounds into the auto-loader. The hunched shoulders
of the gunlayer and trainer . . .

Silence.

And darkness once again. While, within the blink
of a shocked eye, the *Charon* had finally become a
warship.

And the enemy vessel had become a victim. Red,
unimpressive sparkles running momentarily along
the black line of her deck from forward to aft, then
nothing. No explosion, no fire, no panic-stricken
scream for help from our listening radio receiver . . .

Trapp snarled tightly, 'Engage again, Mister. A
proper burst.'

Then suddenly, through the new silence, we heard
the wheezy roar of blowing-off steam and the other
ship started to slew towards us while, at the same
time, the barely visible luminescence under her bow
faded out of sight altogether.

I said thankfully, and a bit surprised as well, 'It's
all right. She's stopping.'

Trapp looked at me and, for a moment, our eyes
met. Then he turned away and gripped the handle
of the telegraph grimly.

'Stop Engine.'

I felt the *Charon* slowing until we lay hove-to side
by side with the enemy and about a hundred yards
off. The Bofors still pointed at her bridge and I knew
the 4.7 would be laid on precisely the same point.
Still no sign or reaction from the other ship. No shouts,
no lights, not even the squeal of davit blocks to suggest they were abandoning. Lifting the telephone I
spoke to Crocker uneasily.

'We're going now. Everything OK down there?'
His voice was confident. 'Aye, aye, Sir.'

'You have the fire control. Remember—anything
goes wrong and you hit her hard. Don't bother about
us, there won't be time.'

It wasn't bravado on my part. If anything did go
wrong then we in the boarding party would almost
certainly be dead anyway. An open rubber boat is
very exposed to the smallest of small arms fire. Our
only insurance would be the unseen threat of the
Charon covering us—and the hope that crews of the
type who ran these tinpot coastals would be more
scared than loyal to their present charterers.

Unless, of course, we met an Arabian Trapp . . .
or tried to board an *ersatz* Afrika Korps troop transport instead. though presumably they'd already be
firing back with everything they'd got.

Trapp muttered irritably, 'Get on with it then,
Mister.'

I glanced apprehensively over at the other ship
for the last time then shrugged. 'Yeah, well . . .'

I slid down the bridge ladder. He came to the top
and looked down at me.

'Twenty minutes. See an' be back in twenty minutes or flash us if you have to spend any longer.'

I nodded and walked towards the shadowy figures
already launching the boat. Five of us were going—
Gorbals Wullie, Seaman Gunner Clark, Mulholland
the big leading hand who'd shown such a resigned
sense of humour the first time he'd seen the *Charon*,
and a Greek fireman called Polly who threw knives
and spoke fluent Arabic. And, of course, myself.
Thanking God that, if nothing else, at least I had four
of the hardest, most devastating thugs who'd ever
donned Royal Naval uniform as back-up men.

Just as I started to swing over the rail Trapp called,
'Good luck, Mister. An' don't you do nothin' you
reckon could get dodgy.'

I grinned back, hoping nobody could see my hands
trembling in the dark.

'I won't, Captain.'

And I really did mean it. Every last dry-throated syllable.

The uncomfortable, exposed feeling became stronger and stronger the closer we rowed to that eerily silent ship. Even Gorbals Wullie at the oars kept craning round uneasily to cast a wary glance as we neared, while Clark and Mulholland crouched in the bow, stens ready cocked and trained on the line of her rails.

We bumped alongside forward of the gently trickling engine discharge, conscious of the muffled beat of the still slowly turning machinery from inside the scarred, rusted hull. Polly the Greek looked at me queryingly, 'You want I should call them, Mistair?'

I shook my head. 'We'll get on deck while the going's good. Too bloody open down here.'

He stood up unsteadily on the shifting bottom boards and heaved. I heard the grapnel clang shatteringly through the silence as it struck the steel deck, then the Greek took in the slack and tugged. It held firm.

Wullie muttered gloomily, 'Well ah dinnae like it. They cannae all be deid, can they?'

Mulholland didn't take his eyes, or the air-cooled barrel of his sten, off the rail above. 'What, with about twelve of a crew aboard, mate—one per shell that we fired? Surprisin' them thick sods on the Bofors even 'it the bloody ship . . .'

I snapped tightly, 'Stop chattering. I'm going up, then you next, Mulholland. Then Clark, Wullie and Polly, smart as you can.'

I took one last, immeasurably longing glance out to where the *Charon* lay, now completely invisible against the jet-black backdrop of the land, then shinned awkwardly up the few feet of knotted rope which hung over the rail. As my eyes rose above deck level I searched in sick anticipation for the least sign of movement. Suspended as I was, with no way of dodging or protecting myself, I was totally exposed to a roundhouse kick in the face or even a leisurely, neatly placed shot clean through my sweat-beaded forehead.

But the decks of that ghostly enemy ship were utterly deserted. Not a movement other than the flutter of a scrap of paper caught under the hatch batten opposite, and the monotonous clack . . . clack . . . clack . . . of a halyard swinging against the mast in time with the slow roll of the hull.

Scrambling shakily over the rail itself I dropped thankfully on one knee, unslinging my sten with fumbling fingers. Hastily I slammed the cocking handle back, then waited, eyes anxiously probing every dark and secret shadow on the well deck.

'Hurry up, Mulholland. Hurry *up* f'r . . .'

A grunt from the rail, then the big leading hand vaulted heavily down beside me and nervously brought his sten to the ready. Seaman Gunner Clark next, screwing himself quickly back over the scuppers to take the boatrope and make it fast while Wullie also half-climbed, half-fell inboard and snarled 'Fuck it!' in far from secretive forgetfulness.

Clark muttered petulantly, 'If I'd wanted ter be a flamin' monkey I'd've joined the bloody Commandos . . .' and I grinned to myself despite the unease that was gripping my belly.

Gradually the damage inflicted by our brief burst from the Bofors became apparent. Above us the square, ugly little wheelhouse—almost as cab-like and antiquated as the *Charon's*—now dropped drunkenly to one side, splinter-riddled and with fresh, whitely-gleaming scars to show where the one pounder shells had blown it apart. Anyone who'd been keeping watch up there, I reflected grimly, certainly wouldn't be around any longer to welcome us aboard.

The slowly spiralling silhouette of the equally *Charon*-era funnel, but sagging forward now with an untidy tin-opener rim where it had been shot away, and the barely perceptible smoke rising almost vertically into the still night sky in ironic contrast.

A jumble of shattered, torn-up hatch boards, all spilled over the coaming under a shroud of ripped and blast-frayed canvas. An unseated ventilator staring mutely at us like a dead eye from the scuppers. A once vertical steel ladder now leading crazily from the fo'c'slehead straight over the bulwarks and into the sea.

I stood erect quietly, 'They have to be aboard somewhere. Some of them *have* to be, dammit.'

We fanned out warily, moving aft in a line towards the accommodation. Still no movement, with only the trickle of the discharge and the sighing of the steam and the steady *clack* of the halyard to break the unbelievable silence.

Until suddenly . . .

'*God!*'

I whirled, finger frozen on the trigger with the shock of it . . .

The fat man sat with his back against the scarred upstand of the coaming, legs splayed comfortably before him and hands folded primly across the bloodstained belly. The long peaked Afrika Korps cap still sat square over wide, unblinking eyes which watched us with blank surprise while the insignia of a German *Wehrmacht* Feldwebel showed plainly against the washed-out khaki sleeves.

Gorbals Wullie stared back at him, looking a bit shaken, then stepped cautiously forward before prodding the fat man resentfully with the muzzle of his sten. The dead soldier keeled sloppily sideways and lay, still gazing up at us with that detached, bewildered look while quite a lot of him slipped sinuously from under the clasped hands.

I muttered tightly: 'Shell splinter. Probably a guard —to keep the crew on their toes. Which also suggests they're Libyans.'

Wullie grinned toughly, anxious to prove his image was buttoned-up tight again. 'Ah wasnae scared, ye ken. It'd take mair than a deid Jerrie tae worry Gorbals Wullie an' that's f'r sure . . .'

'*Here!*'

I moved fast towards the shout, skidding to an abrupt halt round the corner of the starboard alleyway. Mulholland and Clark were already waiting, legs straddled apart and stens trained unwaveringly on the

group of men who stood motionless against the rail.
There were nine of them, some dressed in the flowing
white burnous of the traditional Arab, two in dirty
boiler suits and one—obviously some kind of officer
—wearing a reefer jacket and pyjama bottoms.

Nearly all of them looked scared half to death. Yet
there was something . . . a feeling about the group. An
unease which didn't quite seem to fit . . .

'Any of you speak English?'

One of the Arabs—a tall man with the hood of his
burnous pulled forward to shield his features—turned
his head and stared hard at the rest of the group.
Apart from that, silence.

Polly the Greek moved up beside me and I caught
the hopeful glint of a blade. I snapped angrily, 'Put
that *away*, dammit! Tell them they have been caught
working against the Allied cause and, because of that,
our submarine is forced to sink their ship . . . understand?'

Polly shrugged, looking a bit disappointed, then spat
some rapid, guttural sentences of Arabic but apart
from a few startled glances, they still seemed strangely
quiet and subdued, almost apathetic even. I started
to wonder how in God's name the Germans had managed to instill such passive acceptance into a normally
voluble and protesting race.

Wullie wasn't happy: 'Ah dinnae like this either,
Mister Miller. There's somethin' no' quite right about
they lads.'

I frowned uneasily. 'I know. Polly, ask them how
many German soldiers were aboard when they sailed
last . . .'

The gleam of blued steel swinging towards me from
the tall Arab's robe coincided with an almost explosive
scattering of the rest of the suddenly activated group.
Mulholland, already whirling, roared urgently, '*Watch*
that big bast . . .'

One frozen horrifying imprint of the Schmeisser's
muzzle staring like a metallic Cyclopean eye into
mine, along with a terrified, overpoweringly resentful
conviction that Arabs don't bloody *have* long BLOND
HAIR F'R GOD'S SAKE . . .

Instantaneously, shockingly, the chattering cacophony of prolonged sub-machine gun fire at point blank range, slamming my ear drums, echoing frenetically from every angle and turn of the alleyway. Chattering muzzle flashes ripping the gloom into kaleidoscopic, petrified images . . .

And then a long, bottomless silence.

Until.

'Two, Mistair . . .' The Greek's voice was very satisfied. 'I theenk two German soldiers aboard thees ship, maybe?'

I blinked shakily at the tall Arab who now hung backwards over the rail in front of me, the billowing white robe streaming in gently undulating folds from his upside-down shoulders. I couldn't see the upper half of the folded corpse—I didn't want to, anyway—but the immaculately-creased khaki trouser legs and the *Wehrmacht* gaiters encasing the desert boots told me all I needed to know. Those, and the Schmeisser machine-pistol lying at my feet.

Which also solved the mystery of the mutely reluctant sailors.

For one bewildered moment I still thought it was Polly who'd fired with such savage, uncontrolled over-kill. Thirty rounds into one close-range target. Coldly triggering until the whole magazine ran out.

Then Clark demanded incredulously, ''Aven't you never fired one of them things before, Jock?'

And Gorbals Wullie, still wreathed in drifting clouds of cordite smoke, muttered unsteadily, 'Jeeze but ah didnae even ken it wis a *machine* gun . . . me usually bein' a razor man masel'.'

Eight minutes later we were back in the boat while the Arabs, with great alacrity and finally unrestrained babbling, were lowering theirs.

I shouted urgently, 'Wullie. Where the *hell* are you.'

'Here now, Sir.' He leaned over the rail and passed a big canvas bag into the boat. I took it from him suspiciously. 'What's this?'

Flopping heavily down beside me he grinned sheepishly. 'Mah shopping list, Mister Miller. Frae the Captain.'

I peered inside. Even in the darkness I could see the gleam of silver and I remembered Trapp's suggestion, made what now seemed a very long time ago to a certain admiral. Regarding fringe benefits . . .

'Cutlery,' I muttered grimly. 'And what else?'

'A coupl've braw wee filigree napkin rings. An' one o' they sextant things f'r navigatin' with.'

He grinned again and shrugged. 'Ah took a glance on the bridge. Yon skipper'll no' be needin' them again anyroad.'

I snapped bleakly, 'Well . . . oh, shove the bloody boat off then, Clark.'

But it did take a bit of getting used to.

Being a pirate, I mean.

Not long afterwards Trapp said into the voice pipe, 'C'mon up, Chief. The mate's gotta fixation we're just as likely to sink oursevles as well as the Ayrab when 'e fires that bit've a gun of his.'

I looked at him resentfully through the gloom of the wheelhouse. I was still sweating with the reaction from my too-close brush with death aboard the coaster, while the effort of struggling back to the *Charon* had finally turned the roll collar of my white submarine jersey into a soggy noose despite the chill of the North African night.

'It's not a fixation,' I glowered sullenly. 'It's just that I don't think you've any idea of the recoil of those 4.7's. And if this senile hulk can't stand it then we're likely to go straight down without warning.'

'She's solid,' Trapp retorted airily. 'Tight enough to be classed A-1 Plus at Lloyd's. Anyway, get on with it, Mister—I aim to be forty miles away before it gets light an' I never claimed the old *Charon*'s exac'ly a flyer.'

I gripped the rail with one hand and the phone with the other. 'Ready PO?'

'When you are, Sir.'

A deep breath for about the fiftieth time that night. 'Target—port side . . . One round . . . FIIIRE!'

The explosion, almost directly under us, sounded as though the shell was coming in, not going out. A sharp, ear-slamming report which literally rippled the deck beneath my feet as the sound wave supersonicked outwards and the *Charon* seemed suddenly to shrink while, in the same split second, shaking herself in violent outrage.

I felt her keeling over to starboard under the shock of the recoil as the round left us like a sheet of ripping canvas. Every flat surface aboard, vertical or horizontal, appeared to fuzz under a displaced layer of rust particles, one eroded wire stay parted with a terrifying *twang* at the same moment as the wheelhouse clock and barometer fell off the bulkhead. A pane of glass fragmented in a shower of tinkling, flashing diamonds while, from the engine room, the demented roar of a fractured steam line added to the bedlam. Four drums of lubricating oil secured along the taffrail lurched crazily against their lashings then, in immaculate line astern, trundled majestically through the distorted starboard rails and straight into the sea.

I registered the flash of the hit, precisely on the distant coaster's waterline, in almost absent surprise while still fumbling to collect my reeling senses. One glance as a cursing, half-blinded figure in a vaguely white boiler suit dived into the steam now billowing up the engine-room companionway, then Gorbals Wullie, finally dead shattered, 'Jee*esus!*'

A complete fog of atomised rust now, and soot and dirt from a thousand landfalls, ballooning upwards to knee height while coughing, choking men stumbled for support. I called frantically, 'Crocker! You all right down there, Crocker . . . ?'

The phone splutterd doubtfully. Then, 'Think so . . . can't see a bloody thing right now but the gun's still 'ere. Far as I know any'ow, Sir.'

This time I didn't take a deep breath. I didn't dare to. 'Reload when ready, PO.'

Trapp strolled over, flicking fastidiously at the patina of red which covered him from head to foot, and smiled deprecatingly.

'Din't I tell you, Mate?'

He beamed proudly. 'You wouldn't hardly notice we'd gotter gun on board, would you. No apart from a bit o'dust here an' there, any'ow . . .'

And so it went on. For five weeks we continued our own private war. Sometimes lying up in those secret places of Trapp's during the long sweltering days and, on the more uncomfortable occasions when we'd been caught too far from shelter, just steaming along with apparent dedication to the Axis war effort while the *Luftwaffe* flew low over us and the Lounging Party waved. And, I think, while all of us grew very much older in a very short time.

We sank ships. More coasters, almost carbon copies of ourselves, dhows loaded down to the gunnels with arms and *Wehrmacht* food supplies, even the small caiques which really seemed to prove that the Afrika Korps were scraping the bottom of the logistics barrel.

It became almost a job of work. Some of them we boarded and left no doubt in the minds of their terrified crewmen that the dark, low shadow to landward of them was a British submarine. Others—usually those that we suspected of carrying radio, we just opened fire on from the night, without any warning at all.

We killed a lot of merchant seamen in those five weeks, though probably in no greater numbers than more conventionally delivered bombs or torpedoes would have done. And—whether Arab, German, Italian or even Vichy Frenchmen—they were the enemy while they sailed those nocturnal routes.

Or so I kept telling myself, anyway.

Because there was also a steadily growing collection of cheap silver accumulating in Trapp's cabin, and a few other miserable valuables assiduously retrieved by the crew of the *Charon* from ships already with the mark of death on them under the open sights of our 4.7 . . . And they seemed to make it a dirty war. Even dirtier than it really was.

Almost a trade, in fact.

Certainly not a patriotic, non-profit making crusade

for the Allied Cause. Not by the self-employed and still unsettlingly unpredictable Lieutenant Commander Trapp, RN, do-it-yourself warship supplier and buccaneer without equal.

But, as with any other business venture, the accounting had to come one day. We all knew that. Even Trapp with his hypersensitive nose for danger, and his almost uncanny gift for survival must have expected it.

That eventually the auditors—in the shape of an Axis-grey warship—would finally decide to examine the *Charon*'s books . . .

Chapter Eight

Ironically she was an Italian. What they termed a VAS—boat . . . *Vedette Anti-Sommergibile*. A highly efficient submarine hunter and probably drafted into the Libyan theatre for precisely that task—to seek out and destroy our phantom red herring.

Which made it that much more of a grim joke, really. Because even when they were approaching us, and the subject of five weeks of frustrated searching was sailing blatantly across their sights, they still didn't realise that was precisely what we were.

Not at first anyway.

But when we sighted her, a low-lying rakish silhouette closing with us at an inescapable Fiat-powered nineteen knots, we knew right away that the *Charon*'s moment of truth had finally arrived—and a moment of truth which was ninety feet long and sported twin 17.7-inch torpedo tubes as well as her rather less worrying 20-mm machine guns and thirty depth charges on her after deck.

Tactically speaking it meant that broadside to us, with those menacing torpedoes temporarily impotent, the Italian warship could prove fair game. Providing we could surprise her before she transmitted a desperate 'enemy contact' alert to the *Luftwaffe*.

But at longer range, bows-on to us and presenting an almost impossible target while at the same time keeping her torpedo tubes at instantaneous readiness, the threat from that approaching VAS-boat was—in a word—lethal.

Which meant that we were—in another succinctly picturesque term—dead!

Either way, and steering on any point of the com-

pass, our fast approaching visitor was undoubtedly
determined to engage in a close and almost certainly
revealing scrutiny of the *Charon*'s less apparent modifications . . .

Trapp dropped the glasses and snapped, 'Warship,
Mister!'

I said, 'Oh Lord!'

Then we both galvanised into the routine of preparing to receive boarders which we'd practised so many
times before but never—until this moment—been pres-
sured into carrying out for real.

'Flag,' Trapp growled, head buried in the signal
locker. 'What Flag d'you reckon then?'

'Libyan,' I yelled, trying desperately to disentangle
the telephone wires so's I couldn't accidentally order
the chief engineer to fire and the 4.7-inch to stop engines. 'The Lounging Party's already rigged out in
Arab gear anyway.'

Not that it made all that much difference. Gorbals
Wullie, now promoted permanently to a machine gun
on the foredeck, didn't look any dirtier than he usually
did anyway, even though his thin, ferrety features
were liberally stained with boot polish. But Trapp, as
ever when crisis threatened to strike within seconds,
stopped raking through mounds of bunting and looked
at me stubbornly.

'Why not Eytalian?' he asked cleverly. 'Them bein'
Eytalian as well, it'd help make 'em less suspicious.'

I closed my eyes tightly for a moment and counted
up to five. 'Do you speak Italian, Captain?' I asked in
a slow, controlled voice.

'No.'

'Neither do I. So don't you think it'd seem a bit
funny to them, calling an Italian ship where none of
the crew actually speaks Ital . . .'

But I'd made my point. The hard way, as usual.

'Get layin' about proper,' Trapp roared at our Gilbert and Sullivan Arabs. 'Get lookin' like real bloody
Wogs an' don't expec' me to do all your thinkin' for
you!'

The handset from the gun called, '4.7 closed up,
Sir. Loaded one round HE.'

I glanced hurriedly through the slit. The VAS-boat
was closing fast, still about two miles off and with a
high white flare of foam under her Vee'd bow, but
through the binoculars I could make out the figures
already grouped around the cylinders of her tubes

'Acknowledge.' I said, feeling my mouth dry with
the realisation of what was to come 'And . . . Arthur '

'Sir?'

'This is the big one. And even if she stops, she'll
take off again like a whippet at the first sign of anything wrong . . . You'll only get the one round in to
make damned sure she doesn't.'

The handset retorted, with enormous aplomb. 'One
round it is then. Aye, aye, Sir Jus' you say the word,
Sir.'

I thought, 'Thank God for Crocker.' With feeling

But then, just as my nerves had really started
twitching at the sight of that distant Nemesis about to
overtake us, Trapp wandered out of the wheelhouse
with an enormous, flowing Arab headdress on an 1
posed outrageously in front of me

'I been savin' this f'r a special occasion, Mister
Suits me, does it?'

And finally I'd had enough. Savagely I glared at
him from my cramped corner of the bridge and
snarled, 'That's it! Oh, that's bloody it, Trapp! We're
about to engage a warship that can blow the guts
out've us before we've even started to turn with this
wheel-heavy crap barge an' you   . you caper about
like a flaming débutante dressed up for her first fancy
dress ball.'

But he didn't say anything, not right away He just
stopped grinning all of a sudden and looked at me a
bit surprised

I yelled in hateful frustration 'Good God Almighty,
man, but doesn't anyone on this rotten ship even *care?*'

And only then did Trapp say, ever so quietly, 'Care,
Mister .   . Care about what? King an' Country an'
that, eh? And freedom an' stuff?'

I felt my hands shaking with the outburst. 'There's worse things, Trapp.'

'I *know*, Mate. I know all about them things. I been bloody livin' with them for damn near thirty years.' He seemed to hesitate for a moment, then went on, 'Y'see, Mister, maybe freedom's different things for different men. Take you now—when your war's over you'll go back to your big new ships an' your nice, cosy regular runs. You'll 'ave your monthly pay cheque an' your chief officer's chair in the saloon f'r breakfast, after your four-to-eight watch on a big, comfy, glassed-in bridge . . .'

I didn't answer. Maybe because I knew he was right. Always assuming I would live long enough, that was—and maybe the Italian Navy would cancel even that faint possibility within the next five minutes.

But Trapp continued as though we still had five hours, or even five days.

'But me an' my boys, an' the old *Charon* herself— we don't have nothin' to look ahead to after all this is over. Not unless it's more runnin' and more hidin' from every ship with a grey funnel an' a bloody gun. Because people fight wars to protect what they've got, Mister . . . an' all of us have already lost everythin' we ever had. Includin' our pride and our self respect, an' the kind of freedom that allows a man to walk past a police station without feelin' a clutch at his guts . . .'

He glanced bitterly at the distant warship and, at that moment, I thought I recognised the same resignation in the grey eyes that I'd seen on that first night when we went into action. Then tenderly, almost lovingly, he allowed one weatherbeaten hand to rest on the scarred teak rail of the *Charon*'s bridge.

'But when you say we don't care, then you're wrong, Mister. Only your values are different to ours, an' we aren't so worried about whether or not tomorrow comes—it's hardly worth that anyway, when you think about it—but while it does, then we 'ave to look after this clapped-out old bucket by runnin' contraband, lootin', even fightin' other people's wars f'r the money to keep her afloat . . . because whatever you think of her she's the only world that me an' Al, an'

Babikian an' Gorbals Wullie and all the rest of 'em
have got left to care *about*.'

For what seemed a very long time we looked at
each other and, perhaps for the first time, there was
an understanding between us that we'd never had before. And then the captain blinked and sniffed
abruptly before breaking into a familiar, unabashed
glower of irritation.

'Well, get on with it then, Mister. We gotter job to do
an' no spaghetti-barge is goin' to cancel out Edward
Trapp's contract with Their Lordships of The Admiralty . . .'

But somehow I didn't mind his irascibility any more.
It was reassuring, in an odd sort of way.

Peeping hurriedly through the slit I saw that the
VAS-boat was now only half a mile off and still coming
fast. Time to start laying the gun which would deter-
mine whether Trapp's tomorrow was ever going to
arrive again for any of us.

Flicking the handset I snapped, 'Range—Wun thousand, wun hundred yards and closing. Bearing—wun-
zero-niner relative . . .'

I was hardly aware of Trapp's voice complaining
morosely: 'Your trouble is you're gettin' like the bloody
cook, Mate. Always bloody arguin' . . .'

Grimly we watched the little warship until
it overhauled us, running just astern and to starboard of
our wake but still on a slightly converging course which
kept those ugly, menacing tubes trained perfectly on
the *Charon*'s track.

I couldn't see the Loungers on deck but I knew they
were waving like hell by now, just like Trapp was. Like
all good Libyan seamen anxious to curry favour with
the Axis would be doing as well.

While all the time I kept reciting the decreasing
ranges and bearings to Crocker on the gun, even
though I realised uncomfortably that we were still completely defenceless, the 4.7 being unable to train far
enough aft to lay on that otherwise tempting target. It
was our friendly U-boat episode all over again.

Close enough now to see her crew clearly, white
uniforms crisp above the dazzle-camouflaged hull
colours. A group of heads turned towards us above
the upper bridge screens, torpedo-men waiting beside
her tubes—not too tensely it seemed—while the gunners maintained an easy, almost casual traverse to
sweep our length with the stubby barrels of the 20-mm
twins.

All part of the daily routine up to now. Curiosity,
probably a slight incredulity at the shuddering, wallowing apparition the *Charon* presented. But no suspicion
. . . and still overtaking, narrowing that critical angle.
Only a little farther and she would have to correct her
heading, present her broadside to us to avoid collision
with our rusted counter.

'Come on,' I whispered tightly. 'Come on, c'mon . . .'

But suddenly, frustratingly, the bows of the VAS-
boat dropped sharply as the tinkle of her telegraphs
carried plainly across the water and her speed de-
creased to match our own laboured progress. Now only
an occasional splurge of broken foam under the chine
of her bow showed as she ploughed precisely in company with us, still shielded by the *Charon*'s blind spot.

'Ahhh . . . dammit,' I snarled while Trapp stopped
waving enticingly and sniffed. 'What d'you reckon,
Mister . . . I could swing her a couple of points to st'bd.
Bring your gun to bear that way.'

I shook my head urgently, hoping he wasn't going
to argue. Not this time. 'No. Soon as she sees us cutting
across she'll fall back and start taking a serious second
glance . . .'

The inevitable Tannoy hissed into life from astern.
'*Capitano! Come si chiama questo battello . . . ?*'

'Battle?' Trapp frowned ferociously, 'Is 'e challengin'
us, then? 'Cause I gotter few ideas about that my-
sel . . .'

'*Battello,*' I corrected hoarsely, 'Boat, I think.
They're probably asking for the ship's name. Get Greek
Polly to rattle a few rounds of Arabic back while
Babikian's crowd clear away the panic boat—I can't
do a damn thing unless she overtakes a bit more.'

' 'Ow much d'you need, Mister? Maybe the old

Charon's got a few tricks up her sleeve when it comes to a bit o' nifty manoeuvring.'

'A good ten degrees to starboard with her head, then we're clear to shoot, but for God's sake don't . . .'

But I was too late. Trapp flung a sharp, 'Hang on to your hat, Mate,' over his shoulder and headed resolutely for the wheelhouse. I grabbed the handset desperately and yelled, 'Crocker! Crocker, are you there?'

'Sir.'

'Stand by with the plates an' wait for the word. I'll delay 'til you've got a few degrees either way to traverse, then it's up to you.'

'Aye, aye, Sir . . . Range set on one thousand yards, Sir, and standin' by.'

Trapp using the old voice pipe in the wheelhouse now, independent as ever. '. . . so when I rings down, Chief, I want you ter slam them brakes of yours on like we was hittin' brick wall . . .'

'*Attenzione! Attenzione . . . !*' *Oh hell!* One officer on the VAS-boat's bridge hanging over the screens more determinedly now, the microphone of the Tannoy to his mouth. A whitesmocked rating, collar flapping, swinging urgently down her port ladder towards the torpedomen . . . nothing casual about that bloody dangerous follower from this moment on.

A sudden, nerve-racking *Clang* from the telegraph. Trapp ringing it to 'Stop!' Immediately the vibration in the deck died away as Kubiczek hit the valves down below then, following through with the mildewed brass handle, Trapp swung her right back to 'Full Astern.'

'Hard a starboard.'

Joseph No-name spinning the wheel skilfully, black face frowning in concentration with a touch of sweat glossing the wrinkled forehead. 'Hard a st'bd . . . Wheel's hard to starboard, Captin Suh!'

A hiss of steam from below, then a rumble of pistons as the *Charon*'s screw began to reverse. A high spit of soot from the broomstick funnel, hanging like an exclamation mark above the bridge just before the whole ship started to shudder agonisingly as the big propeller bit harder into astern torque.

I lurched forward, caught off balance. The Italian

ship started to overshoot too. Hitting a brick wall was
a very apt simile.

Trapp again, standing like a statue with eyes fixed
unblinkingly for the first swing of our bows. 'Get ready,
Mister. She'll come round bloody fast now . . .'

White caps on the VAS-boat's bridge galvanising
into sudden movement. One head bent over a voice pipe
while the Tannoy emitted a last, plaintive clatter as the
mike was dropped heedlessly on its cord.

The *Charon*'s bows swinging faster and faster as the
combined action of her rudder and screw twisted her
creakily to starboard while still moving slowly ahead.
The angle of maximum traverse closing steadily while
I chanted almost automatically, 'Eight degrees to go,
Crocker . . . seven . . . six . . .'

A remote, vaguely familiar chattering from astern
while, shockingly, someone started hammering mani-
acally against the armoured steel of the bridge . . . Oh,
God, they've opened up on us . . . Glass shattering as
the wheelhouse windows cave inwards . . . Geddown,
Trapp . . . TRAAAAAAAAPP*!*

One fleeting glimpse of bodies huddled together
under the wheel then the rage started to boil over inside me. Heedlessly I dragged myself up, only vaguely
aware of the snarling scream of ricochets as the VAS-
boat's gun traversed along our forward bulwarks . . .
Everyone hugging the rusted steel deck except one—
Gorbals Wullie, by God—shrieking outrageous Celtic
oaths as he flung the cover away from his machine gun
. . . 'The tubes, Wullie,' I bellowed, 'Get the men on
her torpedo tubes . . .'

A throaty, high-powered roar as the Italian opened
her throttles, surging ahead with the bows rising like a
high speed lift and the whorls of white water spinning
convulsively in her wake . . .

Ahead! Driving straight into the line of our gun
sight . . .

Wullie, black with fury and boot polish, shuddering
under the recoil . . . seamen on the accelerating warship spinning and tumbling around her after deck.
One man hanging slackly over the oil-drum cylinders
in her port side depth charge rack . . .

. . . Three degrees . . . Two . . . One . . .

'Plates, Crocker . . . Open FIIIRE!'

Almost coincidentally, a crash from under me. Steel against steel. The *Charon* revealing her fangs at last. Only a shocking, lifelong memory for that Italian skipper now as the hull opens up to unveil impossible British gunners hunched grimly over open sights. And a precisely machined eye, exactly 4.7 inches in diameter staring bleakly into his . . .

The shattering report that was so familiar by now. The *Charon* fuzzing all over as she reared away. Rust, dust, the same old displaced film of age hanging chokingly in the air . . . and then the hit, the two explosions fusing into one at such close range.

Our first round took her neatly under the bridge, a bright flash seeming to lift the whole box section vertically—still with those white-capped men grouped in attitudes of frozen disbelief—then the flash blossomed into a black and red puffball while the men and the lattice mast and her radio aerials and everything else near her midships section withered away. Still under full power but now with no control she started to skid sideways, a runaway satellite with bits and pieces scattering astern in a crazy, curving trail of smoke.

Desperately I swivelled, eyes probing for the wheelhouse and for Trapp.

Crocker's stentorian snap. 'HE . . . One round . . . Reload!'

Gorbals Wullie, still firing like a maniac with the deadly accuracy of a man who's at last found his true talent. 'Poofy bastids . . . Poofy bastids . . .' Still no originality though . . .

'FIRE!'

Slam!

More dust, more bloody segments falling off the ship —our ship.

Then—frightfully—an instantaneous, eyeball-searing flash from outboard and the shock waves of a huge explosion skittering across the water towards us. Whirling in uncontrollable terror I was just in time to see the gigantic mushroom that marked the end of the VAS-boat's erratic wake before there was a second underwater detonation that seemed to shrink the very sea itself . . . to contract and then abruptly expand again into a soaring, sparkling plume of spray. And then another . . . and another . . .

Which meant that our second round had really hit the bull's eye. Maybe a torpedo warhead, maybe a chain reaction in her magazine. Then her depth charges, already armed, sinking slowly downwards in company with the tangled, eviscerated hull until they reached their pressure-triggered depth . . .

I lifted the handset and muttered in a flat, dazed voice: 'Cease firing, PO . . . Check, check, check.'

But it wasn't really necessary. There wasn't anything left to shoot at any more.

And then I sensed a movement behind me. From the wheelhouse.

Slowly, with sick apprehension, I swivelled once again.

Joseph No-name's white eyes blinked doubtfully at me from the shadowy gloom as he felt himself cautiously all over, while a second figure—wearing an outrageous, debonairly-askew Arab headdress—crawled tinklingly on hands and knees with the slivers of shattered glass still slipping from his shoulder.

'I told you, Mister.'

Trapp grinned up at me with enormous delight. 'Din't I *tell* you, then? Treat her gentle an' the old *Charon*'ll screw her ass around like a ballet dancer at an orgy, Mate . . .'

And so our secret war continued.

We never did find out whether that dead Italian skipper managed to transmit an 'enemy contact' report before the *Charon* killed him but Trapp, with his usual reluctance to waste anything, even turned that incident into another, rather more gruesome shred of circumstantial evidence to perpetuate the British submarine myth.

We'd found one body floating amidst the wreckage of the VAS-boat.

We fished it out without a mark on it—a young Italian midshipman killed by blast. Under Trapp's

bleak direction we stripped the pathetic, blank-eyed
corpse before dressing it again in British submarine
rating's uniform. Then he slipped a Royal Naval
lifejacket over the slack shoulders—the type worn by
gun crews during a surface engagement—and gently
eased the body back into the sea.

And finally Gorbals Wullie riddled the bobbing,
hunched cadaver with machine gun bullets, paying particular attention to the head and features . . .

We sank more enemy supply runners but, gradually,
they got fewer and fewer. By the end of October the
Axis sea routes were being attacked so savagely by
the Malta-based antishipping strikes—made possible
in the first instance, only by the sacrifice and the gal-
lantry of OPERATION PEDESTAL—that Rommel's lo-
gistical support had been reduced to a mere trickle,
and that mostly flown in by the *Luftwaffe*.

Then came El Alamein and, on November 2nd, the
bloodiest tank battle of the war. Tel el Aqqaqir. The
Afrika Korps armour was smashed and Rommel started
to retreat. Falling back through Mersa Matruh, Sidi
Barrani, Sollum, Bardia, Tobruk . . . the battlefront
steadily moved westwards.

And the *Charon* retreated with it. Or advanced. It
depended on which course we happened to be steering
at the time.

While Trapp's piratical hoard of tawdry, second-
hand fringe benefits steadily grew after each ship we
boarded, looted and then coldly sank. And even though
I now understood why he had such an obsessive need
to reinforce what he nonchalantly called 'The old
bucket's pension fund. F'r after the Skull an' Crossbone
season's over . . .' I couldn't shake off a growing conviction that Trapp's greed might, one day, overcome
even his talent for survival.

And that—even more unsettlingly—when he
stopped surviving, so would the rest of us.

But, with what could only be considered miraculous
luck, the *Charon* and her antiquated gun and her ir-
reverent crew rumbled and bumbled her corkscrew
course from one nearbrush with the *Kriegsmarine* to
the next.

Only they, and the *Luftwaffe*, didn't have much time to waste on an Arabian idiot boat like us. Because *they* were too bloody busy hunting for a British submarine which apparently dissolved at will, like an aspirin tablet in a glass of water.

Until—inevitably—something went wrong.

And my nightmare exploded into harrowing actuality.

She was big, much bigger than anything we'd tackled before. Even through the rain-reinforced darkness I could see she was, maybe, three thousand tons gross and ocean going. Obviously not just a coaster creeping nocturnally from one inlet to the next but one of the few enemy freighters which had managed to dodge all the way across from Italy without meeting the Maltese ship-busters.

And now she was homeward bound, presumably. Hopefully heading north-east out of Benghazi, evacuated before that wreck-strewn harbour also fell to the advancing Eighth Army, now hard on the heels of Rommel's weary, sand-parched troopers.

But this was one target we couldn't afford to take chances with. Undoubtedly equipped with a radio transmitter which could blow the ears off the German Naval Signals Station at Gabes, one descriptive scream for help would bring every homicidally frustrated *Kriegsmarine* hunter-killer on the North African coast homing in on us. And—all of a sudden—searching for a submarine with a rusty hull, a broomstick funnel and a packing case on the forward well deck . . .

Our first unannounced round took her directly on the bridge. Almost immediately, probably with only a dead watchkeeper and a corpse at the helm, she started to swing towards us, smashing ponderously into the vicious winter sea and throwing long, flaring gouts of spray outward and upwards to catch the brisk westerly gale and drive back over her fo'c'slehead in a drifting, luminous cloud.

'Reload . . . On . . . FIRE.'

'Reload . . . GerrabloodymoveON . . . FIIIRE!'

I felt the slash of the spray as the *Charon* virtually stopped short herself against a curling, tumbling sea.

Trapp was standing beside me, face impassive and with the salt water streaming down his granite features to form dappling little pools in the folds of his black oilskins, reflecting hundreds of fiery diamonds in the millisecond duration of each muzzle flash.

My handset again. More urgently. 'Go for the waterline and engine space, PO. She's not stopping yet.'

Fire aboard the blinded freighter suddenly. Sickeningly. A yellow and orange glimmer first from the stark black silhouette of her wrecked upperworks. Then the glimmer died, and flared up again a little brighter, individual tongues of flame visible this time as they reared and snaked upwards, fanned into an even greater rage by the wind of her own passage. A ship burning itself to death.

'Come *on,* Crocker. Get those gunners moving down there!'

Another uncomfortable sea slamming in under our bluff bow, creaming subversively towards us out of the blackness and throwing the *Charon* heavily to port . . . Weather's getting up fast, now. One heavy sea shipped into the open plates of number two and we could swamp her. Time to break off the action an' get the hell out of here.

The runaway ship getting larger and larger as she still headed towards us, now steaming almost at ninety degrees to her original course . . . Jesus! Virtually on a collision course, for that matter, unless we could stop or avoid her.

Suddenly.

Trapp running for the wheelhouse door. 'Hard a PORT!'

Everything happening simultaneously. Terrifyingly. Except for one thing—'Crocker. What's wrong with the bloody gun down there . . . ?'

The *Charon* shying to thirty degrees with a crash of run-amok crockery from the galley . . . Trapp lunging for the voice pipe now. 'Chief! Gimme all you got f'r . . .'

The other freighter still converging on us, the white water under her flaring bow plainly visible now with the flames throwing a roaring white light over the tumbling wave crests around her . . . 'Crocker, do you read? *Crocker* . . .'

At last. Breathlessly. 'Sir. We took a wave inboard. S'like a bloody fish tank down 'ere an' more . . . more comin' all the time . . .'

I glance up, eyes straining against the blackness. The target still coming, but so are the seas.

'Secure from the gun. Close up the plates an' get the hell out of it, PO . . . Bofors gun—Open *Fire!*'

Pom . . . pom . . . pom . . . pom.

Flashes bright against even the glare from the fires. Shadowy spouts of foam under the target's bows as the *Charon* rolls convulsively, throwing the barrel of the quick-firer downwards. Cordite fumes whipping aft over the bridge, clutched by the rising gale then a roaring, tumbling sea clambering inboard over the well deck with the Bofors gunners up to their waists in water . . . Christ, but the old scow's hardly able to force her head round and the other ship's so close now her bloody fo'c'slehead's looming over our bridge . . .

Then relief, even from the imperturbable Trapp. 'She's stopping, Mister . . . finally losing way on her.'

I closed my eyes and started to shake. 'Cease firing!'

No bow wave ahead of the burning ship now, only a tumult of orange-tinted foam clawing angrily at her slab sides as she coasted to a rolling standstill less than two hundred yards off our starboard quarter . . . still too damn near for comfort but . . .

I froze, staring at Trapp's expression.

Every line and every crease on the grim, wet face was clearly visible. Plain as an actor under a spotlight as it reflected the glare from the blazing German freighter while that same unearthly brilliance etched every wire and spar and plate aboard the *Charon* with the same, betraying clarity.

Exposing us for precisely what we were—a surface raider. And apparent as such to any watcher within a mile radius of us.

Even more recognisable to those black, stampeding enemy figures silhouetted against the writhing flames on that boat deck only a cable's length away . . .

'Stop engine,' Trapp called abruptly. And very coldly indeed.

Then I just stood beside him, out on the *Charon*'s bridge wing with the wind tugging at our oilskins in unheeded frustration, and watched that solitary un-damaged lifeboat—crammed now with hunched, ter-rified survivors—slowly descend to the clutching waters until, with a squeal and rattle of blocks, they released the falls and the overladen craft pulled des-perately clear of the stricken ship.

Hopefully I muttered, 'They're abandoned, Captain. And the fire's going to attract every patrol boat for miles, even if the weather's too bad for flying. I'd sug-gest we get out of it pretty damned quick.'

But he didn't answer. Not for a minute. Apprehen-sively I glanced at his hands on the bridge rail—they were gripping the scarred teak until the white of the knuckles showed under the dancing glare.

Then he turned towards the wheelhouse and snapped tightly, 'Slow ahead. St'bd ten the wheel . . . steer on that lifeboat, laddie.'

I saw Joseph No-name's eyes staring back at us, pink and flickering, then he acknowledged, hesitantly: 'St'bd ten . . . Ten've st'bd wheel on, Captain.'

I fought the horror welling up inside me, knowing already what he intended to do. 'You can't, dammit! Not deliberately . . . not like this.'

Trapp didn't look at me. 'We both knew it was bound to happen one day, Mister. Even the admiral knew that . . . an' he still give me the contract.'

'*Contract!*' I gestured outboard with a shaking hand. 'The *hell* with your bloody contract, Trapp. Those are *men* out there, not units to meet some kind've sick efficiency bonus target . . . Seamen, dammit! Like you an' me, for God's sake . . .'

Taking grip on my rage I said, almost pleadingly. 'Look, the freighter's done for. She's going down by the head already. There's plenty of time to clear the area before light . . .'

'An' then what?' He swung on me so violently I took an involuntary step backwards. 'Well, I'll tell you, Mister. From the moment them survivors step ashore we're a marked ship—so I has to call the whole thing off. Steam back to Malta with a charter I cancelled myself an' damn all to show for all the gutwrenchin' times I seen good ships sunk . . . not even enough capital to hide the *Charon* away until this bloody war of yours is finished. 'Cause she can't risk trading again now. Jerrie'll be lookin' for her wherever she goes . . .'

There was a rumble from across the water and I sensed, rather than saw, the dying ship lurch farther down by the head. 'So you're going to kill those men then. In cold blood. Just to keep this ship of yours in business.'

He looked at me bleakly. 'I been killin' men since the first day the Navy sent me here, Mister. So what's the difference, doin' it at close range with a machine gun?'

I gazed at him for what seemed a very long time. Then I felt my shoulders sag in defeat. 'If you don't know the answer to that, Trapp, maybe they should have issued you with an SS uniform. Along with that lousy contract of yours.'

'Or shot me! Because that's what they might as well 'ave done when they threatened to take the *Charon* off me, Miller. I told you already—she's all I got . . .'

There was a sudden thunder of tortured, overstressed bulkheads from the burning ship. I whirled in time to watch the flames clawing frantically, hysterically towards her arcing mastheads, even brighter and more revealingly than before . . . and one stark glimpse of the lifeboat, now only seventy yards ahead of our slowly closing bows with the huddled, pathetic press of bodies etched black against the reflection from the burning sea.

Just before the freighter capsized. Monstrously. Tumbling faster and faster sideways to meet the water in a roaring, hissing agony. High gouting spurts of spray and smoke and steam and . . .

. . . and then the light went out.

Only the darkness and the green glow from our binnacle, and the occasional ghostly whitecap sweeping past were left. And the horror of what was about to happen.

Trapp called flatly from the blackness, 'Stop engine. Steady as she goes . . . I'll need that searchlight, Mister. St'bd wing.'

I felt the nails biting into the palms of my clenched hands. 'Not directed by me, Trapp. This is one contract I'm opting out of.'

There was a silence then, uncharacteristically acquiescent. 'I remember I done that once—opted out when I didn't see no future in things. But it's a luxury I can't afford again, Mister . . . *Babikian!* Second Mate to the *bridge.*'

I said bitterly, 'Which makes you a calculating bastard too, Trapp. He's the one spineless kid on this ship who'll do precisely what you tell him to. Only who have you got figured to actually pull the trigger . . . Wullie? Joseph No-name? Al Kubiczek? Maybe you'll find they aren't quite so dedicated to the killing trade as you reck . . .'

'*Me!*'

The voice was like a whiplash. 'I will, Miller. 'Cause I plan to survive no matter what, An' survivin's the one thing—the only bloody thing—I ever been any damn good at it the whole of my lousy life . . .'

And then he was gone, sliding down the ladder to the foredeck. And the machine gun. Babikian came and stood beside me, his brown, effeminate features unhappy even through the darkness. I watched as he hesitantly gripped the wing searchlight control while deliberately avoiding my eyes. Then I turned away bleakly. There wasn't any use my saying anything. Not to him.

The *Charon* was stopped now, wallowing sluggishly as the short seas broke against her. The lifeboat lay maybe twenty yards off, a dim, corkscrewing shape visible only against the welter of foam which framed it. I thought sickly of the apprehension of those invisible seamen as they crouched helplessly, watching the silent, menacing bulk of the *Charon* and wondering why we were still waiting there . . .

There was a sharp, heated exchange from the well deck as the cover was dragged away from the machine gun, then a small figure detached itself from the group

and walked deliberately away. 'Youse can please
yersel's but ah'm no' havin' anything tae dae wi' it . . .
No' when they lads havnae a chance tae fight back.'

I glimpsed the dull gleam of oiled metal as Trapp
swung the barrel of the gun coldly, experimentally.
There was another low mutter from the other crewmen
but it was cut short by the chilling *Click* as the MG was
cocked. Then Kubiczek, desperately: 'Aw f'r Chrissakes, Trapp. You ain't the kinda guy who c'n . . .'

A high pitched cry from the blackness. Full of a
terrible, slowly dawning fear. *'Kapitän . . . Bitte? Was
ist los . . . Wer ist da . . . ?'*

Trapp's powerful frame hunched suddenly, over the
firing handles. I started to run for the ladder, unable
to stomach it any more. *'Traaaaapp!'*

A savage, tautly-stressed command from below.
'Searchlight.'

I yelled hysterically, 'No, Babikian! Not if you ever
want to . . .'

'Light, DAMN YOU!'

The second mate flinching as if he'd been struck.
One tormented, shuddering sob—before a white finger,
dazzling in its brilliance, lancing crazily across the
tumbling facets of the surrounding seas as if found,
then lost, then settled starkly again on the white,
staring faces in a pitching overcrowded lifeboat.

And the machine gun started to chatter raucously,
obliterating the disbelieving screams from outboard
. . . ripping high, fountaining spurts of foam while the
path of the bullets tracked closer and closer to that
pathetic target as Trapp uncertainly corrected his aim.

And then, with unforgettable clarity, I finally saw
what those survivors from the sunken freighter really
looked like. Those slim, bedraggled and smoke blackened figures clinging to each other with all the fear and
terror that only a nightmare could create . . . but very
slim. And very, very frail . . .

I roared uncontrollably, 'Hold it, Trapp! They're
kids. Women an' *kids!'*

Closer and closer. Ripping feathery splinters from
the sea . . .

Then the gun stopped firing. Abruptly. Just before

the vectoring burst had actually reached the boat . . . and there was only the sigh of the wind and the soft crash of the sea against the *Charon*'s rusted flanks. And the sobbing, still unutterably shocked sounds from a lifeboat full, presumably, of German families. Evacuees who had so nearly died because they'd become involved with the unprofitable side of Trapp's war business.

Someone—I think it was Kubiczek—snarled violently. 'Cut that goddam light up there.'

I did catch one fleeting glimpse of Trapp's expression, as he climbed heavily back up the ladder just before Babikian hit the switch. It was that of a man who'd just awakened from a hideous dream. Dazed, bewildered, almost lost.

Then the searchlight left that drifting, unharmed lifeboat to its own private misery. Until it reached the shore some time the following day. And finally the German Navy learnt the real truth about their phantom submarine.

Suddenly, out of the welcome blackness, the captain's voice.

'Let's go home, Mate,' he said.

Ever so quietly.

Trapp seemed to change after that. For a while, anyway. There was an air of apathy about him for the rest of that wild night as we steamed at our tortuous, wallowing eight knots away from the immediate area of the sinking.

Not that he was any the less crafty in his approach to a problem. For instance his idea of going home still wasn't the same as anyone else's would have been under the circumstances—because where most skippers would have done the obvious and laid off a northerly course of Malta, Trapp just pointed the *Charon*'s battered bows due west and aimed towards the most likely place for us to run into the enemy.

Only he didn't even grin that usual irritating, clever little-boy grin of his when I pointed out the fact that I wasn't terribly enamoured with committing suicide. Not just for the hell of it.

Instead he shrugged as if it didn't matter any more, and said meekly: 'Please yourself, Mister. But if I was a Jerrie, an' lookin' f'r me, then I'd draw a straight line on my chart between where we sank that boat an' the nearest British waters—which is Malta . . . an' then I'd send every bristle-head aviator in the *Luftwaffe* to search along it with a bellyful o' high explosive.'

And of course he was right. This was one instance where the quickest way to go was by the longest route. I appreciated that the moment he said it. And we were still as safe as we'd ever been until that lifeboat actually made it to the Libyan shore.

Which seemed to make it even more ironic, in a way—that the German Navy did finally catch up with us less than four hours later. And purely by chance, at that.

Or maybe I should have expected it. Maybe Trapp had deliberately relinquished his right to a winner's place in the Survival Game.

The moment he took his finger off the trigger of that machine gun.

Chapter Nine

But from the start it had been a bloody awful day.

First there had been the sinking. Then the machine gun episode. Then there was the lousy weather. And Gorbals Wullie getting clapped in the brig . . .

Wulli . . . ? Well, maybe he did ask for trouble, using that dearly beloved razor of his, but we were all under a strain by then and Seaman Gunner Clark wasn't the easiest of people to get along with at the best of times.

Though I think the change in Trapp had something to do with it, too. Perhaps he hadn't quite forgotten the way the little Glaswegian walked out on him during the affair of the survivors. Either way Gorbals Wullie was the first man to be placed under close arrest aboard His Majesty's Armed Merchant Cruiser *Charon*.

It started after breakfast. The kind of breakfast which should have earned the cook a permanent place in the brig alongside Wullie. We'd been served with what the tin said was Afrika Korps issue *Kalbskoteletten*—what my tentative German suggested meant veal chops and which I was pretty damn certain shouldn't have been boiled, whatever they were.

And then the crew, gunners and *Charon* originals, had hung around in a gloomy, despondent group beside the hatch cover of number two with the rain misting over them in a fine, relentless spray while I'd stood up there on the bridge wishing Trapp would speak instead of hunching, silently remote, in the lee of the wheelhouse.

Until there was a sudden agonised yell from the deck and I'd rushed to the rail to see Seaman Gunner Clark staggering back with a bright crimson flood mixing into the soggy wetness of his jersey, and most of his

142

right ear still lying where he'd originally started from.

While Gorbals Wullie, shrieking in berserk fury, was being pinned down by Leading Hand Mulholland and two of the Greek seamen, all trying apprehensively to avoid the flashing arc of a rather too-familiar blade.

'Ah'll scunner yon Navy lad,' Wullie howled. 'Ah'll cut yon Sassenach bastid intae Oxo cubes, ah wull. So Manchester United's the best fitba' team, is it? An' the Celtic's just a bunch o' fu . . .'

'God!' Clark muttered, shocked as well as slowly bleeding to death. 'All I said was 'is Celtic woul'n't stand a chance in a proper football league. Not a proper *English* one f'r . . .'

'Ah'll bloody *kill* 'im. Ah'll carve the poofy wee chancer intae . . .'

Then Mulholland hit Wullie with great accuracy—and a very large fist. Whereupon the fighting Scotsman retired into semi-consciousness while Al Kubiczek clamped a pad of oil-soaked cotton waste over the place where Clark's ear had been and growled disgustedly, 'You goddam Britishers! Hell, but if you can't fight the goddam Krauts then you gotta start to fight each other?'

I turned and looked towards Trapp. He still hadn't moved from his corner so I said tentatively, 'Wullie's cut Gunner Clark's ear off, Captain.'

Trapp sniffed gloomily. 'Which one?'

'St'bd side . . . Oh for God's sake, what d'you want to do about it?'

'I dunno. Get the medical chest out've my cabin, then throw 'im in the brig.'

'Who—Clark?'

'Wullie. Too stroppy by far, that one. Doesn't have no respect f'r authority . . .'

'Listen,' I reflected heavily, 'to the pot calling the kettle black.' Glancing over the rail again I saw that the chief now had a hammerlock on the sobbing, agonised gunner while PO Crocker was dabbing the place where the ear had been with an iodine-soaked pad of cotton wool, perhaps not without a certain amount of relish.

Wullie, half-conscious, was still muttering vaguely,

'Where's mah blade . . . Ah feel bare naked wi'oot mah wee blade . . .'

'We haven't *got* a brig,' I said wearily, just about at the end of my tether with the lunatic world of the *Charon* and her homicidal crew and her temperamental master. 'And anyway, if you lock Wullie up and a torpedo hits us, he hasn't got a chance.'

'If a torpedo hits us, Mister, then none've us has a chance . . . Lock him in the paint store forr'ad an' stop arguin'.'

I took a deep breath, then shrugged. If he'd been difficult before, he was utterly impossible now. 'Aye, aye, Sir,' I snapped and turned towards the ladder. Trapp called after me again, with typical inconsistency.

'What's for dinner?'

'I really don't know,' I snarled bitterly, 'But whatever it is, your bloody cook'll boil it.'

Two hours later we saw her. Less than two miles off and even then barely discernible through the driving rain.

But one thing was ominously clear even in those first few, disconcerting seconds—that low, grey shape over to starboard was an infinitely more threatening adversary than the long-gone VAS-boat had ever been. And she was as German as Adolf Hitler's forelock.

'*Schnellboot*,' I rapped. 'Twin 21-inch torpedo tubes an' forty-odd knots . . . Forty *knots*, dammit! We haven't a hope of scoring a hit with the gun at even half that speed.'

Trapp levered himself out of his corner for the first time in hours. Already I was flat on the deck with my eyes glued to the peephole and the phone in my hand, listening to the now familiar sounds of running feet as the crew closed-up to the gun.

'What else has she got then?' he asked, almost disinterestedly. And as soon as I heard that tone in his voice my nerves started to jump. 'Oh Lord, please don't let him go all placid on me. Not now. Not when we need all the Machiavellian ingenuity that only an underhand schemer like Trapp can provide . . .'

'I dunno. One 37-millimetre forward. Twin-twenties

all over her like sticks've bloody rhubarb—but it's those tubes that worry me. And her speed.'

Trapp sighed as if talking to a child. 'It doesn't matter how fast she goes, does it. Not if we get 'er to stop long enough f'r one round up the hawsepipe. What Flag're we flyin' right now?'

'Libyan.'

'It's probably as good as any. D'you reckon she knows about us, though?'

The phone reported briskly, '4.7 closed up, Sir.'

'Acknowledge. Wait, Crocker . . .' I glanced hurriedly at the driving mist, '. . . With any luck—no. It's lousy visibility. Pretty unlikely that boat's been picked up yet.'

Trapp scratched his head thoughtfully, but there still wasn't any of that snap, that earthy aggressiveness which had marked our previous encounters with the enemy. I laid the binoculars on the S-boat. Even as I focused on her she started to turn towards us, while the bows gradually rose until she was aiming quite deliberately at the point where I was kneeling, or so it seemed.

For a sickening moment I stared at the recessed cut-aways on either side of the German's fo'c'slehead, waiting for the first sign of the compressed air cloud which would signal the release of a torpedo salvo, but she merely kept closing with us. The only sign of aggressive intent was in the seamen running forward to man the 20-mm heavy machine gun in the sunken gun pit.

Shakily I muttered, 'She doesn't know about us. If she did we'd be dead by now.'

Then I stiffened . . . maybe we did have one heaven-sent chance to hit her while still under way. A small target maybe, but her angle of approach for the next few minutes was such that—heading virtually at ninety degrees to our gun—the German warship was making very little lateral movement, not even zig-zagging, which underlined her lack of suspicion. And Crocker had already proved himself an extremely lethal gunner.

I snapped urgently, 'Crocker. S-boat, bows on . . . what d'you reckon?'

No hesitation, only a grim acknowledgment. 'Pass the bearing, then say the words, Sir. I'll pre-set the range to fifteen-hundred yards an' you shout jus' before the bastard is on.'

'Roger.' I glanced queryingly at Trapp. 'It could be our best chance, Captain. Maybe our only one.'

He still looked about as concerned as he had been when Clark's ear fell off earlier. The approaching *Schnellboot* was already a mile and a half away and coming fast. We only had about a minute to decide.

'Come on, Trapp,' I sweated. 'Come *on!*'

He shrugged. ' 'Ave a go if you fancies your chances, Mister. Not that it makes all that much diff . . .'

'Range—two thousand, nine hundred and closing,' I called, ignoring the rest of Trapp's moody philosophy. 'Bearing—zero-niner-fife and constant.'

Just for a moment I thought guiltily about Gorbals Wullie, now enclosed in the locker steel coffin of the paint store forward and blissfully unaware of anything wrong. Until it struck me that, if we had to go, then going in a blinding flash and without any previous warning was the best death possible, so I forgot all about our aggrieved Celtic supporter and concentrated on the job in hand.

'Range—two thousand, fife hundred . . .'

Still unswerving, still intrigued rather than suspicious. Maybe I'd been wrong all the time about Trapp's divine right to Survive. Maybe we all had it. Or maybe it simply applied to the *Charon* herself. And God only knew that she was so old she must have rated *some* special protection . . .

'Two thousand yards . . . Stand by the plates, Crocker.'

'Standin' by. Range set to one thousand, fife hundred, Sir.'

Please don't swerve now, *Herr Kapitän* . . . Steady . . . steady . . . that's it . . .

Sweat trickling down my temple, tickling unmercifully but I daren't take my eyes away from the rangefinder . . . Still coming like a lamb to the slaughter, bows high enough to see the scarred black flare of her chines with the white spray cascading away in a drumming, jetting cushion . . .

'Eighteen hundred . . . Seventeen . . . Still bearing zero-niner-fife . . .'

Trapp raising his binoculars. What the hell's he looking at now. And why the sudden interest when he's as good as opted out of the engagement anyway . . . ?

Get readyyyy, Crocker boy . . .

'Sixteen hundred yards. Plates . . .'

'Hold it, Mister!'

Damn!

I hit the phone before my bar-taut mind had time to re-assess the situation. 'Check, check, *check!*'

Furiously I swivelled round on the deck, knowing we were already too late. No time to re-calibrate and the S-boat still closing at a speed which would force her into a wide, impossible-to-track curve at any moment.

'What the *hell?*' I bellowed in shock, disappointment and almost ungovernable rage.

Trapp grinned down at me. It was the old Trapp, the impossible Trapp. Intriguing, mercenary, and totally unashamed.

'It's jus' that I gotter idea, Mate,' he beamed, ignoring the fact that the German Navy was within a Schmeisser's burst from us by then. 'About how I can increase the *Charon's* retirement fund . . .

'We'll *capture* that bit've a warship out there instead. An' then sell her. To the Royal Navy.'

'Capture it? he says,' I muttered to myself, over and over again while one hundred and fifteen feet of potentially hostile, armament-packed *Schnellboot* circled round and round our still blithely steaming hull.

'Capture it . . . That?'

But I was still suffering from shock and the shattering effect of a high-tension nervous system brutally short-circuited into frustrated inactivity. Apart from which I half expected to see the S-boat take off at any minute, as a general warning was sent out to all units of the *Kriegsmarine* about a certain suspected Q-ship operating in the area.

To say nothing of having suddenly discovered that

I was serving under the only warship commander in
the Royal—or anyone else's Navy for that matter—
whose tactical and strategic approach to a forthcoming
engagement was based purely on the size of capital
investment and likely resale-value of the enemy he was
about to fight.

And then the S-boat formed in company with us and
it was situation normal as far as our element of surprise
went—they being too far astern for us to throw anything bigger than spanners at them.

Second standard approach almost immediately.
The loud hailer. *'Achtung, Kapitän . . . In welchen
Häfen legt das Schiff an?'*

Trapp waved his hand at me urgently, looking ri-
diculous as ever in that damned silly Arab headdress of his. 'What's the bristle heads sayin' then?'

I shook my head stubbornly. 'It's your bloody idea,
Trapp. Why don't you ask them to speak English.'

I didn't really mean it but it *was* my turn to be
awkward. But he just shrugged philosophically then,
before I could stop him, roared, 'Nicht sprechen Dutch,
Effendi . . . but I spik a leetle Engleesh maybe.'

Gazing bleakly aft I could see the German commander on the S-boat's streamlined bridge. He seemed
to turn and say something to the rating beside him and
gestured at the *Charon*. A fragment of laughter drifted
across the water and I wished for the fifieth time that
they'd move a little farther ahead. Steaming where they
were they made as impossible a target as if they'd been
patrolling in the North Sea. Then the Tannoy crackled
into faultless Oxford English.

'What is your destination, Captain?'

Trapp frowned down at me. ' 'Ow about Derna, eh?'

I shook my head violently, nervously. 'No f'r God's
sake. Derna's to the east—we're heading *west*.'

'Ah,' Trapp said, suitably impressed. Then he raised
his voice again.

'Tripoli, Effendi . . . if it is the will of Allah.'

The German commander lifted his binoculars and
scanned our bows where the *Charon*'s name, for obvious reasons, had long ago been erased. Then, irritably,

'Report your ship's name and signal letters, Captain.'

'That's *it*,' I growled hopelessly. 'All they need to do is check us out by radio and . . .'

But Trapp just rattled an unintelligible, vaguely Arabic sounding reply before finishing meekly, '. . . but I no spik the English letters, Effendi. My miserable ability does not give me that power.'

Glancing downwards I saw Babikian and the rest of the Panic Party hovering, not entirely without good reason, beside the lifeboat. I wriggled over to the ladder and whispered hoarsely, 'F'r Chrissakes get ready to put on a decent show . . . if we get that much time.'

Then the *Schnellboot* snapped metallically, 'Your international code flags. Hoist them immediately . . . *Verstehen?*'

While the flared bows of that lean, predatory warship stayed precisely in line with our counter. Still ready to haul off at the first suspicion.

Trapp bowed from the waist like a Gilbert and Sullivan opera character, then dived into the wheelhouse. 'Oil,' he growled to Babikian as he shot past the ladder. 'Get me a tin've old oil an' *jaldi*.'

The *Charon*'s selection of code flags were virtually indecipherable anyway, but by the time Trapp had finished dipping them they looked more like black treacle sandwiches. Then he hoisted them, went back to the bridge wing and looked every inch the inadequate, nervously apologetic Arab ship's master.

'That's given 'em a problem, eh,' he winked at the same time.

Until.

'Heave-to! Stop your ship immediately and prepare a boarding ladder, Captain.'

I glared up at Trapp spitefully. 'Given who a problem, did you say?'

While the unsuccessful tactician said petulantly, 'Right, Mister. If that's the way 'e's goin' to be then we'll pull the old hard ast'bd, full astern dodge aga . . .'

'*No!*' I whispered violently. 'Soon as they see you start to sheer across they'll do precisely what that

Italian did an' try to get the hell out . . . only these
S-boats can take off from a standing start quicker than
we can even get the plates down.'

'So what, then?' In resentful disappointment.

'You'll have to con them into pulling alongside of
their own accord. And with their pants down.'

Sharp commands from astern now. Coldly efficient.
'Achtung Geschützbedienung . . .'

Then the Tannoy. 'Stop your ship immediately . . .
Schnell! Or I open fire.'

'Do it,' I hissed, but Trapp still hesitated, looking
aggrieved.

'FEUER!'

The first burst from the foredeck-mounted 20-
millimetre was short, sharp and to the point. Most of
the wheelhouse roof a foot above Trapp's head
jumped abruptly into the air, then came back down
again in splinters.

'Bloody 'ell,' he said, looking shattered for the first
time, then dived for the telegraph without any need for
acting. I elbowed myself urgently towards the ladder
again and waved at the white-faced Panic Party. 'Abandon as soon as you can an' f'r God's sake remember
you're Arabs. Jus' look scared to death and don't
answer Jerrie if he speaks to you . . .'

Then Trapp came wriggling past me like a great fat
slug, heading for the peepholes in the wing, and I followed, grabbing for the handset.

'Crocker. Same as before. You'll have maybe half a
minute to get your first round smack into her . . .'

'Belay that, Mister!'

I froze, a nasty thought entering my heard. Before
Trapp added, with implacable determination, 'We're
goin' to capture that Jerrie warship, I already told you
now, din' I, Mate? So you jus' pass the word to hold
fire when them plates go down 'cause I'm not havin' no
trigger-happy matelot spoilin' the *Charon*'s chance of
prize money . . .'

I informed him, very clearly and reasonably, 'You
are mad, Trapp. Stark raving, utterly and completely
out of your mercenary, suicidal little mind . . .'

And so on. Until the Panic Party had disappeared

below deck level in a squeal of unmaintained and rust-tightened blocks, the whole boat jerking seawards in heart-stopping, unequal runs until there was a sickening splash before, almost miraculously, Babikian's crew reappeared on an erratic course for nowhere in particular, oars flailing like carpet beaters and the cook in the bow clutching what seemed to be, of all things, a large knitting bag.

And by that time I'd run out of breath and invective so I just finished weakly, '. . . screwed-up, mismanaged, cantankerous shower've dead-beats I ever collided with in my whole bloody life!'

'An' I'm the last person to deny you may very well 'ave a point there, Mister,' Trapp allowed generously. 'But now you c'n jus' tell Crocker he's still got to hold his fire, an' that's that.'

And, the way he said it, told me without any doubt whatsoever that within the next few minutes I would either be the part-owner of a good condition, second-hand German *Schnellboot* plus twenty-odd *Kriegsmarine* sailors.

Or dead.

But then the enemy made their first mistake. Instead of keeping their guns trained on the apparently deserted *Charon* they laid them almost jokingly on Babikian's boat. Or almost jokingly. Because I didn't actually see any of our Panic Party laughing too hard.

For a few minutes nothing seemed to happen. The *Charon* just rolled sluggishly in the uncomfortable sea as most of her abandoned crew clung to the tossing little chip of a lifeboat and stared apprehensively up into the barrels of the S-boat's machine guns, while Trapp and I waited on the bridge in tense silence.

There was obviously a certain amount of disconcerted discussion going on across the water however, as two white-capped and immaculate German officers debated our somewhat over-hasty abandonment. Then —abruptly—one of them wheeled to the bridge ladder and snapped a sharp command.

Immediately several sailors ran towards a locker and started dragging out a deflated rubber raft while others grabbed machine pistols handed out by a petty officer. 'They're going to board us,' I said hopelessly.

And then there was the jangle of bridge telegraphs and, ever so slowly, the enemy ship started to move ahead. Straight into our line of fire.

'They've fallen for it,' Trapp gloated. 'One 'undred thousand quids' worth've motor boat an' they've fallen right into it.'

'Crocker,' I snapped. 'Stand by but hold your fire. I say again . . . Hold your fire until I give the order. Understood?'

Only the slightest hesitation, then, 'Understood, Sir. Hold fire.'

A swirl of water under the *Schnellboot*'s counter and she stopped again. Directly abeam of us and less than fifty yards off.

'*Go,* Mister!' Trapp roared.

'PLATES!'

There was a deafening crash as the *Charon*'s hull yawned wide. Every face aboard the German ship swung towards us in paralysed, staring shock . . . and Trapp bellowed at the top of his voice, '*Achtung,* you bastards! One more outa you guys an' you all get yours.'

'Cagney!' I thought disbelievingly. 'Pure James Cagney for God's sake . . .'

But whether that *Kriegsmarine* commander actually understood Trapp's Hollywood-inspired gangsterisms or not, one thing was most certainly crystal clear to him —and that was the muzzle of our gun which, at that range, must have looked like the mouth of a railway tunnel.

And with an express train likely to appear out of it at any moment.

No one moved on either ship. Not a muscle. While those of the *Charon*'s crew in the lifeboat sat like paralysed marble statues under the S-boat's 20-mm barrels. Only the occasional rattle of a rowlock broke the silence as a wave snatched at a rigidly held oar, and the muted grumble of the German's power-packed exhaust competing with the muffled, reciprocating thump of our own idling engine down below.

Until, finally, the tall, uniformed figure on the *Schnellboot*'s open bridge stirred himself and, after a remarkably cool, assessing glance at the order of battle, lifted the Tannoy mike.

And called, quite matter-of-factly, 'Stalemate I would suggest, Captain. Perhaps we should now shake hands and break off the engagement, eh?'

Trapp frowned at me, a bit taken aback for once. Then he leant out over the rail and cupped his hands. 'You gotter be joking, Herman . . . I c'n convert you to a flush-decked rowin' boat with one round an' you know it.'

Awkwardly I stood up. There didn't seem a lot of point in hiding any longer. But I still clung to the hand-set to the gun as if my life depended on it. Which it did. That German commander was one adversary who wouldn't make a second mistake.

Then the Tannoy confirmed my opinion. 'I agree, Captain. But I would also assure you that, before you can do so, my excellent machine gunners will have massacred every last man in your lifeboat. Concentrated firepower, you understand? Even the pressure of a dead finger on the trigger will accomplish that.'

Babikian sobbed tremulously, *'Pleese,* Captin . . .'

Trapp ignored him loftily. I muttered urgently, 'He can, Captain. Those 20-millimetres are lethal. A five-second burst from that lot an' there'll only be a bloody hole in the water . . .'

But Trapp just shrugged and cupped his hands again. 'OK . . . So shoot the bastards. The back wages I owe 'em, you'll be doin' me a favour. Tell you what, Mister —I'll be so grateful I won't even shoot back at you . . .'

This time he really impressed everybody—especially Babikian and company in the lifeboat. The Germans didn't look at all happy either but that was understandable too. Trapp's callous attitude must have made even Heinrich Himmler seem like a Salvation Army welfare officer by comparison.

For my part I just stared at him.

'Psychology, Mister,' he answered my unspoken question. 'That lifeboat's the only ace they hold . . .

an' if they think I'm not worried by it, then they might
as well chuck their hand in.'

But there was something else in his face. A look of
. . . fanaticism, almost. Or was it just plain, ordinary
greed? I whispered sickly, 'Only you aren't bluffing,
are you, Trapp? You really are prepared to martyr
those poor bastards out there. Just as long as their
deaths can show a profit.'

He raised one eyebrow at me deprecatingly. 'How
d'you make that out, Mister? Killing the second mate
an' them won't put no money in my pocket, will it?'

'The way your mind works it could,' I snarled, trying
not to believe it myself. 'Because when they're gone
then, like you said, that German skipper's got no cards
left to play. You still get the S-boat, one way or the
other.'

'I tell you it's a bluff, Mate. Not business—just a
game've poker . . .'

Then the Tannoy crackled into life for the last time.

'Very well! I concede to your ruthlessness, Captain.
Might I propose we hold a parley of war?'

Trapp's eyes betrayed nothing. Then he grinned the
old, unashamed grin. 'See, Mister? Just a game of bluff,
that's all. Jus' like I said it was.'

Then he turned to the rail. 'Welcome aboard, *Herr
Kapitän*. But—before you comes visitin'—might I
propose that them torpedomen stands well away from
the triggers, an' that you arranges to have the rest of
your guns pointin' nice and peaceful into the sky.'

Settling comfortably in the corner of the wing he
inspected the *Schnellboot* appraisingly with a dealer's
eye.

But I, in turn, didn't stop gazing at him for a very
long time.

Because I couldn't help wondering—about precisely
how far he really would have been prepared to go.

And exactly how much *I* would be worth in terms of
the *Charon*'s profit and loss account, for that matter.

As a negotiable cash asset.

Trapp suddenly decided to be formal, so we waited

for the S-boat commander to be brought down to his matchbox sized cabin.

'Now you remember an' call me "Sir",' he said, hastily shoving a pile of six month old magazines off a chair on to the deck. 'Seein' this is Admiralty business we're on.'

I glared at him. I hadn't forgotten the lifeboat yet. 'As far as you're concerned isn't it just plain "Business"? Sir!'

Then there was a movement at the door and the tall German from the *Schnellboot*'s bridge stepped past Joseph No-name and across the coaming. Removing his cap he placed it under his arm with impeccable correctness but I could see, from the thoughtful look in his eyes, that he'd heard out brief and undoubtedly intriguing verbal round.

I also watched him quickly assessing the boxes of cutlery and other loot stacked against the bulkhead. Then he seemed to smile faintly, suggesting there was rather more to this particular German than just a handsome Teutonic face.

'Duttmann!' he snapped crisply, *'Korvettenkapitän* Max Duttmann!'

Trapp looked tremendously impressed. 'That's pretty high up in your Navy, in't it?'

'He's a Lieutenant Commander,' I said wearily. 'Same as you're supposed to be.'

'Ah,' Trapp nodded, then shoved the chair over with his foot. 'Then siddown, Commander. It's goin' to be a long trip back to Malta.'

Duttmann smiled again, almost imperceptibly.

'Do you intend to steam on the surface, Captain . . . or submerged?'

For a moment we both stared at the German officer disconcertedly, then Trapp started to grin. 'You're quick to catch on, Mister. I'll give you that much.'

'But not quick enough,' I added meaningfully.

Duttmann glanced at me coolly. 'If I had been, then you would both be dead men by now. Along with the rest of your crew . . .'

'Miller,' I said. 'Lieutenant Miller, Royal Navy!'

The German nodded courteous acknowledgment

then gestured, wryly apologetic, towards the boxes of
salvaged silver behind Trapp. 'I can only claim wisdom
after the event, gentlemen. Though I admit I was always a little uneasy about the theory of a mysterious
submarine which no one actually saw. While it seemed
out of character for the crew of any conventional
British warship to have such a passion for collecting
. . . ah . . . mementos of the ships which they sunk.'

Trapp shrugged. 'We're not very conventional. An'
that's why *you're* a prisoner of war an' not a corpse.'

Duttmann frowned. 'You hope for prize money then,
Captain?'

'Let's just say I don't like to watch a lot of capital
investment bein' wasted. Now, I already plotted my
courses home. You'll stay aboard here with most of
your crew while my Mate takes over your ship . . .'

But the German hadn't finished probing.

'Then presumably you don't intend to finish this
war without getting something out of it. Something
more . . . ah . . . practical than your country's gratitude?'

Trapp looked at him. 'Damn right I don't,' he
snapped.

'Damn *right* he doesn't!' I reflected with feeling.

Duttmann smiled softly and, in that moment, I realised exactly what it was about him that made me so
uneasy. Because in the tall German's eye there was
precisely the same look I'd seen so often before in
Lieutenant Commander Edward Trapp's.

Calculating. Buccaneering. And very mercenary.

'In that case how would you like to finish it with
several million *Reichsmarks,* Captain,' our guest said,
quite casually.

'Say, roughly, one and a half million pounds Sterling . . .'

'Jesus!' Trapp muttered for maybe the tenth time.
'One an' a half million quid . . . *Jesus!*'

I leaned back against the bridge rail and watched
him striding back and forward, back and forward, with
his head down and a frown of stunned disbelief on his
face. Then he said, 'Jesus!' again and I turned away

resignedly to stare at the *Schnellboot,* still rolling uncomfortably under the eye of our gun, with her despondent crew sitting wearily on her decks, hands held
stiffly behind their heads.

While Leading Hand Mulholland was entertaining
the astonishing *Korvettenkapitän* Max Duttmann in
Trapp's cramped cabin below us—with a glass of Tiger
beer and a sten submachine gun.

Suddenly Trapp ground to a halt and stared penetratingly at me. 'What do you think, eh?'

'I've already told you—I think you're mad as a
bloody hatter.'

But I didn't waste a lot of passion over the simple
statement. He would still do what he wanted to, anyway. 'Oh, I know *that,*' Trapp said, not offended at all.
'But I'm talkin' about the bristle head . . . do you trust
'im?'

I chewed my lip pensively. It wasn't an easy question to answer. I couldn't help having a sneaking respect for the tall German's coolness and, after meeting
Trapp, I realised that men could have many reasons
for opting out a war.

'I'd say he's predictable,' I shrugged. 'Where
money's concerned I think Duttmann's predictable.
Like you.'

Trapp grinned unashamedly, 'You mean he's happy
to put personal gain before loyalty to the glorious
Third Reich, eh?'

'Something like that. Plus the fact that he's already
as good as resigned from the Axis war effort either
way.'

'An' what about you?'

I hesitated, feeling a recklessness I'd never been
aware of before. Maybe I'd been with Trapp long
enough for some of his bloodymindedness to rub off on
me . . . and I'd never really forgotten my row with the
admiral all that time ago, where I'd been elected
scapegoat—and drafted aboard the *Charon* because
of it.

'I don't know enough about Duttmann's proposition yet. I'll tell you when I do.'

He gazed at me for a few moments, then nodded

cheerfully. 'Then let's go an' see a man about a pension. But a million an' a half *quid* . . .'

'The Afrika Korps are withdrawing all along the line, gentlemen. Their presence in this theatre of war is virtually finished. In fact a number of Germans already believe that the Third Reich itself is doomed . . . myself among them.'

I studied him closely. If he really did feel like that it made the perhaps rather-too-docile surrender of the S-boat more easy to understand.

But I still asked pointedly, 'How d'you know so much, Duttmann? They still hold a big slice of North Africa and you're not privy to the secret views of your High Command.'

'No—but you yourself will realise that even comparatively junior officers occasionally have to carry out tasks which, by their very nature, suggest obvious conclusions.'

'And your conclusion?'

'That contingency plans are now being implemented to evacuate Rommel and his Staff . . . several boats of my own Flotilla are already engaged in the escort of vital shipments to the European theatre.'

Trapp wriggled irritably. 'What about the money, Max?' he snapped, with devoted singlemindedness.

'Not money, Captain—gold. Several tons of gold bullion.'

Trapp started to say 'Jesus' again so I broke in hurriedly. 'Where from?'

Duttmann shrugged. 'As you pointed out, Lieutenant. I'm not privy to the *Wehrmacht*'s secrets. But probably sent out with the Korps originally, to assist in converting our Arab hosts to the German way of life. Though I would also imagine that a number of bank vaults along the line of retreat are now open and very empty. No army likes to leave a powerful weapon in the enemy's hands.'

'Weapon?' Trapp asked, looking surprised.

'In this case a devastating one, Captain. Enough gold to equip two *Panzer* divisions . . . build destroyers . . . commission an entire *Staffel* of fighter planes . . .'

Trapp broke in grimly. 'An' that's just about what they'll have guarding it, Mister.'

The German shrugged. 'Not quite. One company of infantry probably, plus an armoured escort.'

I started to feel a tingling suspicion, a very uncomfortable one. 'So how do we get it from them, Duttmann . . . Start a one-ship *Blitzkrieg* against the German Army?'

He smiled softly. 'No. We will merely have to ask them for it.'

Trapp slammed upright. 'An' they'll hand it over jus' like that,' he snarled furiously. 'Probably help us load it aboard too, while they're at it?'

Duttmann nodded calmly. 'Precisely, Captain. Commencing at sixteen hundred hours tomorrow afternoon.'

I said, very clearly indeed, 'You're a clever bastard, aren't you, Duttmann? Playing for time in the hope that one of your chummy ships'll turn up to rescue you. Only you're not quite clev . . .'

Then I stopped. Abruptly.

Because all of a sudden, I realised that *Korvettenkapitän* Max Duttmann had meant every word he'd said . . .

Back on the *Charon*'s bridge again. The S-boat's crew now looking like wet rats sitting around their deck while our own crowd didn't seem in all that much better shape . . . except Crocker. On the phone he'd assured me, quite cheerfully, that he was only too delighted to point guns at Germans all day. Especially unhappy ones.

Trapp was back in his entranced rut. 'Jesus!' he muttered, 'One an' a half *million* qui . . .'

I snapped irritably, 'Oh f'r God's sake!' and he looked hurt.

'It's a lot've money, a million an' a hal . . .'

'It's also suicide, Trapp. Go along with Duttmann and you've put yourself right outside the pale. Everyone's Navy will be looking for you. The *Kriegsmarine* because they'll be out for blood and the Royal Navy

because you just happen to have a contract with them
. . .'

'No I don't,' he said positively. 'I tore that up myself, the minute I went soft on that boat-load of kids.
We were on the way home, remember?'

I nodded reluctantly. He did have a point there,
though whether the admiral would see it was open
to doubt.

'Anyway,' Trapp continued, enthusiastic in a way
that only avarice could engender, 'if we take that gold
then Hitler can't *spend* it, can 'e? An' accordin' to
Duttmann's argument that'd be as good as us sinkin'
a flotilla've Jerrie destroyers or shootin' down a whole
bloody squadron of Messerschmitts, wouldn't it?'

I frowned. Trapp's ideas, when it came to matters
of finance, had a crazy way of sounding logical—and
there was no doubt that the lunatic environment of
the *Charon* was beginning to affect my own reasoning.

But it still sounded all too simple. Too straightforward.

Which probably meant, in the *Charon*'s topsy-turvy
world, that the whole bloody operation would finish
up as a shambles.

'My meeting with you,' Duttmann had said wryly,
'was purely by chance, gentlemen. You'll perhaps
remember I told you earlier that my *Schnellboot*
flotilla is partly engaged in escorting vital material on
its return to Germany?'

'Aye,' Trapp had muttered, fascinated.

'Well, my present mission is to meet and escort
an Italian merchantman from a rendezvous at sea
to a point on the Libyan coast. We are due to meet
her at the rendezvous at zero six hundred tomorrow
morning.'

'So why bother with us, Duttmann? If you had
another job to do?'

He smiled ruefully. 'I was curious. You looked a
little . . . ah . . .'

'Peculiar?' I nodded. It made sense.

'And what happens when you an' the Eytalian get to
this place of yours, then?'

'The Army will be waiting. They will have brought the gold for shipment. Back to Taranto, I understand.'

I shrugged, 'So what?'

This time Duttmann smiled very broadly indeed. It was the same kind of boyish grin that Trapp always used to sugar *his* particular death pills.

'Supposing our Italian friends were . . . delayed,' he said carefully. 'And this ship—the *Charon*—were waiting to load its future cargo instead?'

I stared at him. Then I stared at Trapp. And Trapp just sat and stared at both of us with a great, slowly blossoming grin like a bloody sunflower appearing on his face.

'*Korvettenkapitän* . . .' I said with a sinking heart, '. . . you are even crazier than *he* is. Do you really believe that this fractured old wreck can blithely steam alongside half the German Army and expect them to mistake her for an Italian freighter, jus' because we paint *Leonardo da Vinci* or something on our bows and fly an Italian Ensign . . . ?'

Duttmann still kept smiling, but this time a little wryly. 'I gather, Lieutenant, that the German Navy and the *Luftwaffe* have been doing precisely that for several months now. I did myself, remember?'

I collapsed in my chair, shaking my head disbelievingly. 'But the gold, dammit! Whoever's in command of that armoured column isn't going to just hand it over without establishing our identity . . . our bona fides.'

Trapp started to hug himself in pure delight. But *he* would. It was his kind of dream coming hideously true. Duttmann just shrugged.

'If you were an Afrika Korps major waiting for an Italian ship, and it arrived precisely on schedule and at top secret rendezvous . . .'

'. . . and it was escorted by what is unmistakably a German warship, would you have any further doubts, Mister?'

I blinked at Trapp and shivered. It suddenly seemed cold, up there on the bridge.

'It's outrageous!' I said for the tenth time. 'The

whole bloody scheme's impossible, criminal lunacy and indisputably doomed to failure.'

'But what d'you *really* think?' he said encouragingly.

'Oh, it's worth a try,' I muttered.

Weakly.

Chapter Ten

By the following morning the weather had cleared, with only the slightest chop to ruffle the surface of the sea.

I stood beside Duttmann on the *Schnellboot*'s open bridge and wallowed in the exhilaration of slamming across the dawn-washed Mediterranean, conscious only of the deck drumming under my feet and the wind tearing at my face, and the throated, pulsating roar of seven thousand-five hundred horsepower diesels driving us at forty-two knots.

Occasionally I couldn't help glancing up at the red and white ensign, board-flat under the slipstream and with the black swastika arrogantly reminding me of my present circumstances . . . an international, entirely private alliance which made even the concept of HMS *Charon* pale into insignificance.

But only *if* we could believe the word of a man wearing an enemy uniform . . .

I stole a glance at Duttmann beside me. Still in his peaked cap, he seemed the typical Nazi—blond, handsome and with a calculating aplomb which suggested fanatical dedication . . . but to what?

Was the German S-boat commander really opting out—or was he playing some complicated game with Trapp as his opponent?

The Survival Game.

In which Trapp had already slipped back from the top of the league table . . .

He saw me watching and smiled. 'Still doubtful, Lieutenant Miller? About whether you can trust me or not?'

I shrugged. 'Only until we sight that Italian freighter of yours. Then I'll know.'

'But you are worried, eh?'

I turned and gazed pointedly at Leading Seaman
Mulholland standing, legs apart and riding the
bumps easily, at the after end of the bridge with his
sten gun held casually on Duttmann's back . . . and
at a heavily-bandaged Seaman Gunner Clark on the
after deck, covering the few members of the S-boat's
crew whom Trapp had allowed to remain on board
for this opening phase of OPERATION PANZERHEIST.
Mostly the German's torpedomen . . .

And I settled the stock of my own sten more comfortably into the crook of my arm and said quietly,
'No, *Korvettenkapitän* . . . if anyone should be worried, then it ought to be you.'

We sighted the ship just after six a.m. A distant
smudge on the horizon at first, it shortly grew into
the silhouette of an unmistakably inoffensive and quite
small freighter, then finally, as we roared towards it,
a vessel flying the Italian flag.

'Satisfied, Lieutenant?' Duttmann asked.

'Let's take a closer look,' I said. 'But without stopping. Nasty things can happen when you stop alongside little merchant ships.'

He eyed me expressionlessly for a moment, then
turned to the voice pipe. '*Steurbord fünfzhen* . . .'

The *Schnellboot* heeled into a smooth, blasting
curve which took us cleanly down the Italian's side,
about half a cable off. It was almost a carbon copy
of the *Charon,* apart from being about fifty years
younger, but her crew were lining the sides, waving
with obvious delight to see their Ally turning up to
escort them . . .

I raised the beautifully balanced Liebermann and
Gortz binoculars. A fat man with a heavily braided
cap was leaning out over her bridge wing, watching
us with a big smile on his face. I lowered the glasses
as we rounded her threshing counter. The name and
port of registry across her stern said *Virgilio Andreotti . . . Napoli.*

'Right, Duttmann,' I snapped, dropping the binoculars. 'She's all yours.'

He took her out again, about half a mile away from the still steaming freighter then, as the *Schnellboot* started to come round in a slow, sweeping swing, he gestured aft.

'Do you mind?'

'Right, Clark.'

The gunner warily lowered the barrel of his sten and, immediately, the German ratings clambered expertly into the seats beside the attack controls. Duttmann glanced grimly towards the Italian, now coming quickly on to our bows, and bent over the voice pipe again . . .

Silently I beckoned to Mulholland and he raised the sten until it was pointing directly at Duttmann's unsuspecting head. Then I lifted the glasses once more and laid them on the fast approaching ship.

They didn't know what was happening for a few seconds. One by one the crewmen along her rails slowly stopped waving and stared at us with uncertain attitudes until, abruptly, one man started to run aft, shouting something to the fat skipper on her bridge. I saw him wheel and grip the rail in front of him, frozen into a pose of disbelieving stupefaction . . .

Duttmann snapped upright and his poised hand slashed down.

'Torpedoes . . . *LOS!*'

Whooosh . . . whooosh . . .

'Backbord dreissig . . .'

We heeled away in a slamming, bucketing arc under full helm while the twin tracks of the torpedoes emerged from the watersplashes ahead of us and screamed towards their target on bubble-bursting, converging lines. One stark glimpse of the Italian seamen, some still transfixed against her rails, others running desperately for the far side of the deck, away from the horror that was overtaking them. The fat man on her bridge not moving at all, maybe because he realised hopelessly that there wasn't any point in running but not knowing *why* f'r . . .

The first explosion lifted the *Virgilio Andreotti's* entire afterdeck up in the air. Along with her bridge, wheelhouse and funnel.

The second hit, immediately following, chopped thirty feet off her bows and most of those seamen. It didn't make any difference which side of her deck they'd run to.

And then she was gone. Just like that. Straight down by the head with her propellor still turning and hardly a swirl to show she'd been there at all. Until a great, thrashing blister on the surface indicated that the pressure of the sea had imploded into her empty holds, and a lot of wreckage came up to drift sluggishly in an ever-widening circle.

I lowered the binoculars heavily. I'd seen a lot of ships die in the last few weeks but the *Andreotti* seemed to hit a lot nearer home, somehow. More like the *Charon* could have died . . . only yesterday morning . . . under the slam of those same vicious torpedoes . . .

Duttmann asked quietly, 'Now are you satisfied, Lieutenant?'

I looked at him. There was a sadness in his eyes, the same sadness I'd seen so often in Trapp's, but otherwise his handsome, boyish features were deliberately impassive.

'Welcome to the Homeless Club, *Korvettenkapitän*,' I muttered, then I laid my sten on the ledge between us and turned to Mulholland, still standing watchfully behind.

'You can stand down, Mulholland. Go an' have a smoke with Clark and our new-found partners.'

I waited with my back to Duttmann for a minute, watching as the British and German seamen on the afterdeck gazed hesitantly at each other before one of the *Kriegsmarine*-uniformed torpedomen grinned and pulled out a packet of cigarettes . . .

A voice behind me snapped—very coldly, 'Miller.'

I turned. Duttmann held the sten gun—my sten gun —balanced easily in what appeared to be only too familiar hands.

For a moment our eyes met. His were hard. Unforgiving.

And then he said grimly, 'Don't you ever leave a

weapon in a criminally dangerous state on my bridge again, Lieutenant. Do you understand?'

Easing the cocking handle into the 'safe' slot he threw it to me angrily. I caught it, then withdrew the magazine. I shook it so he could hear the rattle of the spring.

'Empty,' I said. 'That was loyalty test number two, Max. You see, you and Trapp aren't the only deceitful bastards in this particular Navy . . .'

On the way back to rejoin Trapp and the *Charon* I glanced curiously at Duttmann. 'You've got twenty-three crewmen on this boat, Max. D'you really mean to say they're all as unpatriotic and . . . well . . . as criminal as our crowd on the *Charon?*'

He shrugged. 'Perhaps patriotism doesn't necessarily mean blind obedience to any cause. Certainly not to Adolf Hitler's. I and my crew have discussed it often. But to refuse to acknowledge the Nazi regime is, by admission, to become a criminal in the eyes of the Third Reich . . . and we are also practical men, Lieutenant. Until now there has been very little opportunity for us to become self-supporting criminals. Not in a worthwhile way.'

'But this is worthwhile?'

Duttmann grinned philosophically. Trapp again. 'For that much money *Reichsmarschall* Goering could be persuaded to vote for Winston Churchill.'

It was a horrible enough thought that there should be two Trapps loose in the Mediterranean; that the bunch of ruffians who passed for a crew on the *Charon* should be so precisely duplicated aboard the *Schnellboot* was almost too awful to contemplate.

'Surely *some* of your men were reluctant?'

'Two or three. But we persuaded them.'

'*Persuaded* them?'

'All done by kindness, I assure you.'

I frowned. Something which had been worrying at the back of my mind suddenly clicked into place.

'I always understood every German military unit carried its own Nazi watchdog. And there was another officer on this bridge with you the first time we met . . .'

'My late First Lieutenant,' Duttmann said impassively. 'He was a very dedicated Nazi until *Oberbootmann* Röder discussed politics with him in the middle of last night. But Röder's father lives in Buchenwald at the moment. If he lives at all.'

'*Was* a Nazi?'

'Overboard now. With a piece of signal halyard knotted very tightly around his neck . . . So you see, Lieutenant Miller,' he added, almost as an afterthought. 'There are only twenty-two criminals aboard this ship. Apart from yourself.'

'Whaddyou mean, you can't cook spaghetti?' Trapp exploded. 'Everyone c'n cook bloody spaghetti . . .'

Back to normal. Certainly with the red-faced and equally furious cook.

I glanced at my watch. Just under an hour to go until we raised the Libyan coast and Duttmann's secret rendezvous with the Afrika Korps. Over to starboard the *Schnellboot,* again fully complemented with her original crew—less one—crawled painfully slowly in company with us while, in the freshest white paint to be laid on the *Charon* for half a century, the legend on our stern now read *Virgilio Andreotti . . . Napoli.*

Meanwhile Trapp had busied himself with improving on the more subtle details of our new character.

Only . . .

'I am a *Greek* gentlemans . . .' the cook yelled back happily. 'An' Greek gentlemans do not never cook the spaghetti in the 'Otel Majestique I bluddy tell you . . .'

'But 'ow c'n you expec' us to look like an Eytalian boat an' . . . an' *smell* like an Eytalian boat f'r . . .' Trapp positively begged in frustration, 'when not even the bloody *cook* c'n cook flamin' spaghetti . . .'

We finally arrived off the pick-up point at half past three in the afternoon.

It was a bleak, arid inlet with a short, stone landing stage and nothing else for miles around other than heat-shimmering desert, baking black rock and the scorpions.

There was no sign of the Afrika Korps. Nothing. Only the desolation and the sand. And the fear.

Acting on Duttmann's advice we secured alongside the derelict quay, while he lay a hundred yards off-shore, engines temporarily shut-down with his bows facing seawards defensively. The *Schnellboot* ratings stayed at their guns and reloaded tubes.

Sweating and cursing we laboured to knuckle the *Charon* round until she too was pointed on an evacuation course . . . but not too far round. I still wanted our broadside to cover the landward end of the jetty —the only obvious area suggested for a vehicle park.

And then, silently, we closed-up to our guns as well. Crocker and crew below us in the oven-like space of number two hold and the Bofors team boxed in their imitation packing case which wouldn't even give them protection from a Luger bullet.

Duttmann came ashore when we were finally ready. The impression the Afrika Korps formed would be up to him.

And then, German and British, we waited.

And sweated a lot more.

No one spoke. Not even Trapp.

But perhaps it was only then that we'd really begun to realise the true enormity of the gamble we'd committed ourselves to.

Twenty past four . . . half past . . . Leaning over the bridge wing I felt the sweat trickling down my bare arms and forming in little pools on the rail. This time there wasn't any necessity for concealment on my part . . . only for the guns' crews.

Which posed our first major danger. If the Army insisted on coming aboard . . .

Duttmann and two of his seamen, both armed with Schmeissers, stood waiting silently on the jetty. Even Max seemed to be wilting a little under the heat, or perhaps the tension had a lot to do with it as well. I called softly, 'You sure this is the right place?'

He glanced up, looking worried for the first time since we'd met. 'Perhaps the RAF . . . ?'

One of the German ratings suddenly said, *'Bitte! Warten Sie einen Moment, Kapitän . . .'*

Duttman broke off abruptly and listened. I lifted my head and stared hard at the crests of the dunes about two miles away, hurriedly bringing my glasses to my eyes. And then I heard it too—the distant roar of engines.

'They're coming,' Duttmann called, hardly concealing the relief in his voice. I didn't answer—but relief wasn't exactly my primary emotion right then.

Trapp came out of the wheelhouse and leaned over beside me. 'They wouldn't have let 'im clean the toilets in the 'Otel Majestique,' he muttered bitterly. 'Bloody cook!'

'They're coming,' I passed on, wishing he'd forget about the cook.

Trapp sniffed irritably. 'About time too. No wonder they're losin' the war if they can't even be on time with our million an' a ha . . .'

'Stand-to, Crocker,' I snapped into the phone. 'This is it now.'

'Where d'you plan to stow the stuff, Sir? Can't hardly have them liftin' the lid off this little lot down 'ere, can we.'

'After end of number one, PO. We've opened the hatch abaft the Bofors case . . . your boys'll be sleeping on eighteen carat pillows tonight.'

He chuckled on the other end of the line. 'The stuff that dreams is made of . . . Standing-to now, Sir.'

'Acknowledge. And I hope to God I don't have to call you again until we're out of here.'

Crocker's voice was calm and reassuring. 'If you do, I promise I'll answer. An' bloody fast!'

I placed the handset on the deck beside my sten, carefully making sure that I could grab either if I had to. Then I raised the glasses again and started to count the vehicles as they came over the dunes, trailing a hanging cloud of sand.

A half-track leading, then what seemed to be an eight-wheeled heavy armoured car. Two more half-tracked personnel carriers . . . two heavy trucks . . . another light, fully-tracked tank of some kind bringing up the rear . . . and nothing.

So that was our golden column. No fifty-ton *Panzers*,

thank God, but a hell of a lot of light weapon fire-power plus, maybe, something a lot bigger on that armoured car and the tank. I gestured urgently to Duttmann on the jetty. 'What d'you reckon, Max?'

'Watch for the Puma *Panzerspähwagen* . . . the ar-moured car. She's our latest model—carries a five-centimetre gun and can exceed fifty miles an hour flat out. The tank's an old Mark II, maybe a two-centimetre gun . . . no real problem.'

'Not unless it actually fires at you,' I reflected grimly. But the armoured car—the Puma—looked ugly. Positively lethal. I shivered despite the heat on the bridge.

Then the lead half-track was roaring and bucketing towards us down the jettty while the rest of the Ger-man column bumped to a dust-swirling halt, precisely in the area I'd hoped they would.

Immediately the turret of the damned Puma started to revolve until I found myself gazing nervously down the barrel of its unsettlingly large gun. Whoever was in command of that particular armoured car must have had a very rough and faith-eroding war up to now.

Other than that, however, the representatives from the Afrika Korps didn't seem particularly uneasy. The troops tumbled stiffly out of the personnel carriers and commenced desultorily to set up a landward defence perimeter, only occasionally throwing curious, slightly incredulous glances at the *Charon* while thinking, sym-pathetically that their Italian Allies must really be scraping the bottom of the maritime barrel for mer-chantmen.

Even the crew of the small tank appeared only too glad to crawl out of their steel box and relax in the shade of its camouflaged hull. But I still kept my eyes mainly on that eight-wheeled Puma . . .

Then the officer in charge of the column jumped down from his half-track just below our bridge and saluted the waiting Duttmann—a mini-edition of Rom-mel himself, complete with leather coat and sand gog-les hanging casually around his neck to leave dust rings shadowing the pale blue eyes.

'*Heil Hitler!*'

Duttmann saluted back, but it was a Naval gesture without the stiff Nazi arm. '*Guten abend, Herr Major,*' he said calmly.

The major gazed up at us for what seemed a very long time with an expression of open disapproval mingled, perhaps, with uneasy doubt. I stared back woodenly, aware of my heart thumping madly, then Trapp beside me grinned and nodded.

''*Eil 'Itler!*' he said. '*Viva la Duce! Un bicchiere grande di birra, eh Majore?*'

The German major looked blank while Duttmann closed his eyes. I whispered frantically, 'F'r cryin' out loud . . . I thought you couldn't speak Italian.'

'I can't, Mate,' Trapp muttered, still keeping the fixed grin in place. 'Except to ask if 'e wants a glass've beer . . . that bastard's getting suspicious as 'ell.'

'*Verzeihen Sie, Herr Major* . . .' I snapped hurriedly, feeling my throat drying up but forcing myself to continue in what I hoped to God was Italian-flavoured German. 'My *Capitano*, he is saying would you care for a glass of beer?'

I saw the two seamen behind Duttmann ever so casually swivelling until their Schmeissers covered the major. Whatever else happened I didn't have any more doubts about the loyalty of Max's volunteer expatriates. Then the desert soldier smiled a little bleakly and nodded. '*Danke, Kapitän.*'

And to my intense relief turned to Duttmann. I strained to follow the rapid German conversation. 'You really are satisfied with this ship, *Korvettenkapitän*. This *Virgilio Andreotti?*'

Duttmann nodded, then said something in a low voice. The Afrika Korps major swivelled his head to stare at Trapp for a moment then, abruptly, gave a rumbling guffaw. Duttmann smiled too, in an apologetic sort of way at us, while Trapp's return grin looked as though it had been chipped out of granite.

Until the major held out his hand in great good humour. 'Then may I see your papers and your orders. The quicker we clear out of this crap-oven the better . . .'

Duttmann produced a sheaf of papers and, together,

they strolled towards the half-track. As soon as they'd turned away Trapp's grin faded into a black, outraged scowl.

'What did 'e say about me?' he demanded furiously. 'Duttmann said somethin' about me, din't he?'

I got ready to take a cold beer down to a German officer; there wasn't another man on the *Charon* I could trust not to go and put his foot in it.

'I don't know what he actually said about you,' I retorted spitefully. 'But whatever it was, Trapp . . . it just *had* to be the bloody truth.'

They started to load the gold aboard at 1700 hours precisely.

No German soldiers even attempted to come aboard. Duttmann had made it quite clear that no fraternisation was to be tolerated between the *Wehrmacht* and the *Charon*'s . . . the *Andreotti*'s crew . . . on the grounds of strict security.

I watched as the first, disappointingly small sealed boxes were carried up our gangway from the truck, then handed over to a tight-lipped Greek Polly, so chosen because he was about the most Italian-looking character in a cosmopolitan selection.

But, small or not, each of those boxes were worth around twenty thousand pounds. It was the first time in my life I'd seen Trapp literally unable to speak. Not even to argue.

It was the best thing that had happened to me all day.

At 1710 hours something else happened which made me feel a lot happier.

The eight-wheeled armoured Puma went away.

But Duttmann whispered tightly. 'They've only gone over the dunes on a reconnaissance patrol. They'll probably be back shortly.'

It still made me feel better. Not to have that damned suspicious gun pointing at me.

By 1740 hours the first truck was empty.

The *Charon* was now worth roughly one and a half million pounds Sterling.

Or as Trapp said, positively hugging himself with barely-contained glee, 'That's our share. Now all we gotter collect is Duttmann's.'

At 1750 hours I took the *Herr Major* another glass of beer.

At 1756 hours someone shot him.

A great many times. With a machine gun. From the *Charon* . . .

Chapter Eleven

It's still a hazy nightmare. Trying to remember the exact sequence of how things went wrong.

I'd just returned to the bridge after presenting the major with his second drink. It had been tinglingly cold in my hands, I recollect that much, with the sides of the glass all dewy and frosted with condensation.

Trapp had turned to me with the binoculars in his grip. 'We're nearly finished loading an' Maxie boy's gone back aboard the S-boat,' he said, looking like a cat with two tails—and both of them solid gold.

I took the glasses from him and focused on the *Schnellboot*. I could see Duttmann climbing up to her bridge, preparing for sea.

'He's not wasting any time,' I muttered gladly. 'Just as well, too. The quicker we get the hell out've . . .'

And then it happened!

When the door of the paint locker under the fo'c'slehead suddenly burst open with a resounding *crash* and a weird, indescribably grimy apparition stumbled out on to the deck with a crowbar in its hand.

Trapp, myself, the *Charon*'s crew and every German soldier near the ship swivelled in stunned surprise.

While the figure, blinking with the impact of the sudden sunlight, stared in slowly dawning concern at the ring of half-tracks and lorries, and a tank—all with German crosses on them. Plus what must have seemed like half the Afrika Korps pointing guns at him . . .

And muttered: 'Jerries! Och Jesus but we been captured by the bluidy Jerries . . .'

I croaked numbly, 'Trapp? Didn't you think to tell

Gorbals Wullie about this small diversion of yours . . .'

While Trapp closed his eyes. 'Why is it I always 'ave to remember *everythin'* on this bloo . . .'

Just before the disinterred Gorbals Wullie uttered a warlike, totally-forgiving bellow of, 'Dinnae you worry, Captin. Ah'll save youse lads frae them poofy Nazi bastids . . .'

And, dragging the vegetable locker cover from his beloved machine gun, emptied a five second burst into the leather-clad chest of the German major—still clutching a half-full glass of ice cold beer in a disbelieving hand . . .

'Oh, that's really done it!' Trapp snarled. And took off.

I hit the phone. Fast!

'Crocker. *Tank* . . . FIIIIRE*!*'

The plates dropped before I'd even finished. Obviously Wullie's first opening rounds had shattered rather more than just the *Herr Major*'s sweltering complacency.

I prayed hysterically, 'Please, Gun. Please don't jam on us now . . .'

Trapp in the wheelhouse. 'Chief. Gimme all you got an' a helluva lot more . . .'

The sides of the packing case on the foredeck collapsing with a dull crash while, already, the long barrel sweeping up and round as the layer's hands spun burringly . . . Sand-coloured uniforms scattering on all sides as Wullie's bullets chopped fountains of dust in great, sweeping curves across the desert . . . Three tank men scrambling desperately onto the turret of their vehicle . . .

Crocker. Wonderfully . . . *'Fire!'*

Slam!

The tank blossoming into a rising ball of orange with a man spreadeagled on top of it, twisting hideously slowly into the air . . . 'Bloody spot *on*, Crocker. Go f'r the half-tracks, go f'r the half-tracks!'

'Reload . . . on . . .'

Someone screaming in agony. The driver of the dead major's command vehicle . . . *'Ich verstehe nicht . . .*

ich verstehe nicht . . .' Half his right shoulder blown away . . .

'Fiiiiiire!'

Slam!

And the Bofors now, traversing and firing at the same time. *Pom . . . pom . . . pom . . . pom! Pom . . . pom . . .*

But shots coming in suddenly, cracking and whining haphazardly. A group of soldiers on the perimeter struggling to swing their heavy Spandau machine gun around to face their own allies . . . us. Everyone still white-faced with shock.

An engine screaming in high revs as the empty truck pulls away in a cloud of dust . . . the Bofors takes it cleanly and it howls halfway up the side of a dune to fall over with a crash of splintering glass, then starts to burn. No one gets out of the cab.

More firing now. From the distance. What the *hell . . .*

Trapp, roaring like a madman. 'Duttmann! They're joinin' in with the S-boat, Mate!'

I whirl to stare seawards. Already under way the low grey torpedo boat cruises slowly along the line of the shore, every gun blazing. So poor bloody Duttmann's really cut his hawser now, killing Germans. Killing his own countrymen. But he must have prepared himself to do that a long time ago . . . when he first lined up on the *Virgilio Andreotti* . . . the real *Andreotti.*

A bedlam, a hysteria of shooting now. Bofors, HMG's, 37-millimetres, 20-millimetres, sten guns, Schmeissers . . . Lugers.

Slam! A personnel carrier erupts into a hanging cloud of sand and black smoke.

4.7's . . .

Greek Polly hugging a German corporal in a huge, crushing grip under the tail board of the lorry, berserk in an arena with a half million pound roof. Another Afrika Korps soldier hurtles past holding a blazing Schmeisser and chops both men to pieces in his excitement . . . then Wullie, bawling like a lunatic, smashes the third man off his feet and against the remains of the truck's cargo.

Splinters of wood and tumbling, bouncing ingots avalanche to spread in a golden pool over the blood-soaked sand.

'Jesus!' says Wullie, staring at it disbelievingly.

Black Joseph No-name running across the deck, crazily waving a huge, glittering knife and yelling at the top of his voice.

'Je*sus!*' Wullie says again, wondering what he's started. Then an arm with a *Feldwebel*'s stripes on it appears calmly over the low bulwarks and something bounces across the deck to snuggle cosily beside Wullie's machine gun tripod.

'Grenaaaaade!' I scream as Joseph alters course fractionally in his mad charge to kick at it. The grenade rolls a few yards then catches in a ring bolt. It goes off as Joseph's impetus carries him over the top of it and I watch the one-legged corpse, still holding the knife, somersault clean over the rail and on to the jetty.

Trapp's bellowing 'Leggo forr'ad . . . leggo aft!' as I lean way out over the bridge wing and empty a full sten magazine into the *Feldwebel*.

'Och *Jesus!*' Wullie says a third time, white as a ghost. Then starts firing again . . .

Pom . . . pom . . . pom . . . pom! Pom . . . pom . . . pom . . . pom!

Slam!

'Reloadan'gof'rtheperimeter . . .'

Fragile Babikian crawling forward, terrified out of his wits. A line of bullet holes appears in the hatch coaming ahead of him and he freezes, flat on the deck with his hands hugging over his head . . . one of the Bofors gunners jerks like a rag doll in his seat then slides sideways to hang loosely, a broken, bloody puppet.

Trapp swinging the telegraph to '*Half ahead.*' Then, charging out to lean over the rail and roar at the paralysed second mate: 'You just gerroff've yer ass an' leggo forr'ad, Mister!'

Splinters erupt in a perfect curve against the wheelhouse, parallel to and three inches away from Trapp's bent figure. He jerks up and says ever so aggrievedly, '*Bloody* Germans . . . I tol' you we couldn't trust 'em,' then disappears back into the wheelhouse to spin the wheel hard over to port.

A heavy machine gun opening up from the top of a low dune eighty yards away. Bullets are hitting us from every conceivable angle now as the deck starts to throb bouncingly under the slowly threshing power of our screw. Nothing *happening* though . . . Our bows still secured to the jetty by a virtually unbreakable manilla umbilical cord . . .

'Babikiaaan!'

The kid sobs, then drags himself to his feet. He's half-way up the ladder before the HMG catches him, belting him sideways, clean over the rail and into the water alongside . . . I start to run and be sick at the same time.

Then a rotund, red-faced juggernaut overtakes me on the well deck yelling in superheated Greek as he virtually tumbles up the bullet-scarred ladder to the fo'c'slehead. One crazy glimpse of a billowing, ridiculously filthy apron before the meat cleaver in the fat man's grip flashes downwards. The last line to the jetty parts with a huge *twang*.

The cook waves the meat cleaver triumphantly at Trapp up in the wheelhouse and shrieks happily, 'So now you need me—your bluddy chef—to 'elp you run your sheep, hah? I tell you when I was at the 'Otel Majes . . .'

I hear the rattle of the Spandau from the dune as I go down to the deck in a long, hopeless dive. 'Geddown, Chef f'r . . .'

And the cook does—sitting down abruptly, still with a look of complete and utter victory on his chubby face. Only there isn't any back to his head now . . .

While suddenly Trapp roars out of the wheelhouse like a berserk bull. 'Get 'em!' he screams in a voice which I've never heard before. 'You jus' get them lousy, black-hearted, murderin' ba . . .'

The 4.7, the Bofors, the S-boat and Wullie's machine gun erupt into one thunderous snarl. The desert

blossoms into a drifting, hanging sand cloud, and,
when it clears, there isn't a sign of a machine gun
anywhere. There isn't even a sand dune any more . . .

And everything suddenly seems very quiet.

Only the desultory crackle of a burning half-track
and the occasional moan of a wounded, half-buried
man disturbs the desert silence. And the throb of the
Charon's engine as we swing steadily away from that
charnel house.

The phone calls anxiously, 'Sir . . . ? Are you OK
up there . . . ?' but I don't answer. Not right away.
Because I'm still blinking dazedly at Trapp.

But he just stands there like a statue, staring towards the fat man in the dirty, bloodstained apron
who sits so uncharacteristically placid on the bullet-
riddled fo'c'slehead.

And there are tears streaming down his leathery
cheeks.

Captain Edward Trapp is actually . . . crying.

It should have been over by then.
It really should have been . . .

I turned away from Trapp feeling a bit embarrassed.
The gap of water between us and the jetty slowly
widened . . . Fifty yards . . . Seventy-five . . .

The phone called again. Urgently. 'Are you all
right, Sir?'

I nodded. He'd find out soon enough. 'All right,
Arthur.'

. . . one hundred yards . . . one twenty.

Then I heard it. The roar of a motor.

At first I thought it was from Duttmann's *Schnellboot,* now cruising slowly about two cables to seaward
and waiting impatiently for us to complete our swing.
And then the engine noise grew louder and I started
to turn in sudden awareness toward the wreckage-
littered shore.

Just as the roar became a throbbing snarl of power
. . . and the eight-wheeled Puma with the five-centimetre gun burst over the tops of the dunes and came

slamminig towards us at a vengeful, weaving fifty miles per hour.

Hopelessly I howled 'Engage . . . engage . . . engage!' into the handset, knowing even as I did so that not even Crocker's superb accuracy could follow the path of that high-speed, jinking approach. The big gun was just too unwieldy, too slow. And the Bofors too light to penetrate the armour of the fifty mile an hour Puma.

But they tried.

Pom . . . pom . . . pom . . . pom! Pom . . . pom . . . pom . . .

Slam!

An enormous plume of sand exploding into the air ahead of the armoured car. Then it stormed through the hanging screen in raging contempt, already skidding to port in a precisely-executed feint which left the spurts of our first Bofors burst kicking impotently at the desert, fifty yards clear.

'Fire!' A second eruption . . . ten yards behind . . . The Puma careers off at a tangent abruptly. I blink disconcertedly, then I see it—the long black pall of burning diesel fuel rolling impenetrably across the killing ground from the shattered light tank . . .

'The smoke, Crocker!' I scream. 'He's going f'r the smoke . . . !'

More ineffectual gouts of dust astern then the Puma rockets into the oily screen to disappear completely, as if miraculously erased from the action. The 4.7 roars again in parting frustration but there's nothing there to lay on . . . I snarl nervously, 'Check . . . check . . . *check!*'

Trapp lunging for the wheelhouse, suddenly snapping out of his daze of grief for the cook. 'Full ahead, Chief! An' open up them valves like you was givin' steam away.'

And we wait. Only for seconds, but it seems like an eternity. While all the time we can hear the Puma, that steady growling engine-noise without any apparent source, any direction. Which way did he turn . . . port . . . starboard? And when he reappears—from what section of the rolling smoke will it be?

Trapp centres the wheel and calls sharply, 'I c'n hear them, Mister. To the right, about ten points abaft the beam.'

I look at him anxiously. I can hear them to the left, a long way over to the left.

'The middle, Captin,' the indestructible Gorbals Wullie shrieks in suppressed excitement from his machine gun. 'Ah hear thon Jerrie motor comin' straight frae the middle o' the smoke.'

And then abruptly, another high-powered engine roar from seaward. We spin round in shock to see the bows of the *Schnellboot* starting to rise in the air as she creams away from us, climbing up on a flaring white wave to full revolutions . . .

'He's runnin' out on us,' Trapp snarls disbelievingly. 'That gutless bristle 'ead's runnin' out on the deal.'

I glared at him spitefully. 'That'll please you then, Trapp. You got all the gold f'r yourself now an' I hope to God you reckon it's been worth all the lives . . .'

'Taaarget LEFT!'

As the Puma explodes out of the smoke, careering towards the jetty and the threshing, ponderous quarry of the *Charon*'s bulk, our gunners exposed like tethered goats in the cavernous steel shooting gallery of number two hold.

Only, this time, the Puma's turret is winking viciously. Deliberately. And with icy precision.

As if in a trance, I hear the handset. Crocker's calm, completely resigned voice. But, for the very first time ever, despairing.

'Sorry, Sir. We guessed twenty degrees wrong . . . never get the old bitch rou . . .'

Then the eight-wheeler's shells pumped into us, seemingly right below my feet, and the deck leapt vertically as the *Charon* shied away over to port under the impact with Trapp roaring above the holocaust, 'They're comin' back, they're comin' *back*, Mister . . .'

Which appeared to be rather an odd thing to say when an armoured car was engaged in sinking your ship. But I was already blast-dazed with the impact of the explosions which were tearing out the gun position below me, and waiting resignedly—just like Crocker had done—for the first round to trigger off our magazine in the lower hold.

Until I had one vision of the Puma, now racing towards me and still firing down the length of the bullet-scarred jetty . . . and then it, and the jetty, and a large area of the desert around the landing place, erupted into a gigantic, hanging cloud of sand with a shocking, searing flash . . .

Just before the lean, power-packed *Schnellboot* roared underneath my bridge wing in a wide, skidding turn with *Korvettenkapitän* Max Duttmann waving a grim salute from her control platform.

Even now she still flew the red, white and black swastika.

Which was ironical really.

Seeing she was probably the first, and the last warship ever to torpedo an eight-wheeled Afrika Korps *Panzerspähwagen!*

It was the very fact that the *Charon* was so ancient and rust-weakened that had saved her.

Most of the Puma's shells had entered the open plates on her starboard side and then just carried on, out through the paper-thin shell of the port side without even exploding.

But some had. Detonating against the gun itself, or the stronger ribs which framed the hold. Searing the bulkheads, buckling and tearing them while, at the same time, twisting the barrel of the mounting of that old 4.7 into a horror of heat-dulled, angled steel.

Leading Hand Mulholland still sat in the gunlayer's seat, right eye comfortably cupped against the molten rubber cushion of the gunsight. But he was a crisp, flaking black all over.

Something lay in a corner, still clutching a live forty-five pound shell which looked as though it had just been delivered from the dockyard—all shiny brass and not even scratched. But the only recognisable part of Seaman Gunner Clark was a scrap of bloodstained bandage where the head might have been once.

Petty Officer Crocker still looked immaculate. From

the waist up. But Trapp had never quite managed to
impress him with the necessity for dressing like a
tramp just because he was serving aboard a tramp
steamer. And judging by the gently reproachful smile
on Arthur's face, he never would have been able to . . .

Trapp turned away and reached for the distorted
ladder to the deck. When he was half-way up and still
not saying anything I couldn't stand it any longer so
I snarled, 'Trapp.'

He froze and then, ever so slowly, he turned to face
me.

And I saw the look in his eyes. While all the resentment and hatred and accumulated spite in me suddenly evaporated into a dull, sympathetic misery.

'It doesn't matter, Captain.' I muttered. 'It doesn't
matter at all. Not any more.'

And the next morning, sixty miles out to sea, we
parted company with Max Duttmann and his now
equally-outlawed crew of *Schnellboot* 248.

We'd split the gold first, lying alongside each other
in a glassy, gently heaving sea. There was no last minute haggling, no mutual suspicion. Just an easy, almost
gay camaraderie which even Trapp couldn't resist.

And naturally there was no mistrust. As Trapp com-
mented, 'It's jus' a straight business arrangement
between gentlemen, Mate . . . an' you gotter have
some principles when you're a Naval officer.'

Max planned to make for the Lebanon. Scuttle his
ship, then disappear—at least until the war was over.
Trapp reckoned there was a future for a big investor
in Libyan oil . . . but not until the Afrika Korps had
ben thoroughly demobilised. Until then he reckoned
the Greek Islands offered considerable promise for a
warship on the run. 'An' a bit've extra profit, even.
While me an' Al an' Wullie an' the rest've the lads
wait f'r the heat ter die down.'

But he'd never change. I'd learned that a long time
ago.

Personally I didn't know what to do. But then
again—I'd never been an international renegade be-

fore . . . Not like the outrageous Edward Trapp always would be, no matter how much profit he amassed.

Even the last thing he yelled across the water between the two ships proved that. Just before Max waved for the last time.

'Remember, Maxie boy. If you ever gets short've cash there's maybe 'alf a million quid still lyin' buried back there in the sand. Worth a bit o' capital investment to get it back, eh?'

The German warship's engines roared into life. Trapp and I stood there on the *Charon*'s bridge and watched silently as the blue water under her stern whirlpooled into threshing foam while she began to turn away, moving faster and faster through the glass surface . . .

. . . and then she blew up.

Shockingly.

In a great, rising column of spray and bits of ship and men . . .

I remember my first reaction. Horror, revulsion, utter disbelief.

Trapp!

Only, when I swung to face him in outraged fury, he just stared back at me uncomprehendingly, almost guiltily.

'I didn't, Mate! Maybe I jus' happened to think about it but I swear I didn't . . . not a *bomb*. Honest to God!'

And I said in terrified apprehension, 'What then . . . ? What the hell *was it, Trapp?*'

Until I recognised the white, gradually dissolving track leading from the *Schnellboot*'s boiling headstone, merging into the distant sea away to the west.

And I said stupidly, 'A torpedo. She's been taken by a *torpedo* f'r . . .'

Then Gorbals Wullie, frozen in mid-step half-way up the bridge ladder, howled, 'Torpedo track . . . Torpedooooo track!'

Without moving Trapp retorted, still shattered, 'We bloody *know* that much, dammit.'

But Wullie shook his head violently, pointing rigidly. 'Ah dinnae mean that one, ah mean the other yin . . .

. . . the one that's goin' tae hit *us!*'

I realised what was happening right away, I think. Aware only of a cold acceptance, flooding me with despair during the last few seconds we had left.

A patrolling submarine. Whether British or German seemed totally irrelevant at the time, we'd made ourselves an equally attractive target for either now.

Probably British, in fact. A supply ship escorted by a *Schnellboot*. A supply ship marked, quite plainly, *Virgilio Andreotti—Napoli*. What better target?

The last I ever saw of Trapp was his huge, suddenly-galvanised form bending over his trusted old voice pipe and roaring in a voice which knew it wasn't any use.

'Get up out've there, Al . . . Get the hell *out've* the . . .'

Just before the whole ship seemed to lift up into the air vertically. And I watched the *Charon*'s fo'c'slehead, and the Bofors gun, and everything else forward of the bridge curling slowly back towards me like a glowing, red-rusted carpet . . .

And the steam and the dust and the pain enveloped me. And the blackness.

But, even while the *Charon* was rolling over on top of me, I still remember screaming unforgivingly, 'You've lost, Trapp. You've finally bloody well *lost* . . .

'. . . 'Cause you can't win forever, Trapp . . . Not at your kind of Survival Game . . .'

Last Watch on Deck

I'd nearly forgotten about Trapp and the *Charon*.

Only occasionally they still struggled up the surface of my mind. Usually during a particularly bad nightmare—along with vague names like Gorbals Wullie and Al Kubiczek, Crocker and Babikian, Greek Polly, Joseph . . . Mulholland, Clark. And a fat cook whose name I'd never been able to understand anyway.

We'd been hit by a British torpedo, as I'd guessed. They pulled me out of the water, but only after waiting patiently for several hours in the hope of another target—when the *Kriegsmarine* came looking for their missing ships.

There were no other survivors from His Majesty's Armed Merchant Cruiser *Charon*.

The really odd thing was . . . that I was found wearing a lifejacket. And draped very securely over a large section of number two hatch cover. Almost as if somebody had deliberately left me like that . . .

The admiral gave me a medal, back in Malta. 'Brilliant strategy, my boy,' he boomed delightedly when I told him about the gold, and how we'd tried to capture it, and all about the Messerschmitts and destroyers that Hitler wouldn't be able to build without it.

I didn't really press the point about what we'd intended to do with it. Though perhaps the admiral already guessed that much himself. But he was a bit of a fanatic as well, and I think he'd understood Trapp much better than I ever did all along.

So he gave Lieutenant Commander Edward Trapp RNR a medal too. Posthumously, and with great ceremony at a parade overlooking Grand Harbour and the still half-submerged wreck of the tanker *Ohio*. I remember thinking about the look in Trapp's eyes that time so long ago, as we'd watched that gallant ship struggle so painfully into Malta. To save a whole war, and without even the prospect of a profit.

The admiral presented me with the medal on Trapp's behalf. When I stepped forward and saluted he looked at it for a long time, then winked.

'The commander would have been pleased with that,' he whispered conspiratorially. 'It's worth nearly two pounds. Cash price.'

And so the years passed . . .

Until, one day, I was sitting in a bar in Singapore chatting to my chief officer about ship's business in general, when I heard two oil-men talking beside me.

And one said to the other, quite casually. 'You know, it's a funny old world, Harry. On survey in Libya a month or so back I came across this old battlefield beside the sea. Usual thing, you know—wreckage and rust and so on . . . but as I walked through it I discovered a couple of blokes there already. Miles from anywhere, remember—God only knows where they'd come from. And they were bloody rude!'

'Oh?' Harry said, 'What did they do then, Bill?'

Bill looked a bit outraged. 'One of them just kept on glaring at me. Absolute tramp he was, too. Wizened-up, hard looking Scotch blighter . . . and then the other one, big weatherbeaten type, turned round and actually *snarled* at me.'

'What did he say?' Harry asked, intrigued.

Bill shook his head disbelievingly. 'Only the three of us, remember? All alone out there in the bloody desert . . . and the big one suddenly yells, "Bugger *off!*" Just like that.'

I turned on my stool. 'Excuse me, but . . . were they digging, by any chance?'

The man at the bar stared at me. 'How on earth did you guess, Captain?'

I smiled.

Softly. Almost wistfully.

'Will you join me,' I asked. 'There's a couple of old friends I'd like to drink to . . .'